# FIRE IN HIS ARMS

"Who are you, Laurel?" His voice was a low, husky purr. "You rise to any challenge that comes your way, heartened, I'd wager, by more determination than good sense. You have a temper that would make the saints above weep and yet beneath all that fire is a tenderness and compassion that strikes at the very soul of a man."

He slid his hand up her neck to cup the back of her head. His thumb stroked along her jaw line. "Why is your heart racing?"

Her heart *was* racing. An even breath was beyond her, and her mind was adrift, set that way by the seduction of his voice and the lure of his body so close to hers.

"Look at me," he whispered.

She did, lifting her eyes to his. For a brief moment, she saw unnameable emotions shimmering back at her, reaching past defenses and resolve and warnings. Deep inside, near her heart, she felt stroked and enticed until he lowered his head and firmly slanted his mouth over hers.

His lips were warm and persuasive, taking command of the kiss, of her mouth . . . of her mind, and leaving her wanting more. The pleasure was staggering. She'd never felt anything even remotely resembling the blazing currents that raced from her mouth and then straight to the pit of her.

His fingers tangled in her hair, arching her neck back, urging her mouth into closer contact. A little incoherently, she recalled that he'd asked her who she was. At that moment, she didn't know. She didn't care to know and damn the fact that she'd never done anything so wanton. Her body acted on its own, as if it had been waiting forever to be claimed by this particular man . . .

# ILLICIT

ELIZABETH ANN MICHAELS

ZEBRA BOOKS
KENSINGTON PUBLISHING CORP.

ZEBRA BOOKS are published by

Kensington Publishing Corp.
850 Third Avenue
New York, NY 10022



First Printing: December, 1995

Printed in the United States of America

*For Paula Weis Bennett—*
*former student, colleague, "little sister," friend*

*My special thanks to the following:*

Herbert Nath, Research Librarian, the Citadel, for sharing his stories and insights.

Catherine Sadler and Janice Grimes of the Charleston Library Society, for their invaluable research.

The gracious people of Charleston, South Carolina, who opened their doors and their hearts.

Ann Brunetti, who inspired me when she least expected to.

And John Scognamiglio, for "blue shadows and black silence."

# One

"I do believe I would like to have the man in my bed."

"Mercy me, Anna Lee Prescot, how can you say such a thing?"

Anna Lee Prescot flicked a black brow upward and spared her friend and companion a derisive glance. "I'm only sayin' the truth, Emmaline."

"You ought to be ashamed of yourself."

"Well, I'm not." Turning this way and that, Anna Lee admired her image in the dress shop's mirror. "From ever'thin' that I've heard about the man, he's sinfully, wickedly, impossibly handsome. *And* . . ." Her dainty chin elevated as she cast Emmaline a glance out of the corners of her eyes. "He's supposedly as lusty as he is handsome."

"How do you know such a thing?"

Anna Lee pursed her lips and leveled a disgusted glare at Emmaline. "You ask the most stupid things, Emma. It's a wonder your mama lets you out at all."

Poor Emmaline blinked back her obvious affront. "I only asked a simple question. I only want to know how you know so much about the man."

Sniffing with what could only be described as disdain worthy of the royal, Anna Lee declared, "Kathryn Rutledge told me. She has a cousin in Virginia who met the man only last year. To hear her tell of it, he's so handsome he had every woman in the entire Tidewater reachin' for her smellin' salts." She paused to pat a deep black curl back into place before adding, "Those Virginians never were too bright. With a man like that, I can think of a great many things far more interestin' to be reachin' for instead of my salts."

Laurel Seymore listened to the outrageous conversation, careful to keep her face void of expression. It wouldn't do at all for her to let her feelings show. Anna Lee Prescot wouldn't appreciate that in the least.

Daughter of a *very* wealthy plantation owner, Anna Lee believed herself to be the undeclared princess of the low ountry—a rare flower of Southern womanhood. She would work herself into a vindictive snit if she were to discover what Laurel was thinking just then.

*Spoiled, insensitive, pampered little cow. You have the morals of a gutter rat.*

It wasn't one of her more charitable thoughts, Laurel silently admitted, and when she went to Mass on Sunday, she would ask the good Lord above to forgive her, but she really could not tolerate Anna Lee's wretched attitude. For all of her pampered, privileged ways, the woman was as cold and uncaring as a stone. To Laurel's way of thinking, there wasn't any excuse for that.

Sitting on her heels so she could adjust the hem of Anna Lee's new gown, Laurel suppressed the irritated sigh she longed to heave. Anna Lee was in a position to help a great many people if she saw fit. She didn't. Her thoughts went no further than the end of her nose, her social conscience no further than her immediate wants. Laurel couldn't help but find such a selfish temperament offensive.

Of course, it was an opinion she kept strictly to herself. Whether she liked it or not, she needed Anna Lee Prescot and her kind. It was those good ladies of Charleston who insured the continued success of Seymore's Ladies' Shop. Without their trade, Laurel knew she and her sister would be in dire straits.

So, she kept her mouth shut, smiled her inane smiles, and nodded politely. The Anna Lees of the world were none the wiser, and Laurel maintained her livelihood. To all and everyone who knew her, she was the epitome of decorum and tact. It was an impression she strove hard to safeguard.

"The fall of the hem is perfect, Miss Prescot," she said, rising from her kneeling position on the wooden floor. "If you'll just slip the dress off, I'll have it delivered to your house this afternoon."

"Well, of course you will," Anna Lee observed, apparently not yet ready to relinquish her position in front of the full-length mirror. She twisted from side to side, viewing herself from every possible angle. "I do look stunnin' in this particular shade of pink."

Emmaline was quick to agree, bobbing her frizzy blonde head up and down in much the same way a feeding chicken might. "Pink has always been your best color, Anna Lee."

"I've always thought so, and I do so like this material." She pulled her gaze from her reflection long enough to peer more closely at the subtly woven pattern in the fabric of her bodice. "This is the most sumptuous satin I have ever seen. Where on earth did you come by it, Laurel?"

Laurel offered another of her correct smiles as she began to unhook the row of buttons down the back of the gown. "That is a trade secret," she quipped lightly.

"Tell me it's imported. I just know it is."

A private humor suffused Laurel's green eyes, making

the deep jade sparkle and dance. "Who am I to disagree with you?"

"I just knew it." Anna Lee's shoulders squared. "Imported satin, from England no doubt."

"No doubt."

Emmaline clasped her hands to her chest. "You'll be the envy of every woman at the Duncan party tonight, Anna Lee."

"Won't I though?" Anna pondered aloud. "I'm goin' to dazzle Major McKenzie right out of his pants."

If Laurel were the blushing type, she would have turned as scarlet as her hair. As it was, she deftly scooped up the yards of shimmering pink satin and draped it over her arm, not even blinking at the mental image she had of this supposed paragon of naked manliness.

Major McKenzie. She hadn't caught his first name. Anna Lee might have mentioned it, but Laurel couldn't be sure. She did have the habit of shutting off her ears when the shop gossip became numbingly boring. The conversations today had been excessively so. Despite the welcome patronage of Anna Lee and Emmaline, Laurel was glad to see the women finally take their leave.

Alone in the comforting quiet of the shop, she relished the temporary respite. And the solitude. There was little time in her day that she could call her own. These few minutes before someone stopped by to browse through bolts of fabrics, or before she resumed work on the day gown she had been making, or before someone rushed in for an alteration were an unexpected boon. However, absurdly enough, her mind teased her with impressions of the man who was purported to be "as lusty as he is handsome."

"Oh, Laurel," she laughed, "what a silly thing you are."

For a twenty-year-old woman, she didn't know much about lust. In fact, she didn't know anything about it, nor desire or passion, either. True, there had been a few men who had tried to press their suits, but their attentions had always made her uncomfortable. In the grand scheme of courtship, she had never progressed past the stolen kiss stage.

Part of her regretted that. She wasn't a wanton, not by any means. If she had wanted to forsake her virtue, she could have done so a hundred times over. Charleston was certainly not lacking for men, and through the years, more than a few had extended to her a fair number of improper offers.

She had declined them all, but that hadn't stopped her from harboring her own private daydreams about one very special man. A man to make her heart trip, someone who would inspire this passion and desire, this lust that had so many of her customers giggling and whispering.

Carefully folding Anna Lee's dress into a large white box, she let herself speculate as to what this man would be like.

"He wouldn't have to be young, or tall, or even handsome. He would, however, have to be honest. Kind, forthright, intelligent. A sense of humor would be greatly appreciated. And he would have to be honorable. I don't think I could be driven to lust if the man weren't ethical and moral."

All in all, she could love such a man. It stood to reason, then, that passion and desire would surely follow. Wouldn't they? If she loved a man, wouldn't she be heartened to seek the pleasures in his bed? She would like to think so.

Ruefully, she collected herself and scoffed at her conjectures, for that was all they were. As far as she knew, her ideal man didn't exist. Even in these modern times she had yet to find a man who didn't believe he owned the rights to a woman's mind as well as those to her body.

She took real exception to this. She was living proof that women could rationalize and reason as well as any man, and, if given the opportunity, could prosper and succeed at any endeavor. That didn't mean she did not wish for a husband. She did, but with her unusual beliefs, it was very unlikely that marriage or children would ever be hers.

So be it. She could not change her attitudes even though there were those who criticized her for not seeking a husband, for not giving herself up to a man's care. She ignored the censure, preferring instead to be dependent upon herself. An unusual philosophy to be sure, but she had yet to meet a man who could make her feel differently.

Perhaps if her childhood had not been cut short by the untimely deaths of her parents, she might view life in another light. Perhaps if she hadn't had to assume the role of a full grown woman long before she had been ready, she might be more inclined to fanciful notions of a knight in shining armor coming to sweep her off her feet.

But the harsh reality was that she had been four days short of her fifteenth birthday when yellow fever had taken her parents. Their deaths had plunged her and her sister into despair and turmoil. Heartache had nearly destroyed them both as surely as any epidemic's fever ever might have. It was only the cold, grim need to survive that had given her direction. The shop had provided the means.

Even now when she thought of how her parents had started Seymore's with practically nothing, she felt an overwhelming sense of pride. They had toiled and labored, and through the years had taken a meager little shop to the status of one of the most elegant clothiers in the city.

"Oh, Mama, Papa."

She turned now to peer about the crowded work room, women's clothing in various phases of assembly stored everywhere. In her mind's eye, she could picture her mother seated at her work bench in the corner, and her father stationed at his desk balancing ledgers. It had taken both of them working long, arduous hours to provide for their daughters, but they had done just that, and with all the love and devotion in their hearts.

"I love you both."

Not a day went by when she didn't think of them. Every night, she prayed for their guidance, and each morning she rose, hoping that she would make them proud. Her chosen course was full of responsibilities and she took each one of them seriously.

There was the shop to see to, the day-to-day work of cutting and sewing and catering to the fashion whims of the low-country elite, the pressures of making a decent wage, of paying bills and taxes. And of course, there was Hope—fragile, vulnerable Hope.

Just thinking of her older sister drew Laurel to the windows in the front room of the shop. There, she scanned up one side of Broad Street and down the other. Hope was nowhere to be seen.

"This dress be ready for me to tote on to Miss Prescot?"

At the sound of Tess's voice from behind, Laurel left off her study of the busy street, reassuring herself that Hope would be fine. "Yes. Anna Lee was in earlier for her last fitting."

"I sorry I am that I miss that," Tess drawled in her *Gullah* accent, the inflection in her voice just droll enough to make Laurel laugh.

"You wicked thing. I noticed you disappeared as soon as you heard Anna Lee was coming in."

"Me, I don't know what you talk about."

"Hah!" Laurel rewound a length of lace onto its wooden spindle, her teasing gaze never leaving the face of the diminutive servant and friend. Not for the first time, she was reminded of just how much character that face contained.

Every one of Tess's forty years was worked into the bold features and deep brown tones. A former slave, Tess had not had an easy time of life, and it plainly showed. Shadows of hard-learned lessons lingered in the mahogany eyes, and about her gently curved lips there remained a trace of wounded pride.

With all her heart, Laurel wished she could wipe away those signs of former hardships.

"You left me alone with that shrew," she complained lightly, gathering up a stack of fashion plates. "Where did you take yourself off to?"

"The parade." Tess busied herself tying a fat, pale blue ribbon around the box containing Anna Lee's dress. Like the tiny blue laurel blossom embroidered into the hem of every gown made at Seymore's, the ribbon was the shop's trademark, and signaled to anyone who cared to look that another Seymore creation was about to be worn by a most fashion-conscious woman. "I never seen me such a to-do; soldiers marching up Meeting Street, folks cheering. I'd think we was all being delivered from the devil hisself."

Tess's comment wasn't far from the truth, Laurel reflected. The cause for all the fuss did indeed have its origins in the city's demand for law and order. Charleston might be the grandest, wealthiest city in the union, but it was also fraught with unruliness and occasional disorder.

The city fathers had long ago deemed that a city fortress was needed. Now, seven years later, the Citadel was ready for occupation, and today, the infantry from nearby Fort

Moultrie had marched into town to act as the municipal strong-arm.

"You frowning," Tess observed, her voice low, her gaze sure, direct.

Laurel returned the stare just as steadily and forced a small smile. "Am I?" She turned away with a shrug. "It's been a hectic day, one thing after another. I've hardly had a minute to myself, and then all this talk of soldiers and parties. Anna Lee went on forever about a certain major she plans to seduce. Which she won't be able to do if you don't get that dress to her."

Tess shook her head and sighed. "I hear you."

Laurel looked to the older woman and saw her open concern. "I know you do, Tess." For a few seconds she simply stared, then quietly prompted, "Don't tarry along the way."

"Shoot, it never cross me my mind." Halfway to the door, Tess jeered, "If Miz Anna Lee Prescot want to charm some poor soldier, then that her business, but I pity the dumb fellow."

Laurel's brows elevated with her laughter. "What a horrid thing to say. We don't know what this Major McKenzie is like. He's probably not the least bit dumb. After all, he is a major, in the United States Army, no less. He has to have some strength and character."

"Above the waist?" Tess laughed her way out of the shop, leaving Laurel once again with the mental image of a naked Major McKenzie.

Brett McKenzie stood in full dress uniform, surveying the assembled guests crowding the lower rooms of the Duncan house. No matter where he looked, there was one more city official pontificating and one more bare-shouldered woman vying for attention. The scene was as ludicrous as it was laughable.

It was, however, Southern aristocracy at its best. Or worst, depending on how one chose to view the thing. He had seen enough in his thirty-six years to recognize political maneuvering when he saw it. The more obvious cause for tonight's assembly might be the army's arrival into the city, but the underlying reasons were far more subtle and had the more prosperous of the city scrambling to get a foothold with the new powers that be, the United States Army.

Brett let a disgusted sigh slip loose. He had little tolerance for politics. His days at West Point had sickened him quickly enough on the practice of currying favors. The exchanges were beneficial to a select few and were usually at the expense of everyone else.

The scenes in the surrounding rooms reflected much the same attitude. Everyone, it seemed, was out to gain something from the government, whether it be protection or a bed partner.

His silver-blue gaze roved to the far side of the room, to the black-haired woman in pink. They had been introduced earlier, but he couldn't recall her name. But then, he hadn't made a point to commit it to memory.

Somebody Lee Prescot. She had been sending him visual messages all evening. Wryly, he wondered just how much more obvious she was going to become before she crossed the room and, in so doing, crossed her own personal barriers of pride and social etiquette.

She was waiting for him to return her silent communiques. Well, she would still be waiting when it snowed in hell. She was beautiful enough, wearing her sensuality like a dissolute shroud, but he chose his bed partners carefully. More to the point, he did the choosing, and he chose not to close the distance between them and accept what she was so blatantly offering.

Tugging at the dark blue, waist-length coatee of his uniform, he straightened from his position near the drawing-room entrance. He wanted nothing more than a dose of clear, bracing honesty. The crisp night air of January would have to suffice.

Casually but deftly, he outmaneuvered a severe looking matron wending her way to his side, the plump-chested young woman in tow no doubt her marriageable daughter. Giving every impression of having been called to some official duty, he made his escape.

He got as far as the front parlor.

"Major McKenzie," a corpulent gentleman called.

Brett turned slightly to find a group of men gathered in the nearby corner, all smiling his way, all wearing looks of anticipation, all obviously expecting him to join them.

"Gentlemen." Left hand resting lightly on the hilt of his sword, he put forth his most military face, complete with a brief nod. His father would have scoffed in disdain.

*They're nothing but civilians, son, screw 'em.*

He could still hear his father's words in his mind, gruff, direct, indicative of the man himself. Samuel McKenzie had fought as hard as any man in the War of 1812. He'd distinguished himself right alongside Jackson as they'd battled the British.

*Remember, son, God and country above all else. God and country.*

There had been no possible way for Brett to have forgotten. Even as a boy, he had known that those words had constituted much more than noble-sounding phrases. Samuel McKenzie had lived by that creed, placing God and America at the pinnacle of his existence. All else, including his family, had been relegated to a resounding second place.

A lifetime of resentment toward his father surfaced within Brett. It took a conscious effort for him to divorce himself of the feeling and attend to the present.

The rotund sir with the balding pate stuck forth his hand. "A pleasure to have you with us, Major. A pleasure."

"Thank you, sir."

"Ephram Wragg's the name, Ephram Wragg. We were never formally introduced, but I recognize you from the proceedings this afternoon."

"Mr. Wragg." Brett had a vague memory of having seen Wragg during the city's official ceremonies to welcome the army into its new post. Unfortunately there had been so many people crammed into the post's inner quad that nothing more than a brief glimpse of the hundreds and hundreds of faces had been possible.

Just thinking of the pompous formalities caused a spurt of annoyance to dig at Brett's patience. The Citadel was a military post, not an austere parlor for some haughty matriarch's social advancement. It took a conscious effort on his part to remind himself that the new army post had been seven years in the building, the effort due entirely to the people of Charleston. They were entitled to their moment of celebration.

"Let me introduce you, Major," Wragg insisted. With jowls quivering in his excitement, Wragg executed the formalities, ending with a repeat of his earlier sentiment. "Yes, sir, Major, we are damn glad to have the army with us here in the city, damn glad."

One of his friends voiced his agreement. "Now maybe

we'll be able to sleep soundly, peacefully. Hardly a night goes by when some bastard isn't setting one part or another of this city afire."

Brett knew that arson was one of the many problems plaguing Charleston—one of the many problems the army was expected to rectify. "Our commanding officer, Major Belton, has been made fully aware of the situation."

"Well, what about keeping an eye on the slaves," Frank Webster suggested. He shot a look over his shoulder and lowered his voice. "We whites are outnumbered here, Major McKenzie. What's to stop the colored populace from rising up?"

"Do you expect them to?" Brett countered, eyeing the distressed Webster with narrowed blue eyes.

Webster sputtered and puffed up his meager chest. "It almost happened several years ago, Major."

"Back in '22," someone added.

Wragg waved his beefy hand in dismissal. "That's an old worry that's amounted to nothing. Now, a real difficulty is this smuggling that's going on."

Mention of smuggling caught Brett's attention. In the many briefings he and his fellow officers had been given, nothing about smuggling had been mentioned. "What exactly is being smuggled in, Mr. Wragg?"

"What isn't?" Wragg aimed a raised finger Brett's way. "Rum, silver plate, cloth, dry goods. It's ruining honest trade, sir. I'd like to see the army catch these blackguards and hang each one of them up by their thieving necks. There's been many a time when I've been tempted to do that myself, many a time."

Brett's black brows flicked upward. "Then you know who is involved in these illegal activities?"

For a second or two, Wragg worked his jaw before he

actually managed to say anything. "Well, no, not exactly, but I've got my suspicions."

"We all have our suspicions," Frank Webster maintained. Again, he furtively scanned the room before leaning close. "We hear the name Jack Diego whispered about."

"In what terms?" Brett asked.

"The vilest," Wragg vowed. "He slips into town on the darkest of nights and unloads his stolen wares."

"Of course you don't know where," Brett surmised.

Wragg's mouth pulled into a one-sided grin. "If we knew that, Major, we wouldn't be having this discussion. The man is wily, I tell you, wily. No one's been able to catch him."

"That's because he's got help," Frank Webster insisted. "Someone is this city is protecting the bastard."

"And making a pretty penny, to boot. That's what we want you to look into, Major. The man's got be stopped. I don't mind paying an honest dollar for honest goods and honest services, but I'll be damned if I'll stand for one more greedy bugger of a merchant reaching into my pocket like a bandit."

The assembled men gave a chorus of muttered agreements. Brett found their expressions as resentful as their voices. They had only so much forbearance to spare and it was obviously being depleted by the day.

"I'll take the matter up with Major Belton tomorrow, gentlemen."

"We'd appreciate that," Wragg commented, "appreciate it a great deal. It's about time we got this city cleaned up, and you can start right there."

Brett followed the direction of Wragg's nod to the dark-haired beauty in the soft pink dress not ten feet off. The woman, Somebody Lee Prescot, had apparently followed him from the other room and now gazed back at him, an open invitation sparkling in her eyes.

"The woman?"

"The dress," Wragg corrected, with an aggravated growl. "Not another dressmaker in the city can come by fabric like that."

The nature of cloth was not something about which Brett could claim any expertise. His interest in women's fashions was limited to the visual appeal of a transparent chemise.

"Where did the dress come from?" He eyed the gown with interest, noting peripherally that the wearer all but fluttered under his continued perusal.

"Seymore's," came Wragg's answer.

"How do you know?"

"Oh, I know, Major, I know. For one thing, Anna Lee Prescot wouldn't dream of wearing anything that didn't come from Seymore's. For another, if you look closely, you'll see an embroidered sprig of blue laurel sewn into the hem of Anna Lee's dress."

Frank Webster added his complaint. "Damn bit of nonsense, if you ask me, but it's got the women acting like a bunch of ninnies. Why, my own wife insists that she have at least one new dress a year and she doesn't want it unless it comes from Seymore's. She can't wait to have everyone see that damned blue flower."

Brett scanned the hem of the pink dress and discovered the embroidered flower peeking discretely out from the folds of pink. "What is the significance of the blue laurel?"

Ephram Wragg scoffed around his laughter. "Just about everything, Major. The shop is owned by two sisters. The older one, Hope, is a pretty little thing, sweet, and as shy as the day is long. But the younger one . . ." Wragg dragged his hand over the skin on the top of his head. "It's the younger one that runs the shop, and I don't mind telling you that she has some very peculiar notions about things—some very peculiar notions."

"Such as?"

"Such as not owning a single slave, such as having no interest in taking a husband like God intended a woman to do, such as sewing her namesake into the hems of dresses."

Brett narrowed his eyes at the delicately wrought laurel blossom worked in pale blue threads. "Laurel? The woman's name is Laurel?"

Wragg nodded his head for emphasis. "That's who you should talk to about all the unusual cloth she's been getting in, Major. Laurel Seymore. See if she doesn't know a thing or two about Jack Diego and all this smuggling."

# Two

"Miss Seymore! Miss Seymore!"

As much as she would have liked to, Laurel couldn't ignore the calling of her name. To have pretended deafness would have accomplished nothing. She knew the owner of the voice to be remarkably tenacious.

Blinking back visions of Daniel Illston scurrying after her, dragging breaths of air into his sunken chest, she stopped in her passage through Centre Market and faced her persistent follower.

"Mr. Illston." She smiled at the innkeeper as sweetly as she could given the circumstances. Even on the fringes of the city's marketplace, the odor of freshly butchered meats and overripe vegetables permeated the air. The smell was just rank enough to make her slightly ill, and she couldn't help but associate the feeling with Daniel's last name, Illston.

Her conscience pricked her, and silently she admitted to just one more transgression she would have to atone for on Sunday. She wasn't being fair to Daniel, and she took herself to task. In his own way, the man was very nice, despite the fact that his rambling, long-winded manner could at times be extremely annoying. His attentions were flattering, but sadly enough, unwanted. She sighed as he rapidly approached.

"I thought I might have missed you," he panted, his thin brown hair lying lank against his skull.

"I'm sorry if I didn't hear you, Mr. Illston, what with all the noise and bustle." She gestured to the various stalls where vendors hawked their wares in voices loud enough to be heard clear into next week. Potential buyers added their voices in similar tones, adamantly disputing the price of everything. "I hope you didn't put yourself out on my account."

"That would never be possible, dear lady. In fact, I was hopin' you would happen by today. I was tellin' Mama this mornin' how nice it would be if you would see fit to join us for Sunday services. That is, if you were of such a mind. That is, if you had no other obligations that would prevent you from doin' so."

Laurel hooked her market basket over her arm, taking the moment to compose her features. Daniel's request was always the same, an invitation to join him for church. Her response was likewise always the same. "I am sorry, Mr. Illston, but you know that my sister and I attend St. Mary's, while you attend St. John's."

Daniel scraped his upper lip with his lower teeth, his brow pulling into a series of deep lines. "Yes . . . ah, yes. Well, then, perhaps I can help you with your marketin'." He looked around as though a bit bewildered. "What are you after, ham, fish, fresh greens? I thought I saw a fine pork leg on the next street over. You were marketin', weren't you?"

With a sinking feeling, Laurel knew what was coming. Daniel Illston would fly off in five different directions at once without leaving his spot. Quickly, she altered her afternoon plans.

"No, actually, I'm on my way back to the shop," she

fibbed. In truth, she had just left the shop and had intended to find a hen for Tess to cook for tonight's supper.

"Back to the shop?" Daniel queried. "Then you must let me accompany you."

"That isn't necessary, Mr. Illston." Already, she had stepped around one of the market's many buzzards and begun to ease her way down the street.

"It isn't any problem. In fact, I insist." He fell into step beside her, his gate uneven as he tried to direct her path, at the same time seemingly trying to restrain her from making any progress. "Are you sure you wouldn't want to inspect the shipment of corn that arrived today, Miss Laurel? Or flour, what about flour? Do you have enough bread at home? Mama says a body can't have enough bread in one's house."

With all her might, Laurel tried to be pleasant. She accomplished that for the most part by saying as little as possible for the entire four block walk. Every step of the way, Daniel posed one question after another with little regard to her interest and even less regard to any discernable logic.

The virtues of a good loaf of bread were followed by the quality of leather on the soles of his shoes, followed by the price of horse manure. The possibility of rain somehow led into a discourse on ale, and that, for some unknown reason, gave rise to the topic of the phlegm that collects nightly at the back of one's throat.

Each new subject sent his voice up in pitch until it scraped on Laurel's ears, sounding very much like a screech. By the time the familiar brick facade of Seymore's came into view, she was biting her lower lip and praying for God to strike him mute.

"Good day, Mr. Illston," she blurted out, desperate to

be away from the abrasive voice. Flinging open the shop door, she gave him a stiff-lipped smile and quickly slipped inside the blessed emptiness of the shop's front room.

Eyes squeezed shut, she leaned against the wooden panel and snapped, "Jesus, Mary, and Joseph! Deliver me from verbose, aimless, well-intentioned men."

"From that I can only assume you prefer to be left to the mercies of bold, taciturn scoundrels."

At the first sound of the deep male voice, Laurel gasped, her entire body jerking back against the door. Her eyes flew wide, immediately taking in the sight of a man standing in the doorway between the shop's two rooms.

The man. Her startled mind struggled to make sense of his presence. She hadn't been expecting anyone other than Hope to be there, let alone this . . . she scanned his tall figure . . . this soldier.

Stars and garters, his impressive uniform with its buff pants and tall, black leather shako declared him to be with the newly arrived army. That alone was cause enough for her to swallow nervously. But added to that was the man himself. At a single glance, everything about him could be summed in one word: *hard.*

Those silver-blue eyes shone like flinty crystals, the edge of his jaw, framed by the high collar of his blue coatee, looked as though it had been tempered from steel. The contour of his lips was as unyielding as his stance.

Gold epaulettes rode wide shoulders and only emphasized a strength that owed everything to muscle and nothing to deceptive tailoring. Her expert eye recognized padding for what it was, and nowhere on this man was there padding of any sort.

The front of his blue, waist-length, cut-away jacket lay without wrinkles because the chest beneath it was as solid as it appeared. The jacket's twin rows of polished brass buttons marched down the length of his chest to form a V because the man's waist was inflexible enough to be narrow. The shadows delineated beneath the trousers could not be mistaken for anything other than firm, powerful muscle. And the bulge at the apex of those thighs? Well *that* was an insolently relentless testimony to the degree of his masculinity.

"Sir," she breathed, forcing her mind and her eyes from their inspection. "You caught me totally by surprise." So much so that she felt only a twinge of embarrassment at having been caught cursing.

"My apologies, madam. I hope I did not give you too bad a fright."

"No, not too terribly." Laurel straightened from the door, her expression turning patently curious.

"Allow me to introduce myself, madam. Major Brett McKenzie, United States Army." He removed his shako to reveal hair as black as his brows.

Laurel's eyes widened at the name. She should have known that he was the very same major that had Anna Lee Prescot ready to spread her thighs. Handsome didn't even begin to describe him.

*With or without his pants.*

The thought came out of the nether regions of her mind. She squelched it ruthlessly, reminding herself that she didn't have any business imagining the man naked.

But oh, what a temptation there was in that.

In a flash, she pictured him bathed in dewy morning light, chiseled muscles cast into stark relief. Would his chest be covered with a crisp mat of black hair, or would his skin be naked to the touch?

Oh, Lord, what was she thinking? She wasn't prone to

carnal musings. She had seen enough in the slave mart to know the what and wherefores of a man's body and not be affected. The male physique was the opposite of a woman's. Yet there she stood, practical, levelheaded Laurel, and all she could think was that a man's body, *this* man's body, was much, much more than her opposite. It was her complement.

Feeling shaken down to the marrow of her bones, she hurried behind the counter to the left. There, she took refuge in the familiar.

"Is there anything I can do for you, Major?"

"Madam?" One inky black brow quirked upward.

Laurel set her basket aside. Once rid of that mundane ornament, her persona once again became that of Charleston's most exceptional *modiste.* Polite, poised, accommodating, she ventured, "I'm sorry there was no one to attend to you, Major." She spread her hands apologetically. "My sister was supposed to have been here."

His brows angled downward. "You have me at a disadvantage, madam. You are . . ."

"Laurel Seymore, owner of the shop."

Those mobile black brows shot up and his gaze seemed to become more sharp, more probing. "My apologies, Miss Seymore." He made a show of bowing slightly, leather hat tucked in the crook of his right arm, left hand riding the hilt of his sword. "I mistook you for a customer."

Laurel fought the absurd notion to dip into a curtsey. She settled for a courteous nod. "Major McKenzie. What brings you here, sir?"

"Duty."

"Oh?" She gave into a spurt of laughter. "Is the army in need of new uniforms?"

He waved her suggestion aside, matching his grin to hers. "Hardly, Miss Seymore. The cause for my visit today is more of a courtesy, to introduce myself to merchants in this sector of the city."

"How very nice of you."

"That may be, but it is also a necessity." Casually, he strode about the shop, inspecting the various wares with a face that gave away nothing. "If we are going to accomplish our goal here, to keep law and order, then it is important that the citizens of Charleston, and both the army and the state militia work together."

"I couldn't agree more." However, military matters didn't signify just then. Once again, she was caught off-guard, struck by the rare male grace with which he moved. No awkward gate or slouching shoulders for Major McKenzie. He was all smoothly gliding sinew and perfect coordination. And he was as impressive from behind as he was from the front.

". . . to report?"

It took several seconds for her to realize he had asked her a question. Mentally railing at herself, she pasted on a sweet smile and compelled herself to a hard-won attentiveness. "I'm sorry, excuse me?"

Fingering a bolt of ipsiboe he repeated, "Have you had any troubles you wish to report?"

Laurel's gaze dropped to the tanned fingers stroking the delicately transparent yellow crepe. "Troubles?"

"Arson, thievery?"

"No, neither." The long fingers continued to stroke; she continued to stare.

"What about brawls or stabbings?"

For the life of her, Laurel could *not* drag her eyes from the fascinating movement of his hand. Again and again his thumb passed over the diaphanous crepe; strong male flesh caressing intrinsically feminine fabric. "Fighting in a ladies' shop?" she breathed.

"In the street or alleyway."

"N-no."

"Murder?"

"No." Where had her willpower escaped to?

"Abduction?"

"No."

His fingers stilled, his eyes riveted to hers. "Rape?"

Breath locked in her throat, Laurel was held immobile, caught in the upsurge of a sizzling current that sprang up without warning. It passed between them . . . silent intimacy gilded in layers of silver-blue, unspoken awareness that lured, tantalized, and dared her to relent to too many unknowns.

The man was dangerous. *Dangerous.*

"Really, Major," she snapped, her voice as waspish as she had ever heard it, "we have been spared much of the crime that has plagued the rest of the city."

"So it would seem." For a long, *long* moment, his stare remained fixed on hers.

For just as long, she stared right back, feeling as if the air had become hot and thick. The sensation made her excruciatingly aware of herself, of him, and of the differences between them.

"You have an impressive shop, Miss Seymore." He came forward as he spoke, stopping on the other side of the narrow wood counter. Slowly, he offered her a smile that was underscored with a brazen challenge. "Impressive wares."

She refused to be bated, to wonder if he had intended a double meaning in his comment about *wares.* "Thank you, sir." And then, because it annoyed her to no end that her heart was pounding and her fingers were actually trembling, she needled, "Are you an expert on the merchandise found in a ladies' apparel shop, Major?"

"Only to the same degree that any other man is."

"Which is a backward way of saying no."

"Which is a straightforward way of saying that with certain ladies' garments, I possess an amazing expertise." Leaning forward, the silver of his eyes glistening with an ardent challenge, he whispered, "Do you still wish to be delivered from well-intentioned men?"

Her heart lunged against her ribs, her skin prickled with sensations of heat, but before she could even think of a response, the front door opened and Hope entered.

Laurel exhaled sharply, not knowing whether she was glad to see Hope or not. With every ounce of her, she dearly wished to verbally flay the arrogant beast of a major. At the same time, the common sense on which she had always prided herself cautioned her that this man was not to be goaded.

"Hope, there you are," she sighed, careful to keep her inner anxiety from showing. "I was worried about you."

Hope waved an elegant hand about in a characteristically vague gesture. "There wasn't any cause, Laurel. I stepped out for only a moment." Her dark brown eyes shifted to the major. Nervously, she tugged at the lace of her collar. "I-is something amiss?"

"Not at all."

"I only stepped out for a little bit, Laurel. Honestly." Hope's face crumbled, her shoulders sagged. "That was all right, wasn't it?"

"Yes, of course. There's no cause for you to worry. Major McKenzie stopped by to introduce himself."

Hope's weak smile spoke as eloquently as her quickly averted gaze. Laurel's heart went out to her. In the best of circumstances, Hope was shy. With men, she was positively timid.

"I've got work to finish up," Hope explained, trying for poise and missing badly. Clasping her hands at her waist, she made for the back room, scrupulously keeping her chin lowered.

"I'll be in to help in a bit," Laurel reassured her.

Not forgotten, however, was Major McKenzie. She could well imagine what he thought of Hope. It was most likely what most men thought when they first saw her, and with good reason. Hope Seymore was an extraordinarily lovely woman.

Beauty such as Hope's was rare. Men had been known to quite literally stop in the street and gawk, wondering if her face was real or that of an angel. Her brown eyes were the same almond shape as their mother's, her mouth a precise Cupid's bow. Skin flawless and pale, its smooth perfection was enhanced by the rich gleam of her auburn hair.

Laurel was well aware that between the two of them, there was no comparison. It was a truth she had accepted years ago. She loved Hope, loved her dearly and did not begrudge her sister her loveliness.

Turning back to the major, she was surprised to find him studying her closely, and that annoyed her. "Sir?"

He didn't say a word. After one final look, he donned his hat, nodded slightly, and departed, leaving Laurel to wonder what he had been thinking.

She narrowed her eyes to glare at the door. Arrogant, irritating beast. Oh, yes, Major McKenzie was a most dangerous man.

* * *

Brett lowered his chin ever so slightly, his eyes glinting as he made his way to the corner of Broad and King Streets. One side of his mouth was curled upward in a faint hint of a grin. That was as much as he would sacrifice to the derisive humor roiling through him, to the taunting irritation inspired by Laurel Seymore, and her fiery temper.

What a surprise she was. She had burst into the shop like a gust of clean, spring air, and from that second on had been an unexpected little marvel, a fount of contradictions.

She appeared to be a proper young woman, but ladies of that ilk did not go about swearing—at least not in public, and never so extravagantly. Despite that, he admitted that her unladylike language had been refreshingly appealing. The resulting contrast was rife with possibilities, not the least of which was just how proper or improper she actually was.

Her manner offered several conflicting answers. She had inspected him as candidly as any well-trained whore, but surprisingly enough, without any signs of feminine guile. There had been no seductive appeal or flirtatious retreat in her gaze. It had remained clear, purposeful, and direct. That very lack of alluring artifice was unique, especially so in such a visually interesting woman.

She wasn't a classic beauty, not by any means. First of all, she was more narrow than rounded, but that willowy figure still had had the power to draw his gaze to the subtle fullness beneath her bodice. He had taken note of the gentle swells and memorized their shape. He recalled them now as he studied the whole of her more intently.

He judged her to stand five feet four, and not an inch more. If he were to draw her close, he wagered that the top of her head would reach his shoulders. He would have to dip his head, and his knees, too, in order to capture her lips.

Liking the notion, he inwardly smiled. She was definitely unique, more so for the piquancy of her features. He'd never known a woman whose eyes were so large or so damnably green. Her lips were neither lush nor perfectly sculpted. Nonetheless, he found himself wondering if they were as soft as they had looked, if they would part easily to the insistence of his tongue.

High cheekbones gave way to a gently curved jaw, and a smooth brow. Taken all together, the lines could have been indicative of a compliant and amenable nature if it hadn't been for the chin. There was sufficient angle and mettle in the thing to hint at a character as stubborn, as willful, as fiery as the red in the woman's hair.

Tight, deep red curls surrounded Laurel Seymore's face. There was obviously no taming the chaotic mass, and from what he had seen, the lady had resorted to the easiest means of dealing with the matter. She'd secured the twists and spirals to the crown of her head with a green ribbon to match her gown and had simply let nature take its course. The result had been a halo of fire.

The tempting thought of being singed tightened the muscles in his gut. Lower, he felt the first stirrings of desire.

Damn, what a tempting problem the lady was. And he had no doubt whatsoever that she was a problem. His inspection of her shop had proven that. To the casual observer, there was nothing suspicious to be found. However, none of the other dress shops he had visited that day could even come close to offering the selection—the variety nor the quality—of merchandise to be found at Seymore's.

The obvious question was where was Laurel Seymore coming by such stores?

At the corner of the block, he gained his horse being tended by one Corporal Ransom of the South Carolina State Militia. "That will be all, Corporal."

The man saluted smartly as Brett mounted and settled comfortably, familiarly into the saddle. His movements sure, he urged his horse toward the Citadel. That didn't prevent him from continuing his mental examination of the Seymore sisters.

He would have to have been a blind eunuch not to have been stunned by the older sister. He couldn't remember ever seeing a woman who possessed such a spiritual beauty. She was exquisite, with her doe-like eyes, pale skin, and generous curves.

And yet, she herself presented another host of contradictions. For all her physical perfection, she seemed impossibly insecure. His mere presence had rattled her, and in defense, she had turned to her sister for obvious reassurance and guidance. Laurel had supplied both with a gentle patience of which he wouldn't have thought her capable.

He had assumed her spirit too tempestuous, her attitude too disinclined for tolerance. And yet, the green of her eyes had softened with emotion while her pure liquid Southern accent had intensified. Miss Laurel Seymore was devoted to her sister.

Was she also doing her a grave disservice? If anyone was embroiled in smuggling, it was Laurel Seymore. For obvious reasons, he discounted Hope at once. She didn't have the necessary strength to be involved in something illegal. He couldn't say the same of Laurel. She was ten kinds of passion seething just beneath a beguilingly calm surface.

And he wanted to test each and every one of those passions.

Damn, but Laurel Seymore was going to be trouble of the worst kind.

# Three

In her head, Laurel heard the pounding of her heart, a broken, frantic staccato that echoed through her body. Like a dark pulsation, it hammered out a warning of hazards waiting for her in the ebony hours of the night, of perils just over her shoulder, of dangers that brought a cry to her lips.

She came awake with a gasp torn from her lungs, sitting straight up in bed, eyes wide and hands trembling. The seconds ticked by for what seemed like forever before her mind connected the dream with reality. In her bed, the dying coals in the grate casting their ruby shadows, she was safe.

She expelled a long breath, relief making her weak. Remnants of her fright danced over her nerves, but she willed them away, telling herself that all was well, that there was nothing to fear.

The pounding on the front door below contradicted her silent assurances.

Her gaze jerked to her windows. It was well past midnight. There were no auspicious reasons for anyone to be clamoring at her door. Fright climbed into her throat once more, and only then did she note that in the distance, a church bell pealed.

"Oh, dear Lord," she muttered, scrambling from bed,

her nightgown swirling about her slender legs in misty folds. She grabbed a shawl and raced from her room, meeting Hope and Tess at the top of the stairway.

"Laurel," Hope breathed, her expression as tremulous as her voice. "The knocking woke me."

"Someone wants in," Tess predicted, holding her candle high.

Hope clasped the lapels of her robe under her chin. "At this hour?" She hesitantly followed her sister down the stairs, hugging the banister with her body. "Oh, Laurel, something's wrong. Don't answer the door."

The insistent knocking increased in volume. The pealing of the church bell continued.

"Should I get the pistol?" Tess asked.

"Quiet, both of you," Laurel ordered, dread and alarm taxing her composure.

From the other side of the door, a boy's voice called out. "Miz Seymore, Miz Seymore, dere's trouble. Dere's fire!"

Laurel's insides lurched. She flung open the door to stare at the skinny boy, his eyes white and rounded in his deep brown face.

"What's wrong?"

"Come quick, Miz Seymore. Dere's fire."

"Where?"

The boy hopped from one foot to the other, pointing for all he was worth toward the center of town. "Broad Street. Near yo' shop. Master Doyle, he sent me to fetch you, said yo' shop might burn. You got to come quick, Miz Seymore."

Hope scurried forward, arms hugged about her waist to stave off the chilled night air. "Laurel, what shall we do?"

The question barely penetrated Laurel's consciousness. In her mind, she was already running toward the shop.

"Tess, I need my cloak."

"You comin', Miz Seymore?" the boy wanted to know.

"Yes, yes." Mentally, she blessed Joshua Doyle whose silver smith shop was across the street from Seymore's.

"Oh, Laurel," Hope wailed, turning in a complete circle to watch Tess run up the stairs. "Where are you going? What should I do?"

"You're going to stay here, Hope."

"Are you sure? Shouldn't I . . .? Are you sure?"

Tess hurried back into the foyer with Laurel's wrap and a pair of flat shoes. "You going to the shop?"

Laurel threw off her shawl and snatched up her ring of keys from the hall table. "Stay here with Hope. Lock up after me."

In her haste and worry, Laurel barely felt the bite of cold penetrating her cloak. She ran from the house, heedless of everything but one overriding thought: to save Seymore's.

The enormity of such an undertaking was daunting—impossible for a woman alone. The buildings on Broad Street practically sat on top of each other. A single spark, a hint of wind and the entire block could go up in flames.

Hideous possibilities flooded her head. Already, she pictured the two-story structure burning. That it was constructed of brick was a big favor, but the wooden roof was still vulnerable. If it caught, the interior would be destroyed. God help her, what would they do then?

Her breath heaved in and out of her chest. Lungs burning with this unaccustomed exertion, she pressed on, wishing for the first time ever that she owned a horse and buggy. Until now, she'd never seen the necessity of owning either one.

The smell of smoke reached her on a brisk gust of air.

Above the rooftops, the sky was tinted gold. Laurel stopped, gulping in painful breaths, and stared in horror.

"No," she whispered. "Oh, please, no."

Without conscious thought, she sent her plea heavenward. She was aware of little else save protecting her business—the very same her parents had founded. How she was going to do that didn't signify. It was simply the impetus that drove her on.

Thickly roiling smoke choked her before she even turned the corner of Broad Street. In defense, she pressed the trailing end of her cloak to her face, but the effort did little for her eyes. Tears streamed over her cheeks as she made her way through the crowd that had gathered, past curious onlookers and soldiers running in every direction.

As quickly as possible, she wended her way down the street, hope and alarm warring within her. It wasn't until she actually had a clear view of the shop's front door that she realized that Seymore's wasn't on fire. It was still standing, but the building four doors down was engulfed. And already, flames were threatening the common courtyard that ran behind most of the structures on the block.

Blinking back stinging tears, she darted down the narrow alley between her shop and the next, having no real idea what she could possibly do. Men from the militia and the army had formed bucket brigades and were doing their best to extinguish the blaze.

Shop owners were just as occupied, dousing their buildings in hopes that wet wooden shingles would prevent the fire's spread. In the chaotic scene, she recognized merchants she had known all her life struggling against a force that seemed untamable.

"Mary," she choked out, reaching with both hands to help the milliner tote a bucket brimming with water.

Mary Nelson's eyes widened in her plump, lined face, surprise registering for a brief instant before fright returned. "Oh, Laurel, I didn't know if someone had sent for you."

"How bad is it?"

"Two buildings are gone."

Something inside Laurel crumbled in defeat. It wasn't a simple matter of the loss of wood and mortar, supplies and wares. People's lives and futures were contained within these shops.

To a person, the merchants she knew were decent, honest, and hard-working. They were, herself included, not the landed gentry. Money and privilege was not theirs as a birthright. What they had, they worked hard to attain and even harder to keep. Her heart went out to those whose livelihoods had been destroyed, no doubt at another arsonist's hands.

"Over here, Mary," she whispered, her throat constricted with emotion. Her target was next door, and the stairway leading up to Mary's second floor shop. Together, she and Mary flung their bucket of water onto the steps.

"I'll see if I can get another pail," Mary said.

Laurel nodded even as she turned back for the well. Ahead of her, several soldiers repeatedly lowered and raised the bucket, dragging up water and dumping it into the containers of those who waited.

Laurel received her share and hurried back to Mary's stairway. She cast a worried look at her own shop and then ducked to avoid fire sparks that rained down from above. The suddenness of her movement sent a sheet of water down the front of her cloak, soaking her clear to her skin.

She barely noticed. She was intent on only one thing:

stopping the fire before it engulfed this building . . . and then her own.

Time became a relative matter as she worked alongside Mary. Again and again, she carried water and tossed it high, or climbed the two flights of stairs and splashed the wooden beams and siding. At some point, a soldier joined them for a bit, but he was called away to help somewhere else. All the while, Laurel gritted her teeth and willed her aching, straining muscles to do what she demanded of them, what was needed.

Dawn beckoned in the eastern sky before she noticed that the fire had been contained. Smoke still puffed upward in gray clouds, but the flames were finally dead and errant cinders had ceased to fly. In all, five buildings were gone. Mary's building was not among them. Nor was Seymore's.

The realization came as a shock, as if after having struggled for so long, she couldn't quite believe that their efforts had paid off. For a prolonged instant, she stood in the cold puddles, bucket hanging limply from her scraped, bleeding hands, and stared about her.

"Is it over?" Mary asked, her own clothes as torn and sodden as Laurel's.

"I think so." She hoped so. Scanning the area, she saw none of the frantic haste and frenzy of the past few hours. People weren't rushing about. There were no lines at the wells.

More tired than she had ever been in her life, she upended her bucket and sat, shoulders sagging, hair lying in a damp tangle down her back. The chill that anxiety had kept at bay all night made itself felt. Tiny pricks of frigid pain attacked her skin.

She needed a hot bath. She needed to get warm and dry.

She needed to go home. However, the energy necessary for all of that was suddenly beyond her.

"Miss Seymore?"

The voice came to her through a fog of weariness, her mind recognizing the deep tones and yet truly unable to digest their presence, now, in the aftermath of the turmoil. With the inside of her wrist pressed to her forehead, she looked up.

"Major McKenzie." The name emerged as both a statement and a question.

Brett came down before her, sitting on his haunches, his knees spread wide to encompass hers. "Miss Seymore, what are you doing here?"

She peered at his soot-streaked face, his features harsh in the early morning light. The glint in his silvery eyes appeared as unyielding as the edge of his jaw. The combination was not promising, and her gaze dropped to the broad expanse of his chest, the once-white muslin of his shirt plastered wetly to the muscles it covered. Absurdly, that observation brought her a measure of reassurance.

"Miss Seymore?" He studied her face with blatant inquiry.

"The fire," she explained.

Brett shook his head, his thick brows lowering. He could not fathom her being here. And yet, from the looks of her, she had spent the past hours adding her feminine strength and energy to the predominantly masculine effort to extinguish the fire.

He raked her with a discerning, disapproving gaze, noting the smudges of ash that stained her face, the wet, soiled condition of her clothes, the pitiful condition of her hands. Annoyance mixed with a reluctant admiration for her spirit. On the one hand he felt the compulsion to applaud her courage, and on the other, he very much wanted to chew her soft little hide for placing herself in such a precarious position.

"You foolish woman," he grated. In one gliding move, he stood straight, bringing Laurel up with him. "You could have been hurt."

Laurel wasn't prepared for the sudden shift in positions. One second she was resting on her bucket and the next she was struggling to stand erect. In defense, she clung to the powerful arms that held her.

"Major McKenzie, really." His hands at her waist kept her steady. They also felt utterly foreign.

She wasn't accustomed to being touched by a man, in any capacity. To have this particular man's hands on her when she was feeling especially vulnerable sent nervous tremors up her spine and down her legs.

"I can stand on my own," she maintained, willing her pulse to a sedate rhythm.

"You shouldn't be out here at all." His hands coursed up her arms, the gesture flattening his lips into an angry line. "You're soaked to the skin." He shot the back of the dress shop an impatient glance. "Do you have a key to get in?"

"Yes."

"Give it to me."

At his brusque command, Laurel bristled. "Why?"

But he wasn't waiting for her to reply. He was already searching through the cloak's pockets. Laurel gasped when she felt his fingers roaming against her thigh.

"Will you wait for a second?" Her voice an octave higher than it should have been, she drew at her cloak, but to no end. The man had already found her keys, then grasped her elbow none too gently and pulled her along beside him.

Hauled would have been a more accurate accounting of his actions, she silently fumed. The arrogant beast. Who did he think he was to push and pull her about as he saw fit?

"Let go of me," she demanded, backing her order with a scorching measure of outrage. Exhaustion had made hash of her patience. She had none to spare for this . . . this autocratic, overbearing, self-appointed savior of women. "Major McKenzie, I insist that you release me at once."

His reply was to flick her a glance of scoffing humor, complete with one imperiously raised eyebrow—that and to unlock the shop's back door and all but shove her into the work room. Such handling ignited Laurel's temper to a degree that matched the fire that had blazed earlier.

She rounded on him, fists clenched at her sides, teeth gritted hard. In the room's dim light, the green of her eyes flashed with emerald sparks of fury.

"How dare you," she raged, her voice low, deliberate, each word shoved out in curt, disjointed syllables. "You have no right to treat me like this."

The force of Laurel's ire hit Brett like a tiny fist striking him in the center of his chest. The underlying power wasn't enough to inflict damage of any kind, but it was enough to capture his complete attention.

Caught by her burst of temper, he studied her intently. He had been right in his assumption that she was ten kinds of passion just waiting to explode. He could feel the depth and zeal of her anger clear across the room.

Shaking off his momentary surprise, he turned away to

rummage through various articles of clothing lying about. When he found what he sought, he returned to her side.

"Take off your clothes," he ordered.

Laurel stilled. Completely. In the midst of her anger, she couldn't make heads or tails of his actions or his command. Outrage had consumed her thoughts, driving them in one direction. His dictate obliged her mind to suddenly shift its course and head down a whole other path. As tired as she was, she was momentarily bewildered.

"Ta-take my clothes off?"

"That's right."

Her mind was feverishly trying to grasp his intentions. "No." Without conscious thought, she clutched the front of her cloak with a tight fist.

He muttered a pithy curse and saw to the fastening of her cloak himself. "You have a most stubborn nature, Miss Seymore."

"What are you doing?" she demanded, horrified that she couldn't prevent him from parting her cloak and shoving it back over her shoulders.

"I'm trying to get you out of these wet clothes and into something dry."

His answer made her blink. Comprehension and relief washed through her only to be cut short when without warning, she found herself standing in nothing but her thin nightgown, its wet muslin molded to her skin like a feeble, useless barrier that shielded nothing.

It was one more shock in a night made up entirely of shocks. Too late, she gasped and wrenched away, thinking to spin around and cover herself, but he took hold of her arms and held her immobile in front of him. Heart thumping in a wild cadence, she held her breath as a powerful awareness grew between them.

Brett openly stared. The misty transparency of the gown clinging damply to Laurel's slim body drew his gaze like a wandering soul to a bright beacon. The lure acted on his senses, his mind, and body while instinct old as time demanded that he look his fill.

Every curve and hollow of her was revealed. Her breasts were high and gently rounded, her waist a trim contour. The flat of her belly gave way to the flaring of her hips and the tapering of her legs. At the juncture of her thighs, a thatch of dark red curls teased seductively.

She was beautiful, the personification of woman calling to everything that was male within him . . . and his response was instantaneous. His body vibrated with the kind of sexual arousal that had him gritting his teeth. Blood poured through his veins in a near-painful rush to collect thickly, demandingly, between his legs.

Slowly, deliberately, he lowered his hand and molded her breast to fit in his palm. Laurel flinched and dragged in a moaning breath. He raised his gaze to hers and saw astonishment and dismay and arousal.

The combination numbed her, rooting her in place while he caressed her as no man ever had. She couldn't think, couldn't move. Everything had taken on a dreamlike quality where reasoning was sacrificed to the pleasurable feel of his fingers slowly, insistently caressing her flesh.

Distant warnings and vague reprimands bounced around in her head. She didn't know this man, she shouldn't be allowing him this liberty. But his touch was an illicit magic, dark and enticing, overriding caution and beckoning to her spirit as if she were his alone.

Unfamiliar sensations of heat raced out from her breast, capturing her breath and making her knees go weak. And still, she couldn't drag her gaze from his, not then nor when he traced his hand over her ribs to her waist to settle on her hip.

"You're beautiful," he rasped.

She could have gone on forever, blossoming under his touch. The pleasure was that unexpected, that unique, that great. Had he not spoken, she might very well have surrendered to the need. But his voice, so low and deep, gave focus to her world again. Reality rushed back.

Swallowing hard, she stepped away, awkward now in the aftermath of such intimacy. A melange of emotions bombarded her from every direction, making it nearly impossible for her to know how to react, or what to feel. Thankfully, he let her go.

He didn't want to. He had been spellbound by the simple feel of her, captivated by her acceptance *and* her reticence. He could understand her feeling one or the other, but the two together were unusual. He wondered what it would take for her to give free rein to her passions. Or if she ever had.

Once again, he was struck by her contradictory nature. She was a puzzle of the highest order. And *nothing* challenged him like a puzzle that had to be solved.

"Here, put these on." He handed her a dress and a cape before he turned and strode into the other room.

She watched him go like one who was dazed, her body responding sluggishly to mental commands. He had told her to change clothes and all she could do was stand there and wonder what had come over her.

Shivering from cold and as a reaction to all that had happened, she finally shed her sodden garments. Once in dry clothing, she felt more like her usual self, although fatigue still clung with a tenacious hold that left her feeling unsettled. Cape in hand, she entered the front room of the shop, ridden by a vulnerability that had her ready to defend herself against the formidable man who looked at her with unnerving intensity.

She regarded him in equal measure. Tall, dark, as imposing in his ruined shirt and pants as he was in full uniform, he was unlike most men she had met. Both he and his actions were dominant and mysterious. In the quiet hush, she felt the full force of him and she trembled, the air between them becoming strangely charged.

She stared for a long while. "Why did you touch me the way you did?" she whispered, needing to know, yet fearing the answer.

"Why did you let me?"

"There didn't seem to be any way of stopping you."

"There wasn't."

One delicate red brow arched. "Do you make a habit of fondling every woman you meet?"

"Are you in the habit of letting any man hold your breast in his palm?"

"No!" Hearing him state it so bluntly was outrageously disconcerting. "I am more circumspect and discriminating than that."

"So am I."

Which meant what? That he only fondled those women who annoyed him? She scoffed and tossed the cape onto the side counter. "I'm sure the mamas of Charleston will be glad to hear that."

"Why so?"

She gave him a blandly wry look. "Your reputation has preceded you."

Tipping his head back, his eyes narrowed ever so slightly. "I wouldn't have thought you'd pay any attention to the rumormongers."

"I usually don't."

"But you did in this case."

"You have a, shall we say, noteworthy manner about you, sir."

"No more so than you." At her expression of inquiry, he lifted one black brow and grinned. "Your reputation has preceded you."

She knew she was considered something of an oddity. Normally it didn't bother her. Tucking a strand of hair behind her ear, she shoved aside the unsettling sensation of self-consciousness.

"I can well imagine what you heard: that I'm independent and opinionated and that as a woman, I don't know my place."

Folding his arms over his chest, he asked, "Do you?"

"Know my place? From a man's perspective, no." Unconsciously, she squared her shoulders in challenge. "But most men don't allow a woman to have a place other than in the kitchen or bedroom. Most don't credit a woman with having a brain."

"Some don't," he challenged back.

"I do."

"So I'm beginning to see. Is that why you don't have a husband?"

That question was delving into matters that were highly personal. Mentally, she threw up her hands. They had very definitely progressed beyond that. "I don't see what that has to do with anything?"

He advanced slowly, his eyes riveting in the murky light. "You don't think like most women. Your opinions are radical, to say the least. Most men would find that unacceptable in a potential wife."

"Perhaps. Then again, I find such narrowminded intolerance unacceptable in a potential husband."

Surprisingly, he burst into a short spate of laughter. "If you aren't the most contrary little termagant." At arm's length, he reached out and tucked another stray curl behind her ear. "You would definitely make life interesting."

His humor hinted at a purely male arrogance. Annoyed, she jerked her head away from his touch. "How generous of you," she quipped in high sarcasm. "I suppose my being 'interesting' makes me more suitable for marriage."

"I wouldn't know. Marriage is an institution to which I rarely give any credence."

Before she could think better, she asked, "Why not? I thought all men sought marriage."

"I'm not like all men. I've made the army my life."

"To the exclusion of having a wife?"

"I'm afraid so."

Laurel frowned at that. By his own admission, he had no desire to marry. This said a great deal about him, and even more about the position of all women in his life. He would use a woman for pleasure alone, but he would never go so far as to honor her with his name.

Suddenly, the advances he had made were offensive. She was embarrassed and angry to have so naively given of herself to a man who obviously thought no more of her than an "interesting termagant," someone who was good enough to fondle, but no more.

"It's time I returned home," she asserted, snatching up the short cape from the counter. She was feeling increasingly foolish as each moment passed. "I'd like my keys."

She congratulated herself on her poise. Not for a second would she let him know how deeply he had managed to disturb her. Collecting her dirty clothes and locking up the shop provided sufficient diversion from the unexpected ache centered around her heart.

"Are you all right?" he asked, the cool morning air saturated with the remnants of water and smoke.

"I'm tired, Major." She refused to look at him, refused to give in to the unexplainable hurt that filled her. "Good day."

She didn't even manage one step before he blocked her with his body. "What are you doing?"

"What does it look like? I'm going home."

"Alone?"

"I'll be fine."

"The hell you will." He looked about the courtyard. "Where is your livestock?"

"My what?"

"Your horse. And your carriage. Where are they?"

"I don't have either."

He stared at her in disbelief and mounting irritation. "You came here on foot, alone?"

His tone was as black as his scowl. Both severed what little restraint Laurel had remaining. Glaring up at him with eyes that betrayed the depth of her ire, she spat, "What I do is none of your concern, Major McKenzie."

"It's my business when you behave like a fool."

"You'd like to believe that for your own convenience." Her back straightened with every last bit of fortitude she possessed. "I will get home, Major, the same way I arrived here—the same way I accomplish everything in this life. Alone and by my own means."

With that, she stepped around him and made her way down the alley to the street. She ignored all and everything around her, intent on reaching home.

"Excuse me, miss," a voice came from behind.

She stopped and leveled an irate glare at the boyish-faced corporal. "Yes?"

He touched a finger to his hat. "Major McKenzie's compliments, ma'am, but I'm to see you safely home."

By will alone did she keep from giving into a scream of frustration. Pursing her lips, she spun and walked on, the corporal beside her. She'd never felt more lonely.

# *Four*

"Excuse me, Major, you've got a couple out here asking to speak with you."

At Corporal Ransom's interruption, Brett tossed aside the list of supplies he'd been scanning, grateful to be pulled from the tedious task. There were few things he disliked more than paperwork. Unfortunately, he had his share to wade through this Sunday afternoon.

Shoving his chair back from behind his desk, he asked, "What do they want, Corporal?"

With obvious doubt distorting his young features, Ransom replied, "Something about pirates and stolen goods, sir."

"Pirates?"

"Their words, sir, not mine."

"I can't help them with pirates, Corporal."

"Yes, sir, but since you're handling complaints about smuggling and theft, I figured they needed to speak to you."

Brett chewed on that for a moment. There was nothing he could do about cargos lost at sea. The army's function in the city was limited to civil and criminal disobedience within Charleston itself. What did this couple expect him to do, sprout rudder and sails and take to the ocean?

At the ill-tempered thought, Brett clamped down on his

annoyance, reminding himself that the army's presence was of a larger scope than simply maintaining order. Whoever wished to see him believed they had a legitimate complaint. They were entitled to be heard.

"Very well, Corporal, who are these people?"

"A Mr. and Mrs. Jackson, sir. And I have to tell you, they're fit to be hog-tied. He looks like he's about to bust a gut and she's doing her best not to give into a fit of tears. And all because of some silk, sir."

Brett's head snapped up, a feral tension rippling over his nerves. "Silk?"

"Yes, sir, stolen silk, or so they claim."

Propping one elbow on the chair's arm, Brett scrubbed at his chin, a humorless grin tugging at his mouth. "Show the Jacksons in, Corporal."

Brett came to his feet and paced the small confines of his bare-bones office. Silently he mused on a possible connection between pirates, stolen silk, and smuggling. Under normal circumstances, the relevance of one to the other was not even noteworthy enough to warrant conjecture. However, circumstances in this case were not normal, and mere speculation escalated to suspicion for one very important reason.

Laurel Seymore.

He'd spent an inordinate amount of time in the last few days thinking about her. Again and again, he pictured the slender beauty of her. He could still feel the utter softness of her breast: warm, vibrant, womanly. Her heart had beat a wild pulse against his fingers. The memory alone was enough to tauten his muscles. Damn, but she was beautiful.

Unbidden, the image of how he had found her came to mind. Sitting in the waning darkness, she had been so tired and emotionally spent that he had been stung by a fear and displeasure for her sake. Then and now, he would have preferred not to have felt anything at all. The resulting concern made him decidedly uncomfortable.

He wasn't a cad, but emotionally he kept his distance from the fairer sex. To enjoy the more secular joys found between an experienced, willing woman's thighs, to enjoy her casual, pleasant company and to provide her with the same was as involved as he chose to become.

Perhaps such a view was a bit hard about the edges, but as he'd intimated to Laurel, anything more than a casual liaison was not for him. A serious involvement with a woman would demand a certain degree of concern. Caring had a way of leading to stronger sentiments such as love, and there was no place in his life for love. Or marriage.

This was a philosophy of long standing with him, one he knew was based on defensive instincts that ran to the very core of him. Whether it was sensible or not, wise or not, contemptible or not, didn't matter. It was simply how he chose to be—and with very good reason.

He'd seen firsthand the heartache that came from a marriage where the husband was a soldier devoted to the army. He'd seen his mother's misery, witnessed the sorrow and anguish that came from knowing that no matter what, she'd always take a second place to her husband's commitment to his duty.

Brett could understand that sense of duty, and it had nothing to do with following in his father's footsteps as a soldier. By nature, he was fierce about all his convictions, giving completely of himself or nothing at all—no half-measures, no wavering or faltering.

His beliefs, his ideals, and his profession were all intertwined. He was committed to the need for a strong national militia. The army was his life and he didn't see how a marriage could survive that, how a wife could endure the kind of bitter heartache his mother had suffered. He would never ask that of a woman.

Irritated that he felt the need to remind himself of this, he took control of his thoughts. Picturing Laurel's slim, fragile beauty was more to his liking. It afforded him a harmless, detached pleasure that indulged his masculinity on its most basic level—aesthetic but uninvolved enjoyment. Remembering her temper only added to the satisfaction.

Where did she come by such fierce emotion? How did a woman walk around containing such fervor . . . and *what* did she do to release it? Other than lose her temper. Everything that was male within him settled on the single most appealing answer.

Independent, stubborn little termagant. He could think of a dozen things he'd like to tell her to do with all that headlong willfulness. Smiling, he thought of another dozen ways he would like to tame it.

He was still wearing that smile minutes later when the Jacksons were ushered in.

"Thank you for seeing us, Major," Mr. Jackson said, once he and his wife were seated.

"That's quite all right," Brett assured the graying pair. Leaning back against the front of his desk, he gave the husband and wife his most professional smile, curt, scant, direct. "Corporal Ransom informs me that you have experienced some difficulty with stolen cloth."

Mr. Jackson nodded insistently, his eyes behind his spectacles bulging with indisputable ire. "Not just any cloth, Major McKenzie, but silk."

"A silk I had specially designed and woven in London,"

Mrs. Jackson added, pressing a trembling hand to the layers of her chins.

"And it has been stolen?"

"Pirated, at sea," Mr. Jackson stated. "Three months ago."

Brett glanced down to the tips of his boots. "With all due respect, Mr. Jackson, madam, there is very little I or the army can do in cases such as this. If the fabric was taken at sea, it could be anywhere."

Mr. Jackson shifted his hat from one hand to the other, the cords of his neck straining into prominence. "But it isn't anywhere, Major. It's here, in Charleston, this very minute."

"How do you know?"

"Why, we just saw it, sir," Mrs. Jackson whined. "Not twenty minutes ago, we were strolling home from Sunday services and there it was, in the front window of Seymore's."

Brett suppressed the scoffing laugh that demanded release. Now why could he have guessed what Mrs. Jackson was going to say? Mentally, he shook the living daylights out of Laurel Seymore. "How do you know this is the same cloth?"

"Oh, it is," Mr. Jackson asserted.

"You're positive?"

"Yes. The pattern was taken from my mother's bridal gown. I sent all the way to England to have it made up, paid for its shipment home in advance. I was plenty angry when we were told the ship carrying my cloth, the *Atlanta Star,* had been attacked by pirates."

"How can you be certain that your cloth was actually on that ship? It is possible that it was never sent, or it was mistakenly transported elsewhere."

Jackson jabbed at the bridge of his glasses with one finger. "The ship's captain confirmed the shipment, and I have a bill of lading at home to prove it."

"And you're sure that pirates were involved."

"What do you call robbery at sea, Major? I call it pirating. Besides, everyone knows that Jack Diego is a devil of the seas."

Brett carefully kept his face void of expression. "Jack Diego was responsible?"

"Yes, sir, according to the captain of the *Atlanta Star*. Sad state of affairs, but I was forced to let it go at that. Until today, I assumed I had no recourse, that the silk was gone for good. But like Mrs. Jackson says, the fabric is right there in the front window of Seymore's. I'd like to know how it got there and what the devil Laurel Seymore is doing with it."

Brett damn well wanted to know, too. "I have no way of knowing that, sir, but I will look into the matter at once."

"I'd appreciate that, Major."

After taking a description of the silk and making note of the Jacksons' address, Brett saw the couple on their way. Then, eyes shining with an unholy light, he donned his hat, strapped on his sword, and strode from his office.

Laurel wrapped a loaf of bread in a clean bit of muslin toweling and added the bundle to the growing collection of food stuffs in her basket. Standing in the tiny kitchen just behind her house, a small smile of gratification flirted with her lips as she reached for another warm loaf.

Stuffing the wicker hamper was something she did every Sunday afternoon. The process was satisfying for its very simplicity. Unpretentious scents of honey and yeast, of molasses and ham and nutmeg; they were aromas that brought to mind the safe haven of home, of the security to be found at a family's kitchen hearth.

However, even more pleasing than all of that was the sense of contentment she derived from knowing her charitable act would benefit so many. The food she gathered each Sunday helped feed the orphans of the city. The good sisters of St. Mary's saw to that. They did their best to relieve the suffering of those who were most helpless.

Being helpless was something Laurel understood. It was a feeling that had been wrought by the death of her parents and to this day made her insides shrivel with dread. To be so powerless meant to be at the mercy of others. Your fate was not your own.

Not knowing if there would be food to eat or a roof over your head was an unhealthy condition in which to live. She wouldn't wish that on anyone, certainly not innocent children. If her simple offering of food could alleviate even a small portion of their plight, then she was happy.

"Miss Laurel," Tess said from the doorway.

Laurel peered over her shoulder.

"You got company at the front gate, Miss Laurel."

"Oh?" Cocking her head to one side, she silently asked who it was.

"A soldier. Major McKenzie."

Laurel's contentment evaporated instantly. In the process of folding a linen napkin over a cheese round, her hands stilled.

"What does he want?"

"To talk to you. I imagine that why he ask for you."

Laurel didn't want to talk to him. She didn't want to look at him let alone be in the same room with him. "Tell the major that I am not receiving callers this afternoon."

Tess's mouth quirked to one side. "If that what you want."

"It is." And she didn't care what he or Tess might think. No explanations were owed anyone, least of all a servant who gave her a parting look of serious doubt or an army major who had caused her to lose too many nights of sleep. *The beast.*

She had resolved none of the tumultuous emotions left over from their last meeting. Meeting? Ha! Debacle more accurately described it. Every time she thought about the entire scene, she wanted to shrink into herself in mortification.

As carefully as her mounting ire would allow, she continued to pack the last of the food into the basket, willing herself to a calm that seemed beyond her. All because she couldn't shake the memory of Brett McKenzie's warm, hard hand on her breast.

The region surrounding her stomach flipped uneasily. No man had ever touched her that way. And the beast had definitely touched . . . while she had done nothing to stop him. Her only excuse was that she had been wearied to the bone, and modesty had been the last thing on her mind. So he had caressed her like a lover *and* looked his fill, the silver of his eyes taking on a hungry cast that even now caused her throat to tighten.

Every sensation she had experienced then rose up swiftly now. The pleasure, the headiness, the unbelievable awareness of him and herself. He'd tempted her with a taste of passion, then ruined that bliss. His sentiments on women all but relegated her to the status of a whore and she resented that greatly.

In defense against the surge of punishing emotions, she

clenched her eyes shut and dropped her head to the top of her basket.

"Are you suffering some ill effect from your battle with the fire, or is this a new manner of offering up prayer?"

The voice. The beast's voice. She jerked upright and spun around. Major McKenzie stood as an imposing silhouette in the open doorway.

"Go away."

He gave her a one-sided grin. "I can see that your spirit is fully recovered. But you didn't answer my question."

"Nor do I plan to. In fact, I have nothing to say to you at all. Tess should have told you that I am not receiving today."

"She told me."

His temerity was galling. "Then what are you doing here?"

He sauntered into the kitchen as if he had every right to do so, his body appearing too large for the tight space. "What is all of this?" He gestured to the basket.

Barley keeping her ire in check, Laurel snapped the lid shut on the hamper. "It's none of your business."

Her gesture earned her a taunting smile beneath piercing eyes. "Your temper is showing, Miss Seymore."

She didn't need to be reminded, but he had a way of sapping her composure. And he knew it, too, from the look of him.

Gathering her restraint, she dug deep for patience. "I wouldn't have a temper, sir, if you didn't insist on behaving in so rude a manner. You are not welcome here, I have told you to go away. You cannot blame me if I react as any sane woman would."

To her surprise, he threw back his head and laughed.

"Bravo, madam, bravo. Tell me, have you always been this outspoken?"

A score of disreputable replies tumbled one on top of another in her head, each aching to be unleashed. But to do so would only give the man more fuel to feed a fire that he in turn would use on her.

"What do you want, Major McKenzie?" she asked, hoping to get to the heart of the matter. The sooner she did that, the sooner he would be on his way, and she could be on hers.

He propped one hip on the edge of the worktable, one leg stretched out to brace his weight, the other bent at the knee. He appeared to be a man totally and completely at ease.

She didn't trust him for a second.

Leaning forward, he countered, "Why must I want something?"

"You're here." She lifted her hands to indicate the obvious and found her right wrist suddenly caught and held in his much larger, stronger grip.

"That's a nasty cut," he said, studying the injury she'd received while battling the fire.

His move was so unexpected that she stared rather stupidly at their clasped hands for a full count of five. It was five seconds too long. It was time enough for her fingers to absorb the heat of him and for her mind to relish the sensation.

Furious with herself, she tried to yank her hand free. "Let go."

Mouth thinned, he replied by retaining his hold and tracing a path from her little finger to her wrist. "Does it pain you?"

"Only when I'm forced to talk about it."

His brows shot up over eyes glittering with reluctant humor. Some of that humor actually reached his mouth. "Then by all means, let us not discuss it. I would hate to have this visit spoiled in any way."

Thankfully, he let her go and she had to physically restrain herself from giving in to the impulse to tuck her hand behind her back. "Precisely what kind of a visit is this?"

"It could be social."

"It isn't."

"How do you know?"

"Because the term implies that a genial attitude exists. The closest you and I can come to that is tolerance." Folding her arms beneath her breasts, she goaded, "Now, Major, would you please be about your business. I am expected elsewhere."

"With this?" He shot the basket a glance.

She sighed. They had traversed a perverse little circle and were back to exactly where they had begun. And if she didn't miss her guess, they were not going to make progress of any kind unless she allowed him to direct the conversation as he saw fit. Narrowing her eyes, she glared her displeasure at him.

"If you must know, this is food for the orphans. Charleston has a considerable number of children who have been left in frightful circumstances. There are several organizations and groups that offer what assistance they can."

"By collecting food."

"And distributing it as needed."

Brett McKenzie's gaze dropped to the basket again. For several moments he remained quiet. "This is a very noble gesture on your part."

The compliment was completely unexpected, and unwanted. She did not desire praise from this man. Neither did she want his condemnation. All she wanted was to be left alone, free of his disturbing presence.

Crossing the room with a basket of apples, she scoffed, "There is nothing noble about what I do. We all have a moral obligation to those who are needy."

"True, but not everyone takes that obligation seriously."

"Well, I do."

"Why?"

His inquiry was absurd and she gave him a look that said as much. "Because it is the right thing to do."

"Do you always do what's right?"

"I try."

"Do you succeed?"

"Hopefully."

"What if you don't?"

"I can at least go to bed at night knowing in my heart that I did not shirk my responsibilities, that I was true to certain principles that I hold dear."

She finished a bit breathlessly, the intensity of her beliefs adding a flash to her eyes. She was left to wonder what he thought of her demi-tirade. Nothing good, to be sure, and a search of his face offered her nothing except the harsh beauty of his features.

In truth, they were disarmingly distracting. The molding of his lips and the chiseled planes of his cheeks were bold reminders of his indomitable masculinity. The uncompromising edge of his jaw only added to the aura of power that clung to him. Taken as a whole, the face, with its silvery-blue eyes, was the perfect counterpart to the rest of him.

Which, she reminded herself irritably, she had no business even thinking about. The man was the proverbial thorn in her side, here today for heaven only knew what reason.

In the silence that grew, she waited for him to give her some hint as to the purpose of his call. None came. Instead, she realized that in the expanding hush, the atmosphere was filled with an unexpected and sudden intimacy.

Quietly, his voice a rasping murmur, he ventured, "You take your responsibilities very seriously, don't you?"

"Yes." The single word emerged as a whisper, restrained by the warmth in his eyes.

"That's why you helped put out the fire the other night."

"The merchants on that block had much to lose. I couldn't have lived with myself if I hadn't done all I could to help. And, too, there is the dress shop. There are those of us who depend on it for our livelihood. I had to prevent its destruction."

"You honestly think the efforts of one lovely woman made a difference?"

*Lovely.* Oh, stars and garters, the beast had called her lovely. Somewhere in her lungs, the air got stuck. "Yes," she averred, mentally scrambling to recall what he had asked, mentally scrambling to remember that she wanted him gone. "One person . . . one person's effort is never wasted. Sometimes it can make all the difference in the world."

"So you don't believe in lost causes."

"No, I don't. We should never give up, any more than we should turn our backs on evil or injustice. Others might find it convenient to do so, but I can't ignore right and wrong."

What was right and what was wrong just then was a mystery to Laurel. Part of her wanted to stand and ogle the man like a smitten, mindless idiot. Was that wrong?

She didn't know. She'd never had the desire to do anything even remotely as outrageous. And yet, women she knew did much the same thing, and more, on a daily basis. But did that make it right?

Without warning, he stood to his full height, shattering the intimate ambiance that had existed, startling Laurel into taking a hasty step back. Her gaze watchful, she shook off her languid reverie, and mentally berated herself for giving in to such foolishness.

"Major McKenzie, I must ask you to leave now," she announced briskly. "You have detained me past all reasonable time."

"My apologizes, Miss Seymore." He gave a short, smart bow. When he straightened, he wore an equally abbreviated smile. "You have been more than gracious, taking a few moments to speak to me. I will try not to usurp more of your afternoon, but I do have one more thing I'd like to ask."

"And what is that, sir?"

"What do you know of Jack Diego?"

# *Five*

"Jack who?" Laurel replied, her gaze steady, one red eyebrow arched in puzzlement.

"Diego." Brett pronounced the name with special care, taking just as much interest in watching for Laurel's reactions. "Jack Diego."

Laurel whispered the name several times, her face finally brightening when she obviously recalled the significance of the name. "Oh, yes, he's that pirate I've heard about."

"Then you know who he is?"

"Of course." She shrugged delicately and spread her hands wide. "Just about everyone does, I suppose. His name comes up in the shop from time to time."

"In what context?"

"In regard to every notorious, unlawful act that one can possibly imagine." Surprisingly, she ended her description with a trill of laughter.

Brett tipped his head forward ever so slightly. "Something amuses you, Miss Seymore?"

"Yes," she chuckled, waving her laugh aside. "Please, excuse me, but some nonsense has a way of being humorous."

"You think Jack Diego is a bit of nonsense?"

"Of course. The man is nothing but the product of unoccupied minds."

"Some people disagree with you."

She rolled her eyes as she picked up the basket by its handle and hoisted its bulky weight from the table. "Some people believe in fairy tales."

His moves quick and deft, Brett relieved Laurel of her burden. In the process he earned himself an exasperated glare.

"I can carry that, Major."

"Of that I have no doubt." But he had no intention of relinquishing the basket. Women were not meant to bear the strain of physical exertions, especially in the company of a gentleman. He would carry the damn basket.

*And* if the testy Miss Seymore thought she could simply pick up her hamper and traipse off, she could just think again. She wasn't going anywhere until he was finished with her. There were questions he wanted answered, and so far she had satisfied his curiosity on only one point: her reaction to the scene in the dress shop after the fire.

She was still in a pique about the whole thing. That pleased him, for it showed that she had been thinking about their shared intimacy as much as he had. Short-lived as it had been, he couldn't remember an interlude that had been half as arousing. He suspected that she felt the same and in defense, her reaction was to dismiss him.

He silently scoffed at the notion of Miss Laurel Seymore dismissing him. Did she honestly think she could order him away? Apparently so—which left him wondering about her state of mind.

He couldn't go so far as to refer to her as an absurd little woman because he was frankly amazed and perplexed by her reasoning processes. First in rationalizing her assistance with the fire and now again with helping the needy, she displayed an amazing level of honor and integrity. In his experience, both were quite rare in the female of the species.

She was an unusual woman. He admitted that her sense of responsibility and dedication were admirable, but he detected in her a recklessness as bold as the crimson of her hair.

He scanned the slender length of her in her dark green dress—she seemed to favor the color. Its demure white lace collar gave the impression of modest equanimity. It wasn't a trait he would associate with the lady, especially after seeing the flare of passion that had glimmered in her eyes when he had trailed his fingers over her softness. Scarlet and black would better suit her, contrasts that lent themselves to a tempestuous, independent manner.

Basket in hand, he stepped from the kitchen, knowing that the tempestuous, independent young woman would follow. He didn't have long to wait. Laurel emerged from the kitchen in a flurry of activity, delicate hands shrugging her shawl about her shoulders as she hastened to catch up to him.

"What do you think you're doing?" she demanded.

"You are in a hurry to deliver these goods, and we are not done with our discussion." Raising his hand to her elbow, he urged, "Come, I'll escort you and we'll finish talking at the same time."

"You will not escort me," she asserted, yanking her arm from his grasp. A hint of irate color began to stain her cheeks. "I thought I made myself clear about having your company this afternoon. Really, Major, I don't know how much more blunt I can be. You force me to be plainly rude."

Folding her arms beneath her breasts, she tilted her head back to stare him straight in the eye with emerald ire flashing. "I wish you to leave me alone. With my basket. To be on my way. I wish you to mount your horse and be gone."

Brett had known audacity in his life, but nothing could compare to the insolence of this one small woman. For a full ten seconds, he gazed down at her, once again amazed that she was free to walk about. By rights, her kind of boldness should have landed her in someone's custody years ago.

And then another two seconds ticked past and his tolerance for her impertinent behavior dissipated entirely. He had played her game as any self-respecting man would, allowing her a measure of dignity. Damnably, it had been at his expense, his courtesy meeting with her so-called bluntness.

Very well. If it was rude, straightforward *bluntness* she wanted, so be it.

He set the basket down with deceptive care, never once releasing her gaze. His left hand came to rest on his sword's hilt, the line of his jaw hardened. If there had been any trace of humor or generosity in his misty blue eyes, it was gone, replaced now with icy conviction.

"Your name has been linked with that of Jack Diego, Miss Seymore. Not once, but several times, and from different sources. You claim you have no knowledge of the man other than common street gossip, and yet you have in your shop this moment the very same goods that have been reported stolen by this pirate."

He stepped closer, using his height to an intimidating advantage. She was forced to tip her head back to an uncomfortable degree. "What do you have to say for yourself, Miss Seymore?"

"Nothing," came her instant reply.

"Nothing? This coming from a woman who gives the word loquacious new meaning? Don't play coy with me, madam. I know you, too well."

"You don't know me at all," she retorted, her jaw as inflexible as his.

"There is a bolt of blue silk in your shop window. Where did you come by it?"

"Is this an inquisition?"

A nasty smile pulled at his mouth. Softly, his tone precise, he promised, "It can be. If you prefer, we can continue this chat in my office or in one of the prison cells at the Citadel. The choice is yours."

With a certain amount of satisfaction, Brett watched Laurel struggle with the intensity of her emotions. She was furious and it showed from the stain on her cheeks to the heaving of her chest. He waged a quick bet with himself as to how long it would take her to come to the conclusion that she was powerless.

She surprised him by relenting sooner than he had anticipated.

"What do you want to know about the silk?" she asked, every bit of her resentment still very much in evidence in her voice.

"First of all, where did you come by it?"

"From a merchant who came through the city last month."

"What's his name?"

"St. James."

"Is it usual for you to buy your fabrics from him?"

For some reason that tickled her. "No, it is very *unusual.*

I normally send to London or France or New York for the more exotic materials we use."

"Then why did you make an exception this time?"

"The silk is quite extraordinary."

"It is also stolen."

"How do you know?"

"I have it on good authority that the piece was stolen by Jack Diego."

One of her shoulders rose. "It might very well have been, but I didn't know that when I purchased it, Major. I bartered in good faith."

"You were deceived."

She scoffed and sent the nearby bush a punishing glance. "I have no control over the fate of a bolt of linen or a spool of thread before it reaches my shop. I make my purchases and trust that I am being dealt with fairly and honestly, but for all I know, the Parisian velvet I sewed up for the mayor's wife last week might have originally been intended for some potentate's mistress. Does that make me guilty of a crime, or responsible for corrupting an innocent woman? Does that make the gown any less beautiful than it is? All I know is that the velvet was delivered, I paid for it, and I used it."

"Perhaps in the future, you might want to be more discerning in your choice of suppliers."

"With you spying in my front window, I don't think I'll have much choice."

It was wise of her to realize that. He would be keeping his eyes on her. "What more can you tell me about this merchant?"

"Very little. I have seen him upon occasion, but this was the first time I actually made a purchase from him."

"How often does he come into town?"

"I do not keep track of his comings and goings."

"Does anyone else know him?"

"I can not speak for others, Major."

She was saying damn little. Brett had the impulse to grab her up by the shoulders and shake her until he had some straight answers from her. He couldn't say why, but his instincts warned that while she might have been telling him the truth, it was her own version of the truth.

His opinion of her altered once again. With each passing moment, more and more intricately subtle facets of the young woman were revealed. He could now add clever and shrewd to the growing list of traits that defined Laurel Seymore. The question was, where did those stand in relative importance to her honesty or her devotion?

Taking in his surroundings, he looked to her house for clues or answers. The simple white structure was similar to a hundred other *single houses* just like it in Charleston. The gable end faced the street which placed the double piazzas overlooking the fenced-in courtyard. Shrubs bordered a neat and tidy walkway that linked the house to its dependencies.

All in all, her home looked comfortable and relatively uncomplicated. It hinted at nothing even remotely resembling the lady. And from what he could see, it showed no signs of extravagant wealth. The house was that of someone earning a modest income, not someone embroiled in the lucrative business of smuggling.

"What do the gossips have to say about Jack Diego?"

Laurel's mouth puckered at the query. "Nothing good."

"Be specific."

She sighed in heavy annoyance. "He has the same reputation as any pirate, I would imagine. Some claim he is a scoundrel, others insist he is a self-made man, making his way in life by his own merits."

"Do you believe he is a scoundrel?"

"I've never given him enough thought to warrant an opinion one way or another. And even if I did, what I think of him doesn't matter a whit."

"Oh, but you're wrong, Miss Seymore. Your opinion of the man could matter a great deal . . . if you were sympathetic to his cause."

His inference hit home with devastating results. Laurel whirled away only to spin back and face him, her shoulders and spine marked by the kind of insulted rage that knew no bounds.

"You think I'm trading in stolen goods, don't you? You think I make a profit at someone else's expense." She gripped the ends of her shawl with shaking hands and ground out, "You arrogant son of Satan, I would never do anything so dishonest and I don't care how many people assume differently. I have never accepted anything that I didn't earn, I have never cheated my customers, and I have never . . . let me repeat that, *Major,* never *knowingly* sold so much as a button that could have been smuggled in by this Jack Diego."

She stabbed him with an icy glare. "Now, are you done insulting me or do you intend to besmirch my dignity as thoroughly as you have my honor?" She didn't wait for his reply. Instead, she snatched up the basket. "I will have the entire bolt of silk sent over to your office, Major. It will be my loss, but I will consider this entire episode finished." With that, she swept out of the courtyard.

* * *

Pearly mists swirled across the moonless sky. Murky clouds rolled in off the rivers. Solid forms appeared misshapen, colors were neutralized to lifeless grays. Cold seeped up from the ground and pierced the soles of Laurel's shoes.

Her black cloak pulled snugly about her, she crept silently through the city, head tucked low beneath her hood. Alleys and paths she knew to be harmless by day loomed sinister in the ebony stillness that shrouded her path.

Night sounds came out of the darkness: the howling of a dog, the skittering of rats, the muted beat of a voodoo drum. She paid them little heed, listening instead for more immediate noises: a whispered word, a raucous laugh, the shuffle of feet following her.

Tucking her hand into her pocket, she gripped the handle of her small pistol and felt a measure of comfort. If she questioned the wisdom of her actions, it was only for a short, nervous moment. She knew that at the heart of her purpose lay a truth that transcended danger or foolishness. That truth guided her steps until she reached the entrance to Seymore's.

Only then did she stop. She cast furtive glances in all directions, then hastened down the alley to the yard behind. As quietly as possible, holding her breath for good measure, she unlocked the door leading to the shop's basement and slipped inside.

In the several seconds it took for her eyes to adjust themselves to the low light coming from below, she waited on the narrow landing above the stairs. She used the time to collect her composure and every ounce of her courage.

She'd never before considered herself possessed of an extraordinary amount of courage. She had always done what needed to be done. In that she saw nothing unusual, certainly nothing denoting bravery. But tonight, with Major McKenzie's accusations roiling through her veins, she wondered for the first time just how much inner fortitude she did have.

Enough to descend the stairs?

She squared her shoulders, her course of action a foregone conclusion. She could no more walk away from her chosen path than she could ignore the man who waited below. The two were irrevocably intertwined.

"Laurel love."

His voice came to her just as she reached the compressed dirt floor. She spotted him a moment later, lounging indolently across several bales that hadn't been there that morning, feet propped up on a vat she had never seen before. Such cool nonchalance was his style.

"I've told you not to call me that," she said, her voice low, steady.

He spread his hands wide and gave a smile of sheer devilry. "Ah, is that any way to greet me?" His booted feet landed heavily on the floor with a muffled thud. "It's been more weeks than I care to count. Didn't you miss me at all?"

She knew his chicanery for what it was. "I have enough to contend with without having to put up with your teasing." She studied the array of goods that filled half the basement. "I see you got everything moved in."

"But of course. Did you expect anything different?"

"What I expect is for you to have it all moved out by the end of the week."

"That is our usual practice," he drawled, "but I could be tempted to speed things up if you made it worth my while."

By the light of the single lantern he had lit, she regarded

the indulgent expression that added charm to his already handsome face. A dimple dented one lean cheek and the bold slash of his dark umber mustache emphasized the width of his grin. His eyes, usually sparkling whiskey in color, were softened to a velvet brown.

"Nothing ever changes with you, John. You don't take much in life seriously."

Standing, John shrugged with his brows. "And you, Laurel love, take everything in life far too seriously." Sauntering toward her, he cocked his head to one side, his grin stretching. "Our last run was good, I'm here in one piece, what more could I want in life . . . except perhaps a kiss from you?"

It was always the same with him. So cocksure, so self-absorbed. "I hate to spoil your fun," she began, brushing past him, "but my week has been especially bad."

"What problems could you possibly have? A frayed seam, an overzealous suitor?" His grin became a full smile. "Don't tell me your sister has finally discovered what we've been up to?"

"No, she hasn't." For that, Laurel was grateful. Hope, in her naiveté, had never thought to question the goings on in the cellar, if she was even aware of them. To Laurel's knowledge, her sister never ventured down the stairs, had never even thought to do so.

"If you don't already know, the United States Army has moved into Charleston."

"Ah, I see. That could make things a bit sticky for you."

"It already has. I only wish I could say it was all your fault."

"Why the deuce would you want to do that?" he asked, looking wounded to the extreme.

"To make me feel better." She pressed her fingers into

her temples, knowing her complaint served no purpose other than to relieve her tension. She needed to concentrate on what was truly important. "I may be in trouble."

"Why?"

She arched a red brow his way. "A certain major in the army knows that the bolt of blue silk I bought from you was stolen." She wasn't the type to wring her hands, but she laced her fingers together and squeezed hard. "I knew I shouldn't have bought that fabric. I knew I should have kept our bargain as it always has been in the past."

John closed the space between them. "Who is this major?"

"McKenzie."

"How did he find out?"

"I don't know, but he was dead certain, and he accused me of conspiring with Jack Diego."

"That rascal?" John teased.

"Don't joke about this."

Turning on his heel, he mused, "Should I run this McKenzie through for you?"

"No!"

"That would solve your problems."

She grabbed hold of his arm and managed to plant herself in front of him. "John St. James, I will not have you killing anyone on my account. Do you hear me? I won't! If you so much as get near him, I'll go to the authorities myself and tell them everything."

It was not an idle threat. John could see as much.

In the blink of an eye, his insouciant air dissipated. In its place came a cruelty made all the more severe for its sudden upsurge.

"You forget yourself, Laurel."

The change in him would have frightened Laurel if she

hadn't already known that beneath his mocking facade lay a chilling ruthlessness. Past experience had taught her that. And she had learned to meet his savagery with a grim callousness of her own, or else she would be lost.

"I forget nothing," she grated, each word backed by an unshakable resolve.

"I won't tolerate your whining like a spoiled babe because this McKenzie is asking questions."

"And I won't tolerate threats to his life. You and I have an agreement. You use my basement to store your wares. In return, you pay me in gold. I made a terrible mistake in breaking my own rules, in buying *anything* from you, but it was my mistake. I will not have anyone else suffering the consequences."

She finished on a savage note, eyes blazing with honest intent. For endless seconds, she waited for his response.

He threw back his head and burst into gusts of laughter, all strain and unpleasantness between them dying a quick death. Setting his hands on his trim waist, he looked down at her.

"Ah, Laurel love, you are magnificent. Are you sure you don't want to shed this life you have and come with me?"

Not for a moment did she consider his suggestion. But it was reassuring to realize that he was going to be reasonable. For that she was grateful. John St. James could be extremely unreasonable when he chose.

"I have responsibilities, John. You know that."

"I know that you consider it your duty to conquer the world on your own."

She shrugged one shoulder, letting his criticism slide. "To each his own."

"Ah, Laurel love, what am I going to do with you?"

"Not a damn thing. And don't call me that."

His good mood completely restored, John scooped her hands into his. "I will the very same day you refer to me as everyone else does."

"I call you by your real name. John St. James. It isn't my fault you've rebaptized yourself in the Spanish translation."

"But it sounds so much more romantic, don't you think?"

"Whenever possible, I don't think about you at all."

"You wound me, Laurel love."

"You are a fool, Jack Diego."

# Six

"When did you start to lying?" Tess asked.

Laurel choked on the rich dark coffee she had been about to swallow and coughed out her amazement. Setting her cup down on the dining table, she grabbed up her napkin and gave Tess a pained look.

"Why on earth would you ask such a thing?"

"Because I heard you talk to that major from the army yesterday."

"I didn't lie to him."

Tess's eyes narrowed slightly. "You didn't tell him what all the truth, either."

Laurel sat back in her chair and sniffed in annoyance. "What exactly did I lie about?"

"You said you didn't know Jack Diego."

"I don't. He may refer to himself by that theatrical name, but I don't. His real name is John St. James. I have never thought of him as anything else regardless of how he styles himself."

"You play with words."

"That's not the same as lying."

"But you stretch the truth. You knew the silk was stolen."

Laurel took real offense to this. "I most certainly did not. John never told me where the fabric came from."

"And you never asked?"

"That's right," Laurel vowed a little fiercely. "I make it a point never to ask . . . about anything. I don't want to know what he does. It's enough that he and I have our arrangement."

Tess slumped into her chair and shook her head. "It's a dangerous game you play."

Laurel didn't need to be reminded of the seriousness of her actions. From the very first moment John sauntered into the shop two years ago, weaving grand tales of sailing the coast as a merchant, she'd been at risk of grave peril.

The passage of time had born that out, but in the beginning, when she'd hardly known the man, she hadn't been aware of the extent of the danger John presented. On those occasions when he'd come into town and stop by the shop to see her, she'd believed it had been for romantic purposes. The conclusion had been logical. John did have a way about him and he was certainly handsome enough.

But she'd never considered him as a possible suitor. She'd detected his innate ruthlessness at once, and that, coupled with his humorously dispassionate air, had stemmed any personal interest on her part. Thankfully, he'd accepted that, and beyond an initial bout of flirtation, had never pressed her for more. And yet, every four or five weeks, he'd returned, smiled his dimpled smile, and paid his respects.

The question of why he would even bother had been a riddle back then. She'd found it odd that any man would go to the trouble of visiting for no real purpose. Suspicions had begun to fester within her, but she had appeased her misgivings by thinking that John was simply in need of a friendly face.

What he had needed was a safe location to store his

cargo. What better spot than in the center of town, in the cellar of one of Charleston's most circumspect shops. It was the very last place anyone would think to look.

In retrospect, Laurel still marveled over how readily she'd agreed to his plan, despite how suspicious she'd become of him. But the shop's cellar had stood empty, and the promise of the kind of money he offered had been too tempting to turn down, even when she discovered his alternate identity.

Jack Diego. He was a dangerous man, his uncertain temperament shrouded by an infamous reputation that at times made her shiver. If she let her defenses down, the fear she lived with constantly would rise up and suffocate her.

By day the dread could seep into her consciousness. By night it would claw at her dreams. Only by sheer determination had she learned to control the fear. It was normally tamed to a peripheral tension.

She wouldn't change things for a second, though. She couldn't. The money she earned from hiding John's wares was needed.

"It's not a game, Tess." Sobered by the facts, she stared hard across the table. "You more than anyone should realize that."

"I know," Tess whispered, her voice as thick as the resolve in Laurel's eyes. "But that won't make no difference to McKenzie."

"Let him think what he wants," Laurel whispered back.

"What you going to tell him if he finds out?"

"Hopefully, he won't, but I didn't lie to him. I don't trade in stolen goods and I have never used the money John pays me for my own gain."

"I know, but fact is fact. You helping a criminal."

"What would you have me do?"

"Stop."

"People depend on me.

"Help some other way.

"How?"

"I don't know, but you won't be no good to no one if you land in prison."

A mellow light softened the brittle green of Laurel's eyes. "If I stop, I won't be any good to myself."

For a long moment, Tess stared back, saying nothing, her gaze sad and telling. "I pray to God that He watch over you."

The prayer struck Laurel straight in her heart. Her throat closed up with emotion. She was so used to caring for others that it never failed to touch her when someone so obviously cared in return.

"I'm sure He does, Tess."

From the doorway, Hope asked, "Who does what?"

Laurel looked to her sister, glad for the interruption. So solemn a discussion was not how she would have started her day. Giving Hope her brightest smile, she said, "God watches over me."

Hope slid into her chair, her gaze earnest. "I'm certain that He does."

"See," Laurel chuckled to Tess. "I'm as good as protected."

"God always watches out for us wherever we are," Hope expounded. As she reached for the platter of eggs, she added, "Only I just wish the good Lord looked out for you right here at home, Laurel. I wish you didn't have to leave again."

"I'll only be gone a few days."

"I hate it when you go away.

"Tess will be here."

Over her shoulder, Hope glanced at Laurel's valise sitting in the foyer by the front door. "Why do you have to go all that way?"

Laurel sent a quick intense look to Tess, but the smile she offered her sister was patient serenity itself. "It's not that far—only to Savannah. And we've been through this before."

"I know."

Still, it never changed. No matter how many times she explained her reasons for leaving, Laurel was always faced with her sister's fears.

Reaching for Hope's hand, she said, "Muslin doesn't walk through the front door of the shop on its own. You know that I have to travel sometimes to purchase our fabrics."

Hope nibbled on the inside of her lip.

"You'll be all right, Hope. I promise."

"And busy, too," Tess coaxed. "We got that order for seven new dresses to tend to."

"And don't forget Mrs. Casidy. She's due in today for a fitting and she absolutely insists that you help her."

A hesitant smile came to Hope's face, her spirit obviously bolstered by the encouragement. "I shouldn't be so silly about this."

"You're not being silly," Laurel said. Although she didn't understand the reasons or the origins for Hope's insecurities, she knew they were very real nonetheless.

Laurel would do nothing to disparage those feelings, and yet in good conscience, she tried her best not to nurture them, either. It would be very easy to pity Hope, and in so doing, sap what little strength she claimed as her own. That was the last thing Hope needed.

Gazing at her older sister, Laurel saw through the impossible loveliness to capabilities and potentials that Hope didn't know she possessed. But they were there, and even emerged from time to time. When someone remarked unfavorably on the reputation of Seymore's, or when Hope suspected that she was being duped, then she would come to life with a brief flare of fire. It didn't happen often, but the fact that it did reassured Laurel that her sister was not to be pitied.

Hope could be a strong woman in her own right. If she needed a bit of direction, so be it. If she was shy and reticent, there was no fault in that. Laurel didn't love her any less.

"Let's not worry over this any longer. I'll be back before you know it."

"You promise?"

"I promise. Now, let's have a pleasant breakfast. You have a shop to open and I have a ship to catch."

*You arrogant son of Satan.*

Laurel's remembered words skipped through Brett's mind as he stared at himself in the mirror. Razor in hand, he had to concentrate on keeping his face still. He wasn't about to cut himself all for the sake of a smile.

The woman definitely had a temper. He hated to fall back on old adages, but what they said about redheads was apparently true. They, or at least this one, had a spirit to match the fire in their hair.

Pity she couldn't use some of that vitality to keep herself out of trouble. He was still not convinced that she was not embroiled in smuggling, and he didn't give a damn how much she protested otherwise. She might have done an admirable job of talking her way out of trouble yesterday, but nothing she had said had proven to him that she was as innocent as she claimed.

Her answers had been too glib, her poise too practiced. His gut instinct warned him that both had been skillfully wielded to conceal something. The question was what? Was she involved with Diego or was she operating on her own? He didn't have the answers now, but he would soon. For the right amount of money, people would be more than willing to talk about anything, Diego included. Brett had his informants, and one way or another, he'd discover what there was to discover about Miss Laurel Seymore.

The little termagant. He scoffed as he washed the last of the soap from his face and vowed that she would see the error of her ways if she thought to play him false.

He straightened abruptly, ignoring the drops of water that trickled down into the hair on his chest. Picturing Laurel Seymore in prison was like a kick to the gut.

His reaction unsettled him, to the point that he consciously searched for a reason for feeling the way he did. He came up with the most obvious.

She was a woman.

He pondered that rationale for a bit and found it ample justification for his puzzling concern for Laurel. It was not in his nature to want to harm a woman. That was why he didn't want to think of her as just another lawbreaker who had to be dealt with. That was why the notion of her having to face the consequences chilled his insides.

It wasn't because she had impressed him with her sense of honor and compassion. Nor was it because they had stood in the darkness together, and she had shared a small portion of her body with him. He was troubled for her sake because he was a man and it was in a man's basic disposition to protect a woman.

Thinking that out made him feel a hell of a lot better. Once again his personal universe was back on it normal course. He could go about his duty to God and country as he always had, with a firm understanding of his behavior, especially as it pertained to Laurel Seymore.

As a man he responded to Laurel. But he was first and foremost a soldier.

That was all there was to it.

Period.

As he dressed for the day, he felt renewed by the reminder of his purpose in Charleston. It was his job to keep the law. That meant ferreting out those who would do otherwise and seeing that they were brought to justice, regardless of whether that person was a man or a woman. Regardless of how he personally felt about the matter.

Hadn't he learned at his father's knee that a soldier's personal feelings didn't matter?

*And didn't Mother resent that? Didn't I?*

Waiting near the stables for his horse to be brought around, he shied away from delving into the hurts he'd incurred as a child. Instead, he focused his attention on the small dark woman, advancing his way, carrying a bolt of fabric.

"The man at the gate say you Major McKenzie," she said, her dark face serious, wary.

"I am."

She thrust the blue silk his way. "Miss Seymore say to give this to you."

Brett took hold of the bolt shoved into his chest, recognizing it even though until now he hadn't laid eyes on the thing. The cloth was exactly as it had been described to him.

"Did she have anything else to say?"

The woman gave in to a mocking smile. "Plenty, but not for your ears."

He could well imagine what Laurel had had to say. "You go back and tell—"

"No, sir. I tote this silk to you because Miss Seymore ask me to. But I don't have to be carrying messages because you order me to."

The woman's nerve could have been amusing if Brett had been in a receptive frame of mind for such. As it was, he was more inclined for a verbal flaying.

"Who the hell are you?" he snapped.

"Tess."

"Tess what?"

"Just Tess."

"Are you always this impudent, *just* Tess?"

"No, sir. I simply doing what Miss Seymore told me to do."

"Do you always do what she tells you to do?"

"I usually try."

Brett wondered to what extremes that took the woman. "What do you know about this cloth?"

"Nothing."

"That's about as much as Miss Seymore knows." Only Brett didn't believe that. Damn it, he wanted to know what in hell Laurel Seymore was all about.

"Come with me, Tess."

She balked visibly, wrapping her arms about her waist. "Why?"

"There are some questions I would like to ask you."

"About what?"

Mentally, Brett consigned this small woman to the same realm as Laurel. Both were too contrary for their own good.

The silver-blue of his eyes taking on a flinty cast, he warned, "I will tell you exactly what I told Miss Seymore yesterday. We can have this chat in my office or in one of the prison cells below. The choice is yours."

Of course, he knew there was no choice at all. Tess came to that conclusion in about the same amount of time that Laurel had. She stiffly nodded her agreement to follow him inside. Once she was seated on one side of his desk and he on the other, he began where he had left off.

"What exactly do you do for Miss Seymore?"

"I work."

"At what?"

"Sewing, cutting, waiting on folks. At home I help with cooking and cleaning."

"You help the other slaves?"

"I'm no slave. I a free woman. And there aren't no other servants. Just me."

"You mean that Miss Seymore cooks and cleans?"

"Yes, sir. And Miss Hope, too. We all pitch in."

Brett leaned back in his chair. A woman of Laurel's obvious business success could have easily had more than one servant. "How long have you been with Miss Seymore?"

"Going on six year."

"How long have you been free?"

Tess's brows slowly crept downward. "Why?"

"Answer the question."

She worked her jaw from side to side, fighting an obvious battle with herself. In the end, she said, "I been free for seven year."

"Then you aren't from South Carolina."

"How you know that?"

"Because the law in this state hasn't permitted the freeing of a slave since 1820. Where did you come from originally?"

Cautiously, ever so carefully, she said, "Georgia."

"How did you come to be with Miss Seymore?"

Again, she fell silent, her expression betraying her inner struggle. "When my old master he die, he free all us slaves. I come here on my own. Miss Laurel she take me in."

"Do you earn a wage?"

"Yes, sir."

"How much?"

"Enough."

Brett swallowed the string of curses he was tempted to hurl. Getting information from Tess was akin to swimming upriver against a full current. Possible, but damned difficult.

Letting his impatience show, he stated, "Shall I send for Miss Seymore? Perhaps you'd prefer that she answer my questions while you wait in a cell."

His display of displeasure worked. Tess dropped her gaze to the floor.

"Miss Seymore pay me what she can afford. Some week it a dollar, most time it's less."

"That's very generous of her."

Her gaze snapped back to his. "She's a generous woman. She's a good woman, her heart is big. Not another woman like Miss Laurel."

"I admire your loyalty."

"I'm loyal because it's her due. She's had a hard time of it since the fever take her momma and poppa. She was a little bitty girl then, barely fifteen, but she didn't let that beat her. She pull herself together and keep the shop open even though her heart to breaking with sorrow."

"When was this?" Brett sat forward, his words demanding, his black brows lowering sharply.

"Five year, now. And all this time, she take care of Miss Hope and me and make sure we got enough to eat, that we got a warm, safe place to live."

"Was there no one else to help her?"

"No one. The parents they come to this country from England. And the rest of the folks around here?" She scoffed derisively. "They too busy taking care of their own problems. But that didn't stop Miss Laurel. She set her mind to keeping us out of the poor house, and she done it, too. Works harder in one day than most folk do in a full week. And she never forget those who don't have."

Tess finished on a furious note, her chin elevated, her gaze blazing. "So, yeah, I loyal to Miss Laurel. And if you waiting for me to say some bad about her, then you going to wait 'til judgment day."

Of that, Brett had no doubt. And in truth, he couldn't blame Tess. If all she said was true, then Laurel was deserving of loyalty.

Damn, but a few things were beginning to make sense. Laurel's independent streak wasn't just a quirk. It was the result of being forced to survive. He didn't know many fifteen-year-olds who could endure the deaths of their parents and go on to take care of a fragile older sister and a business as well.

No wonder she was beset with what she considered to be her responsibilities. A sister and a former slave truly did depend on her for guidance, support, and means. It was a weighty burden for a young woman to have carried for so long, so exclusively.

He had to wonder if she ever had a respite, if there was

anyone to whom she turned for relief from the pressure of her responsibilities.

Muted, suffocated words came back to him now. *I will get home, Major, the same way I arrived here, the same way I accomplish everything in this life. Alone and by myself.*

An unaccountable swell of sadness rose up in him, tugging at emotions he reserved solely for his mother and sisters. It didn't make a damn bit of difference that he didn't have any business feeling sorry for Laurel. He simply did.

Jerking to his feet, he clamped down on his wayward thoughts. Damn it all! He had just regained his perspective on the lady. He didn't need to feel discomfited for her plight. She wasn't the first person to experience her share of hardships. People did the same and more every day, and he wasn't wrenched with this kind of deep concern for them.

His indignation went far in restoring his impartiality. Laurel might very well believe herself alone, she might appear to be dainty and frail, but this was one case where looks were definitely deceiving. She may be slender and delicate in stature, but that elegant fragility was banked by unrelenting determination, true sense of purpose, and an unflagging spirit.

Was she using all of those attributes to ill purposes?

Leaning back against the front of his desk, he crossed one booted ankle over the other. "You're right to defend Miss Seymore. I only hope you're as good a friend to her as she's been to you."

"I'd do anything for her," Tess vowed.

"Would you keep her from hurting herself?" Brett delivered the query in a deceptively soft voice, but there was nothing gentle or subtle about his gaze. It was relentlessly hard.

"I don't know what you mean."

"Exactly what I said. If Laurel were doing something that was dangerous to herself or to her sister, would you try and stop her?" *If she were smuggling, would you come to me for help?* he added silently.

He waited and watched. The face that had only seconds ago been alive with expression became a visual void. The body that had practically vibrated with emotion went perfectly still. Tess pulled into herself, silently telling him that she would tell him nothing more.

Inwardly, he sighed. In her silence, Tess had spoken volumes, about herself and about Laurel.

His suspicions came back full force.

•

# Seven

The gold coins she had received from John tucked into the bottom of her black reticule, Laurel slowly wended her way through a small crowd that had gathered outside for the morning's activities. As was typical of the people of Savannah, cordiality was the order of the day. Gentlemen tipped their hats, women offered genial smiles.

Laurel nodded sedately to all in return, comporting herself as the young widow her mode of dress proclaimed her to be. Her leisurely movements displayed hints of a black silk dress beneath a cloaked cape of the same hue. Upon her head, an ebony bonnet was laced with a veil of the sheerest gray netting. To all who cared to look, she was in mourning.

That was the way Laurel intended it to be. Her trips to Savannah were frequent, her venturing into this part of the city fairly routine. She wanted those who saw her to assume she was someone other than who she really was. As Tess had so aptly put it, it was a dangerous game she played.

Her stomach fluttered nervously at the thought. She wasn't playing a game. For what she did, there were those who would gleefully string her up. Major McKenzie would have to get in line behind a great many irate citizens and wait his turn to exact justice on her.

Thinking of him was not a wise thing to do. He was a dangerous man. He could pose a real threat to her if she wasn't careful. He was already a threat to her peace of mind, the beast.

She darted a quick look up and down the street, impatient for the entire business to be over and done with. Her nerves were beginning to tighten and tremble and no amount of silent scolding was going to alleviate that. Even though she told herself that there really wasn't any cause for her to worry, that she had done this very same thing at least a dozen times before, her uneasiness lingered.

Being so pressed for time did not help. To that end, she'd made her inquiries and knew she could not dawdle through any portion of her morning. Alacrity was essential in what she did. It allowed for no uncomfortable questions or dangerous scrutinies that probed too close to the truth.

Into her musings came the sound of scuffling feet and a harsh, guttural voice issuing orders. Laurel turned her attention to the coffle of slaves being herded toward the auctioneer's block.

Carefully, her face scrupulously wiped clean of any expression, she examined the group of black men and women as they were made to stand off to one side. The slave trader had obviously done his job, for to a person, each of the slaves looked fit, clean, hardy.

*Looked* fit and hardy. Laurel knew that wasn't the same as actually being so. There were a whole host of tricks traders used to make their "merchandise" appear in better condition than they actually were.

Laurel's lips thinned as she peered more closely at the silent group, studying, inspecting, judging as intently as any around her. Maybe even more so. To her right, a fat, pompous-looking man dismissed the entire lot after a brief review and proclaimed his disregard for all to hear.

The trader protested.

"Nothin' but the best, ladies and gents. I offer you nothin' but the best." He waved forward a young dark man clad in coarse but serviceable clothing. The slave took up a spot in the middle of the low, raised platform.

Laurel scanned the young man and got the impression that he was more boy than his appearance revealed. She guessed his age to be near eighteen, although his features and his bearing told a different story. They told of hardships met and conquered to the best of his ability. It was there in the tension of his carriage, the deep lines framing his mouth, and the vigilance of his gaze.

"His limbs and joints are pliant," the trader proclaimed, "and he's got nearly a full set of teeth. Strong and young, and free of venereal taint."

But not free of spirit, Laurel thought. The young man might not be able to claim his own freedom but his will and his soul were still unfettered. She could see it in his eyes.

Giving the other slaves a hasty but thorough look, she quickly made up her mind. When the auction began, she placed her bid. In less than five minutes, the young man was hers.

Without batting an eye, she reached into the bottom of her purse and withdrew several coins. She wouldn't go so far as to bless John St. James, but she did offer up a prayer of thanks.

"What's your name?" she asked as soon as she had settled with the trader and her new "property" joined her.

His eyes narrowed to slits, his chin elevated. Hardly moving his lips at all, he muttered, "Julius."

Laurel noted his manner and one red brow arched. "Save all that indignation for another time, Julius. You'll need it." In fact, it would stand him in good stead. "Do you have any belongings?"

"No."

"All right then, come with me. We have no time to spare." She hastened down the street with Julius one step behind. All along the back of her, she could practically feel his restrained anger.

Good, let him be angry. Let him be fierce and willful. As long as he accompanied her without incident she didn't care if he sprouted a second head. But until she finished her business with him he had best be cooperative. Everything would be ruined if he decided to bolt.

To her immense relief, they reached a local mercantile without incident. Julius stood solemn and quiet as Laurel outfitted him with two new pairs of pants, just as many shirts, a thick woolen jacket, a hat, socks, and a sturdy pair of brown leather boots. Once again, Laurel laid out coin, and the items were wrapped up in a bundle for Julius to carry.

Throughout the whole process, he said little, speaking only when asked a direct question. But more than once, Laurel caught his speculative gaze lingering on her. She didn't let it concern her, as her mind was occupied with more important matters.

Feeling the pressure of time weighing heavily, she hurried from the shop, Julius trailing in her wake with his sack under his arm. She didn't stop until they arrived at the docks. Only then did she fully consider Julius at length.

He was strong; both physically and mentally. It was one of the reasons she had chosen to buy him instead of one of the others. For what he was about to face, he was going to need to be strong.

"I'm trusting you to remain here." She tipped her head back and faced him squarely, every ounce of her determination blazing in her eyes. "Do not move from this spot, do not call any attention to yourself. I'll explain it all in a moment. Do you understand?"

At her rushed, imperious tone, thick brows lowered in question.

"I'll only be a minute or two."

Satisfied, Laurel tugged on the ends of her gloves, sucked in a full breath, and entered the small shipping office.

"Good morning, sir," she said to the narrow little man situated behind a makeshift counter. The air in the dank confines reeked of rotting wood and unwashed bodies.

"Ma'am."

Lifting a delicate hanky to her nose, Laurel hid her grimace and effected her most pleasant demeanor. "Sir, I was hoping you could help me."

Minutes later, she emerged from the office, glad to see that Julius was still there. For the first time all morning, she breathed a full sigh of relief.

"Here," she said, holding out a small leather pouch. "There's money in that to see you on your way."

Julius automatically took the pouch, but it was apparent he couldn't make sense of what was happening.

"Yes, I know," Laurel assured him, seeing his confusion. "I haven't given you any warning, and absolutely no choice, but there was no time. I'm sorry about that. I was half-afraid we'd be too late, that we wouldn't get here before the ship sailed. I didn't want to get your hopes up only to have them crash down upon you."

"What?"

Laurel nodded to the nearby ship swarming with activity. "I've booked passage for you to Boston on the *Honoria.* It leaves within the hour." She handed over his boarding papers and also a letter she had penned earlier.

"Keep these with you. One is your guarantee of passage and the other is your paper of freedom."

At that most treasured of all words, Julius started, his eyes flying wide, his lips parting. The belligerent defensiveness that had marked him to that point dissipated. "Freedom? You settin' me free?"

"Yes." Quickly, she unfolded the letter. "It's all legal. I wrote it earlier and inserted your name while I was inside making arrangements for you. If anyone questions you along the way or gives you trouble, you have this to prove that you're free. There shouldn't be any problem. I know of this captain and he is a fair and honest man."

Julius stared at the missive, holding it as if it were a sacred talisman. His eyes scanned the neat lines and the signature below.

"I'm free?"

"From this moment on."

He dragged his gaze up to Laurel, disbelief and wonder and pain warring openly in his face. "I . . . I don't even know yo' name."

She pointed to her signature. "Laurel Seymore, of Charleston, South Carolina."

He nodded, swallowed hard, stumbled about for words, and then finally managed, "Where's mine? Where's my name?"

"Here." A shout from the *Honoria*'s deck drew her attention, and alerted her of their rapidly diminishing time.

"If you would prefer not to go, I'll understand. Tell me now and I'll see what can be done for you."

Julius sputtered out disjointed fragments of words, shaking his head in an amazement so profound that Laurel could feel its impact.

"But I would suggest that you do leave," she continued. "Those I've helped in the past have chosen to do so."

"You done this . . . before?"

"Several times. And it has worked out very nicely this way. If you don't wish to go to Boston, you can still leave on this ship. It docks in several ports along the way. You can get off anywhere you choose, but the further north you go, the better it will be." The green of her eyes took on a sober cast. "And it would be safer for both of us."

She wouldn't dream of telling Julius he couldn't remain in Savannah, but she hoped that he wouldn't, for both their sakes. Savannah was not that far from Charleston. Word had a way of traveling. Should that happen with the social climate being what it was, they could be faced with some very grim repercussions.

"If it's all the same to you," Julius concluded, "I'll go to this Boston."

"Good." She darted a glance to the ship. "You'd best be on your way."

Yet he stood and scanned the huge vessel, not moving, his hands gripping his precious possessions. After a long look, he faced Laurel once more. "I'm free."

He was, and Laurel prayed he would be strong enough to survive that. Freedom didn't mean equality. Julius was going to have to struggle simply to survive, but he would be able to do so as freely as God had intended him to.

She laid a tender hand on his arm. "I wish you luck, Julius."

He nodded before moving away. Ten feet off, he turned back, his brow creased with a series of lines. "Why you doin' this?"

It was one of those questions that Laurel tried never to study too closely. The reasons for what she did were complex, tangled up with common human decency and with the moral edicts of what was right and what was wrong. And yet, gazing at Julius, his face filled with a genuine need to know, she could not evade pondering the reasons.

If she lived forever, she would never understand the rationale behind slavery. To own another person as one would a horse or a shoe, to be within one's rights to be able to sell that person at any time, into any circumstances, to think of that person as a thing, an object not human but inanimate, was barbaric. And it was beyond her comprehension.

Letting her gaze take in the whole of Julius, she felt her insides shrivel a little. She could not fully appreciate the suffering he had endured. The basic facts were common knowledge, but those were pitiful hints of the whole truth.

How could she, who had always been free, truly understand what it felt like to have your every function determined by another? How could she comprehend an existence where you consciously observed and felt and experienced all that went on around you but were considered no more aware than the animals in the fields? That was absolute misery of the heart and soul, and in comparison, the struggles she had had to face were paltry.

As a child, she'd awakened each morning, secure in the knowledge that her parents would be there that night to tuck her in. Death had stripped her of that security, but no human being had. No one had had the right to enter her house and remove her from her mother's breast or cart her sister off to another city or take her father away, never to be seen again.

She was confident and whole because of the love and security bestowed on her from the constancy of a family. It was something she never took for granted, and she damned all the so-called good people who claimed to hold true to Christian values and at the same time embraced the perversity of slavery.

You could not do one and the other at the same time. A person couldn't be truly charitable and compassionate and wholly committed to the essence of love and family, and own another human being. She just didn't see how it could be possible. Or right.

And that was why she did what she did. Because she couldn't live with herself if she ignored the hideous wrong of it all.

"Does it really matter why I helped you?"

Slowly, Julius shook his head. "No."

A sad smile tugged at her lips. "Then you better get aboard."

He considered her answer and then straightened, all the hopes and dreams in the world shining in his grin. "You a good woman, Laurel Seymore of Charleston."

She tried to be, but as she stood and followed his progress up the gang plank, she felt the encumbrance of her integrity and honesty hang heavy on her shoulders. Under the brilliant noon sun, she watched the *Honoria* weigh anchor, stared at the gradually diminishing face of Julius as he waved to her, and all the tension and anxiety of the last few hours pulled at her.

The energy that had sustained her was rapidly dissolving. She wanted nothing more than to return to her room at the hotel and curl up. More than that, she wanted to go home, to her almost ordinary life of sewing, to Hope and Tess, to peace and relative calm.

She'd leave tomorrow. Waiting for her was the shop, the routine, mundane decisions she made every day, the secret meetings with John. And Major McKenzie.

Her lungs constricted about her heart.

Back in Charleston, Major McKenzie waited for her as surely as the *Honoria* sailed out of sight.

Even as she left the wharf behind her and headed for home, she could hear the undisputable ruckus of a commotion. Frowning, she shifted her valise from her left hand to her right and wondered what was going on. The disturbance came to her from the area off to her left, from the very direction in which she had to go in order to reach home.

She gave an indelicate grunt, her thoughts turning sour. Well, if that wasn't just peachy. If one part of the city wasn't erupting into disorder, then another part was.

There was no telling what had prompted this latest discord. A drunken brawl could have spilled out of one of the tippling houses and gotten out of hand, or a dissatisfied customer might have taken exception to a merchant's prices and decided to exact his displeasure in purely physical means.

None of it was new, but the present chaos was closer than she was comfortable with. The nearer she drew to her house, the more ominous the uproar became. Swallowing her trepidation, she silently prayed that Hope and Tess were safely indoors and out of danger.

She turned the corner onto Meeting Street and was met with a sight that choked a curse from her lips.

"Jesus, Mary, and Joseph!" Before her was a full-blown riot, men battling each other into bloody messes while soldiers from the army and the militia tried to restore order.

A lethal dose of irate impatience surged up as she glared about her. Could these men think of nothing better to do with their time? She deemed them all savage idiots, wondering why they always had to resort to violence.

For her unladylike thoughts, she resigned herself to a weighty penance on Sunday, but stars and garters, how was she supposed to respond to this—she gasped as one man landed on his face near her feet—to this brawl? Fighting never solved anything and she resented it highly that she would, for the few more minutes it would take to reach her doors, have to be subjected to its revolting spectacle. And she resented it even more that these brutes could effectively keep her from her house less than half a block away.

She scanned the street choked with all manner of man, trying to see past fists connecting with chins, trying not to give in to nausea as blood splattered from noses and men fell in crumpled heaps. It was obvious she could not remain where she was. She either had to retreat the way she had come and wait for the melee to die down, or chance the short walk to her house.

Why she should have to wait? Who were these people that they could ride roughshod over her intentions? What gave them the right to disrupt the lives of innocent others with their savagery?

Muttering dire warnings under her breath, she took hold of her valise with both hands and hugged the building at her back, daring anyone to get close to her. She'd be damned if she was going to wander aimlessly about the city, waiting for these rude, self-absorbed men to come to their senses—if they had any at all. At the moment, she was being extremely generous in thinking that collectively they possessed the wits of a turnip.

Shouting and cursing met her ears, joining the stench of sweat and hostility, and then the clang of steel meeting steel. Raised swords were a serious matter. She hastened on, a twinge of real alarm clenching her chest. Into her path, two men stumbled and grappled with each other, spittle and blood flying in equal amounts, their breaths strangled, hatred making their faces seem more animal than human.

She reared back, flattening herself against a wrought-iron gate. Instantly, she questioned her own good senses in believing she could make it home. The crowd seemed to have swelled and she looked for an avenue of escape, her only intent now to reach home unharmed so she could reflect on her rash arrogance and repent.

The men lurched away, leaving her with a clear path. She darted forward, her hat askew, her lips drawn back in a grimace of growing fright. All around her, bodies twisted and battled. She did her best to avoid them all. For a few short-lived moments, she actually thought she had succeeded, until she was grabbed roughly from behind.

Her response was instinctive. No conscious thoughts guided her arms. Damning the fact that she abhorred violence, she turned in one fluid motion, swinging her valise with deadly intent, and clubbed her attacker on the side of his head, and shoulders.

For a fraction of a second, his face was nothing more than an indistinct blur. Then he lurched away with a muffled curse, but not before Laurel saw amazement and lust contort his features. The combination made a very unnatural moment all too sickeningly real.

She turned to flee, and horribly, found herself trapped. The blow to the man's head had made him falter, but he had still managed to retain his hold on her cloak. His hand was fisted about the fabric, and when he righted himself, he yanked her closer.

She had no time to prepare or react. The brute stripped the valise from her hands with a single move, his laughter ringing out threateningly. By the time she thought to defend herself, he had pulled back his arm and wound up to smash his fist into her jaw.

The promise of pain brought a cry to her lips. Reflexively, she whirled as far as she could from the coming blow, when suddenly she was torn from the man's grip and hurled aside. She landed face down on the street, her hair a wild scarlet tumble, the air knocked from her lungs. Distantly, amidst the turmoil in her mind and the chaos surrounding her, she considered her rescue. Turning her head to one side, she saw Major McKenzie send her attacker reeling with one powerful blow.

That Brett should be the one to save her was astonishing. Yet there he was, unyielding, powerfully dangerous. She blessed him to Heaven and back.

He didn't waste any time with words. In truth, from the look of him, she didn't know if he was capable of any just then. He grabbed her up by the arms and immediately shielded her body with his own as he maneuvered them out of the worst of the mayhem.

Her face pressed into the wide expanse of Brett's chest, she drew in the scent of him. Never in her life had the muskiness of a man and leather and wool smelled so wonderful. Without thinking, she slipped her arms about his waist and held tight.

"Thank you," she whispered, her eyes shut, a fine trembling beginning to seize her limbs. The quivering was repeated again in her head, for one thought after another ricocheted about in the most absurd and foreign manner. What was he doing here? How had he happened to be in the right place at the right time to save her? Why had he even bothered?

"This way," he ordered, his deep voice like ice.

Laurel lifted her head to discover that they were outside her house. A smile flitted about her lips. She raised her eyes to silently thank him, but her gaze never reached his. Just behind him, a hulk of a man charged with a wooden pike aimed directly at the major's back.

"Look out!" she cried.

Brett turned, simultaneously shoving Laurel behind him while raising his sword in defense. He managed to deflect the worst of the assault, then attacked with deadly precision.

To Laurel's abused senses, his sword was a shining flash of silver. She saw glimpses of blood, but could not find the source as his body moved with a fluid, muscular skill born of years of training and conditioning.

In his face, she saw an unholy light of battle and it was then that she sensed that his entire being—mind, body, and soul—was converged on one point. Brett McKenzie had become single-minded in his quest . . . and that was to save her.

He did so in the next heartbeat. The wretch he had been fighting scrambled away, holding his bloodied side. Laurel was on the verge of flinging herself into the major's arms when he swung back to her, his face a pasty white, his coatee stained with blood.

His mouth contorted in agony, he clenched his eyes shut. And then he dropped to the ground at her feet.

# *Eight*

"Don't you dare die!" Laurel ordered. "Do you hear me, Brett McKenzie? I will not let you."

Not since the death of her parents had she experienced such dread. Her insides quaked with fear and denial, and she was reduced to sitting helplessly by to await the doctor's arrival.

Where the devil was he? It felt like hours ago that she had sent Tess for him, and longer still since she and Hope and Tess had half-carried, half-dragged the major into the house. Getting him up the stairs and into her bed had taken all of their combined strength, but they had managed because to have done otherwise would have surely meant his demise.

His death was still uncertain. His breathing had stopped at one point. In a terror-born panic, she had shaken him as she would someone whom she wished to drag from sleep. Finding his skin so icy had brought weak, scalding tears to her eyes.

She gazed at the thick wad of bandages pressed to his left shoulder. Blood slowly soaked its way through the layers of linen, the scarlet stain a grisly sign that this vibrant, vigorous man was slipping away from her. All she could do was watch the shallow rise and fall of his chest and send up a host of prayers.

"Dr. Mathews is here," Hope said, issuing the portly physician into the room.

"I came as soon as I could," he assured them.

Laurel came to her feet, her face awash with misery, her fingers tightly laced. "He's dying. Do . . . do something."

He spared her a glance then bent to attend his patient.

Laurel stepped aside just as Tess arrived with fresh bandages and another basin of water.

"How is he?" she whispered.

Laurel shook her head. Dr. Mathews was succinct in his assessment.

"Not good, I'm afraid. I'll have to sew him up, but I can't make any promises." He shrugged out of his jacket. "Has he been bleeding like this since he was injured?"

"Yes," Laurel murmured.

"How long ago was that?"

For the life of her, Laurel couldn't determine a time. In her mind it had become warped. She looked to Tess for an answer.

"Thirty minutes."

The doctor scowled. "Then he's lost too much blood, by far. Frankly, I wouldn't hold out too much hope if I were you. You might want to send word to his commanding officer."

The finality of his opinion struck Laurel hard. It reeked of resignation, of meekly accepting defeat. She had never passively submitted to anything in her life; she wasn't going to start with Brett's death.

Anger surged into her veins, singeing her chilled nerves until her skin prickled. All manner of irate thoughts lined up in her head. Who was this . . . this doctor that he could so casually dismiss the life of a man? How dare he make his predictions as if Brett were no more than a slab of meat?

"You listen to me, Doctor Mathews," she snarled, her cheeks suffused with color. "You stop the bleeding, give him whatever medicine you have to, but he's not going to die. Do you hear me? He's not going to die. I'll see to that."

The intensity of her voice carried to every corner of the room, skewering the doctor along the way. He blinked several times in rapid succession, taken aback by the severity of Laurel's command.

"I'll do everything I can, Laurel."

She gritted her teeth, silently vowing that he had damn well better do exactly that. And Brett McKenzie had better not even *think* of dying.

She took in the pallor of his face and her ire gave way to remorse. They had been at odds with each other from the very start, yet he had saved her life at grave risk to his own. The utter generosity of his actions humbled her.

What kind of man did what Brett McKenzie had done? In parting with him days earlier she had called him an arrogant son of Satan. His response to that was to protect her at all costs when he had no good reason to. They were not related, he was not responsible for her. She had treated him as coolly as she would anyone who sought to interfere with her life.

Pressing the heel of her hand into her forehead, she rubbed at the pounding. The headache remained as steadfastly as did her new discoveries about Brett. Underneath all of his autocratic masculine pride was a manner both noble and chivalrous.

It would have been easier for her if she didn't have to acknowledge that. Then she wouldn't have to consider him in a whole new light; then she wouldn't have to grapple with feelings of Brett being thoughtful and kind. But she was too honest at heart to disavow the truth, and so she watched as the doctor bloodied his hands, and she prayed with every ounce of her being for Brett's life.

---

His mother was crying again. In his head, Brett could hear her weeping and he turned toward the sound, his heart sinking. He hated to know that his mother was not happy. It tore him apart to see the sadness she tried her best to hide from him and his sisters.

But he saw through her brave front. She'd never been able to hide it from any of them.

*Don't cry, Mother.*

*You mustn't think badly of your father.*

*He makes you unhappy.*

*In his own way, he cares.*

His father's words echoed out of nowhere. *God and country, son. Always remember that your duty comes first.*

Not knowing why, Brett turned away from the voice and sought solace. Instead, flames climbed up from the ground. The heat scorched his skin. He wanted to escape to safety, but his feet were mired in yards of patterned blue satin. The heat increased, pain engulfed him. He tried to twist away.

*Drink . . . drink.*

He responded to the command for no reason that he could discern.

*Drink.*

The water felt good. It lapped at his senses and bathed his body like shimmering folds of russet silk. Slowly, subtly, the fabric caressed his face, reaching out as though to embrace him. The color deepened, the texture changed. What had been silk became curling tresses of red.

*I will get home the same way I arrived here, the same way I accomplish everything in this life . . . alone.*

Laurel. He didn't want to think of her as alone.

*Drink this, Brett . . . please. . .*

It was imperative that he reach her, that he save her.

*Forgive me.*

Her voice was a balm. On some basic level, it soothed him, captured his thoughts and left him in peace.

Sitting in the silence of her bedroom, Laurel leaned forward in her chair and laid a tender hand on the expanse of Brett's chest. He was unconscious and restless, battling the fever that made him burn with heat one second and shake with chills the next.

Her touch didn't serve any real purpose. It didn't ease his suffering or dull his pain. It didn't promote his awakening and it most certainly didn't heal the wound to his shoulder. Still, she felt compelled to touch him, as if doing so could help him in some way.

She told herself that she was already doing all she could. Again and again, she had bathed his body with cool wet cloths and lifted his head in to her arms to encourage him to swallow small sips of water. Every hour, she checked the binding on his shoulder to assure herself that the injury had not festered. Her ministrations were as much as anyone could do, but they were frustrating in their limitations. Thinking back on Dr. Mathews's parting words didn't help.

"Keep him as comfortable as possible. If he makes it through the night, let me know, and I'll be back to check on him. If not, do as I said and get word to his commanding officer."

The heartless dolt. She had been tempted to tell him what he could do with his offhanded suggestion. Prudently, she'd kept her mouth shut and sent to the army post, but not with word of impending doom. Her message had been nothing short of an order for their physician to attend to one of its officers . . . at once.

A Captain Jeffers had come and gone. While his professional treatment had been much the same as Dr. Mathews's, his manner had been more attentive and kind. Like his civilian counterpart, he could not make any promises for Brett's recovery, but Laurel had received a measure of comfort from his obvious concern.

Releasing a sigh, she withdrew her hand from the hard, warm flesh, letting it drop limply to her lap. Despite the fire in the grate and the brace of candles on the dresser, night crowded the room with shadows that prompted a searching of her conscience.

She blamed herself for Brett's misfortune. If she hadn't taken the riot in the street so personally, the major's life might not now be in jeopardy. He might very well have escaped the entire fracas unharmed. Instead, he had come to her rescue, and why? Because she'd once again been too stubborn and idealistic for her own good.

Balling her hands into fists, she dropped them down to her knees, squeezing her eyes shut in self-reproach. Why did she behave as she did? Why did she have to view each of life's occurrences as a challenge to be met and bested? She could have . . . no, she *should* have fled from the fight, but she hadn't. Without thought to the consequences, she'd puffed up with self-righteous indignation and moral outrage and dared the world to tread on her. As a result, Brett

McKenzie was now engaged in the most serious battle of his life.

She surged to her feet, hating that flaw in her character that brought her to such ends. Once, just once, she wished she could be more passive and accepting, not so willing to blindly charge the gates of hell all in the name of noble intentions. But how did she go about doing that without sacrificing the very ideals of her life?

She leaned her head against the cool surface of the windowpane, her heart as weary as her mind. Both ached with spent emotions that decried her for a fool. She was definitely that, and naive as well for so blithely believing that decency and goodness insured safety and fairness.

Brett McKenzie was proof to the contrary. He had acted decently and in good faith. He was now suffering and there was nothing fair about that.

From behind her, he mumbled incoherently, his face more flushed than it had been minutes before. She collected her basin of cool, clean water from the dry sink and returned to the bed.

As she pressed her hand to his forehead, her heart contracted. His body heat seemed to have increased and his breathing was more shallow. Quickly, she wrung most of the water out of a cloth and began to sponge him down.

"Forgive me," she whispered. She had no right to ask that of him. She did anyway . . . over and over again as the night progressed.

"Laurel?"

At Tess's whisper, Laurel jerked awake in her chair. Alarm flared briefly as she sat straight, her gaze shooting to Brett's still form.

Tess calmed her fears before they could be voiced. "He's not dead."

Laurel slumped wearily. It had been a long night. Dawn's light peeked in from behind the shut curtains. Morning. She looked from the window to Brett. He'd made it through the night. The victory brought a weak smile to her lips.

"Why don't you get some breakfast," Tess urged. "I can sit with him."

Laurel hated to leave him for even a moment, but she knew it was the wise thing to do. Her stomach felt as if it was devouring her insides and her cramped muscles were protesting the hours spent in a chair.

"I won't be long," she said.

Tess squinted one eye shut. "You need to eat, you need to take time for you." Gesturing to the bed, she added, "He going nowhere."

Sadly, that much was true. Rising, Laurel pressed her palm to his forehead. He was still much too warm, but perhaps not so much so as last night.

"Go," Tess urged.

"See if you can get him to take some water."

"I will."

She hugged the assurance close as she made her way to the dining room. Hope was already seated.

"How is he?" she asked.

Taking her seat, Laurel poured herself a cup of the coffee she so badly needed. "Not much improved."

Hope's beautiful face lined with dismay. "Do . . . you think he'll—"

"No." Laurel cut the query off at its roots, shaken at the thought that Brett might not live. "He's survived until now. Neither doctor expected as much. That's a good sign."

In her place, Hope seemed to shrivel a bit, her brown eyes filling with contrition. "I'm sorry, Laurel. I didn't mean to upset you."

Laurel waved the apology away. "You didn't. I'm just tired. And worried."

"Is there . . . I mean, should I be doing anything to help?"

"No. Tess is with him now."

"But what about later? Will I, that is, do you wish me to sit with him?"

Fingering the rim of her cup, Laurel watched the play of emotions tramp all over her sister's face. Normal day-to-day life was at times beyond Hope's capacities. A man severely wounded in an upstairs bedroom had Hope at her most vulnerable.

"Don't fret over that, Hope. I'll stay with the major."

Hope couldn't contain her sigh of obvious relief. "If you think it best."

"I do. Besides, you'll need to be at the shop."

"Today?" Hope couldn't contain her amazement.

"It's Monday, Hope. The shop has to be open."

"Oh."

From that single breathless word, Laurel heard all she needed to hear, and for a second her temper flashed. The past hours had taxed her to her limits. Now more than ever, she needed Hope to be strong.

Doing her best to keep the strain from her voice, she explained, "Hope, we don't have any choice." A tired corner of her mind rebelled, asking why an explanation was even necessary. "Someone needs to tend to Major McKenzie, and someone needs to tend to our customers. I can't be in both places at once. You wanted to help and this is a way."

"I don't like being at the shop by myself."

"I know you don't, but Tess will be there, at least part of the time. She has deliveries to make this afternoon."

Hope openly struggled with the situation, her gaze darting about the room until it finally landed helplessly on Laurel. "Would it really be so bad if we didn't open the shop today?"

Without thinking, Laurel rose to her feet, green eyes glazed with irritation. "Yes, it would! This isn't a temporary predicament we're in. There's no telling how long Major McKenzie is going to need nursing. It could be days, or weeks. What are we supposed to do all that time? Shut the store down? We'll lose every customer we have. What will we do then, Hope? How will we live?"

She swung away, instantly ashamed of her outburst. Tiredly, she rubbed at her forehead, reaching deep for the remains of her inner strength. There was no excuse for having railed at Hope that way. None of this was her sister's fault.

"I'm sorry, Laurel," Hope whispered.

The apology stabbed at Laurel. She hung her head, lifting a hand in an impotent gesture. "Don't apologize to me." She turned to face her sister. "I shouldn't have yelled at you."

Hope sat dejectedly and yet, oddly enough, there was a vague sense of purpose about her. "I know I'm a burden to you, Laurel. I try not to be, but I can't seem to help myself most of the time. I wish it weren't so. I wish I were as strong as you." Her voice lowered. "I'm sorry I can't be."

Second by second, Laurel's chagrin increased. "You do the best you can. In your own way, that is a certain strength."

"You're so much more capable than I am."

"You're capable, Hope, only you don't believe it. I think that's why I lost my temper. I know you can do anything you set your mind to."

"Really?"

Laurel nodded. "You're a smart, able, beautiful woman."

"Then why do I act as I do?"

Giving a shrug, Laurel crossed to Hope's side. "I've always thought of it as a matter of timing. I accepted certain realities early on and all at once. Perhaps you need more time to accept the fact that you are as capable as any other woman. That doesn't mean you're a failure or that you're weak, just lacking in confidence for the time being."

"It means that I have to rely on you."

"I'm your sister." Laying her hand on Hope's shoulder, she vowed, "Someday you'll be as strong as you want. I know it."

Hope tipped her head up to stare deeply into her sister's eyes. For a long moment she remained silent and still. Finally, she came to her feet.

"Where are the keys to the shop?"

Laurel's heart blossomed with pride for Hope. "I'll get them for you. And don't worry, everything will be fine."

"Promise?"

"Promise. Before you know it, Tess will be there to help you."

"Will you be all right here alone with the major?"

"Yes."

"But what if he—"

"He won't." Laurel could not contemplate Brett's death. The thought was vile and abhorrent, and it pierced her heart with an agony she'd never felt before.

# Nine

The days and nights became a blur for Laurel. Any given midnight might well have been noon, a shadowy dawn just as easily dusk. Hours blended one on top of another as she stayed by Brett's side.

Three days had passed and for all that time, Brett had been unconscious. There were moments when he lay as still as the death Laurel feared. At others times, he writhed in fevered pain. She wasn't sure which she feared most. Both had a way of drawing at her soul.

Dr. Jeffers, from the army post, called every day. Frustratingly, his advice was always the same: Keep the man as cool as possible. Laurel had done that very thing. If at times she felt her efforts were useless, she took great hope from the fact that Brett was still alive.

Sitting on the bed beside him, her hand resting lightly on his chest, she rejoiced in a bit of optimism. He was definitely cooler this evening than he had been that afternoon, and he seemed to be sleeping rather than drugged by unconsciousness. She had no way of knowing for sure. Nonetheless, for the last few hours he had not been as restless, and his breathing had been deep and even. The satisfaction in that made her nearly giddy with happiness.

"Major?" She scanned his features, looking for some

indication that he might be improved enough to hear her. "Can you hear me?"

He remained silent, but she didn't let that disappoint her too much. He was on his way to recovery. She could well afford to be patient a little while longer.

Riding the joy of that anticipation, she smiled as she smoothed the loose folds of her robe, her gaze turning to the cot at the foot of the bed. That was where she had been sleeping—or at least stealing snippets of sleep. Brett's condition hadn't allowed for extended slumber, nor did it allow for her to be far from his side. She had brought the cot in because it had been the only practical thing to do. There were no other beds in the house to spare, and hers was fully occupied.

That was an understatement. Looking back to Brett, she mentally confirmed what she already knew to be true: there was so much of him. In her delicate four-poster, he appeared a defiant blade of power invading her soft, feminine domain.

She jerked away from the unsettling thought and set about bathing him once more. Ever mindful of his wound, she drew the cool, damp cloth over his forehead and down the column of his neck. Again and again, her hand passed over the warm muscles of his chest and arms and the lean tautness of his belly.

In the hush of the room, the subtle rasp of the cloth gently dragging at the crisp hair on his chest and the stubble on his cheeks was resounding. In a most unexpected way, it served to remind Laurel of the sheer maleness of him.

She yanked her hand to her lap, deeply shaken by this startling awareness. Stern words of rebuke echoed in her head. The man was ill and in need of help. It was unconscionable that she should be struck by the male perfection of him at this moment, but she was.

Perhaps in her relief and joy at his improved condition, her mind had become besotted. Perhaps she was too tired to be proper a moment longer. In any event, her every nerve was attuned to the physical evidence of Brett's masculinity, and her disobedient eyes looked their fill.

Even as ill as he was, Brett McKenzie was a handsome man. The shadow of beard that darkened the lower half of his face didn't detract from that. In fact, she found it far too easy to picture him with a full beard or a mustache, giving him a roguish air. Both would only enhance the curve of his mouth.

Knowing she shouldn't, yet powerless to prevent herself from doing so, she let her gaze drop to that normally hard line. Riddled by good conscience, she allowed herself only a quick glance before she tore her gaze away. But again, fatigue teased and seduced every one of her feminine instincts until she openly studied his mouth. She'd never noticed before just how sensual his lips were.

A bit frantically, she reasoned that was because his mouth was usually compressed with irritation over something she'd said or done. Then not only his mouth, but his entire face would take on a resolute cast of disapproval that was normally echoed in his stance and bearing: legs spread wide, shoulders unyielding with indomitable strength and determination.

Remembering how commanding he could appear, she helplessly looked lower. Brazenly she took visual inventory, tracing a path from the mat of dark hair fanning his chest to the flat male nipples to the hair that bisected his abdomen and coursed downward beneath the sheet at his hips. The white muslin delineated tapering planes, hard hollows. And a bold male swelling.

"Stars and garters!" She jumped to her feet, mortified at her behavior. "Weariness has robbed me of my common sense." And certainly what little decorum she could claim as her own. There was no other excuse for the decidedly erotic bend of her observations.

Her movements less than smooth, she crossed to the dry sink with her basin, righted a stack of towels, fussed with the sash at her waist . . . and then called herself a hussy. She punctuated the epithet by tossing the thick, unruly plait of her hair back over her shoulder. For her efforts, she felt only a smidge better.

It would have to suffice. She told herself as much as she extinguished most of the candles and slipped beneath the covers of her cot. Sleep was what she needed. Rest would restore her normal composure.

But sleep didn't come. And rest filled her head with the image of Brett's face. With a heaved sigh, she draped her arm over her eyes, recognizing uselessness for what it was.

Into the darkness, she admitted, "I've been closeted with the man for too long."

Propping herself up on one elbow, she stared at his shadowed form wishing she could be irritated with him for so thoroughly disrupting her thoughts. She couldn't though. At least not while he was so dependent on her.

She considered that as she lay back. It was difficult to think of Brett McKenzie as being vulnerable. He was normally so healthy and stalwart that it was odd knowing he was momentarily defenseless. Children were defenseless, babes in their mothers' arms were defenseless, not tall, arrogant, handsome majors with piercing pewter-blue eyes that could cut to the quick.

Brett McKenzie could in no way be confused with a child. Even trying to picture him as a young boy was difficult, and she had no hint of what his childhood might have entailed. It did occur to her, however, that he *was* someone's son.

The realization filled her with dismay. At this moment, a mother and a father believed their son was alive and well.

She came to her elbow again, discomfited and oddly enough, hurt by what she logically knew was a big assumption on her part. She didn't know anything about the major. She was taking it for granted that he did have parents, and that they did indeed care about him. But realizing that these conjectures were unfounded didn't lessen her anguish for two people she didn't even know.

In her heart, she cherished the bond between parent and child. Despite whatever discord might exist between her and the major, she wanted to believe that his parents worried over him, that they loved him as much as she had been loved by her own parents.

Slowly, she lay back, more troubled than ever by the man. Damnably, he had just become very real to her—a strange notion given the fact that he had invaded her house with his *very* real wound and his *very* real presence. But she truly hadn't considered him as more than the man who on more than one occasion had tried her temper, the man who had saved her life, the man whose life she was now trying to save.

To her he had been a person on an impersonal level. By putting him in the context of a family, she had inadvertently given him more of an identity, and she found that very disconcerting. She didn't want to think of him as someone's brother or uncle, friend or lover.

"Dear heavens!" she declared into the muted grays. *Was*

he someone's lover? No sooner had the question entered her mind than she clamped down hard on her train of thought and her reaction.

"For all I know," she muttered, completely disgusted with her lack of self-control, "the man might have a string of women falling all over themselves just to be in his company. He could have a score of lovers. He might have a *harem!* It makes no difference to me."

With that conviction, she willed herself to go to sleep and to dream of nothing. The former she did with remarkable ease, the latter was not so readily accomplished. Her mind spun unwelcomed visions of Brett McKenzie and when she next awoke, it was to the sound of his voice.

She threw aside her covers and approached the bed, distantly aware that she must have slept for hours. Sunlight outlined the edge of the curtains with brilliant force.

"Major?"

He turned his head toward her. It was then that she realized that he was bathed in sweat. His fever had broken. Happiness surged up as brilliantly as the sun outdoors. Never in her whole life had she seen anything quite as lovely as the telltale moisture dotting his face and torso.

Quickly, she reached for a towel and dabbed at his cheeks and arms. At her touch, he stirred and shifted beneath the sheet.

Smiling hugely, she poured a small glass of water, then carefully slipped her arm beneath his neck and shoulders to lift him slightly. "Major, you need to drink this," she coaxed. When he turned his head away, she followed the movement with the glass. "Please, Brett. Just a little."

As if her words had reached him, he turned his head back toward her and pressed his face flush into the fullness of her left breast.

Breath choked off, she momentarily forgot about the glass of water. Through the thin fabric of her robe and nightgown, she could feel the damp heat of his face against her skin, the imprint of his nose and mouth against her nipple.

She was held immobile, shocked at the contact that sent tremors straight down to the pit of her. Her heart lurched and her stomach constricted with a kind of pleasurable ache she'd never experienced before.

Swallowing hard, she gathered her wits, determined to ignore the delightful sensations into oblivion. "You need the water," she ordered sternly, annoyed with him for no other reason than he made her feel things she had no business feeling, and annoyed with herself for succumbing to those feelings.

Denouncing herself for a fool, she shifted his head within the crook of her arm. "Brett, open your mouth and drink."

Much to her surprise, he did exactly that. Eyes still shut, he swallowed what she offered then lay back quietly on the pillow.

Laurel sighed deeply, relieved to put some space between them. At the moment, she felt awkward with her own body. As it had once before, it had betrayed her in a most unfamiliar and carnal manner. Thank heaven he hadn't been awake.

From the middle of the room, she peered over her shoulder to reassure herself that he wasn't. She gasped to find that he was staring straight at her.

"Major." She was at his side immediately, her inner trepidation melting before the startling satisfaction that he was no longer unconscious . . . and before the searing intensity in his gaze. Those shimmering cobalt eyes glittered back at her from between half-opened lids.

"Don't try to move," she told him, her voice gentle and soothing. "Just lie still." Perched beside him, she searched his face. "Are you thirsty? Do you need more water?"

His lips remained firmly shut, his gaze fixed on her face. Laurel realized he wasn't truly awake, but in some cloudy remnant of unconsciousness.

"Can you understand me?" Out of habit, she laid her hand on his chest. "Is the pain terrible?"

With surprising strength and speed, he reached out with his right hand and took hold of her wrist, grimacing at the move. With a stare that never wavered, he watched her as if trying to discern some dark fathomless mystery.

"Brett, you shouldn't exert yourself. You've been badly injured, you need to save your strength."

She might well have been talking to the wall for all the good it did her. Slowly, irrevocably, he drew her close, not stopping until she practically lay atop him, her bent arm pinned between her chest and his.

"Major," she breathed, worried that he might tear the stitches out of his shoulder. "Please, let me up."

If he heard her, she didn't know. Somehow he had managed to free her wrist and wrap his right arm about her.

"Brett. You're going to hurt yourself. You don't want to do that." She tried to extricate herself from his grasp, but found she couldn't move.

Given his injury and his present state of health, she wouldn't have thought him to be so powerful. His arm banded her to him as securely as a steel vise. And against her breasts, she could feel the rippling tension of his muscles.

"Major McKenzie, you have to stop." She put as much force into her declaration as she could muster. It wasn't much though. His heat was seeping into her, rendering her limbs useless while his proximity was doing devastating things to her will power.

His arm tightened, forcing her body closer, her head nearer to his. Her lips hovered over his and appallingly, she realized he intended to kiss her.

In ragged puffs, his breath fanned her cheeks. Through narrowed, unfocused eyes, he studied her. "Sweet." His voice emerged as a grating whisper against her mouth.

The breath she stole was his, her gasp drawing the scent of him into her lungs, into her body and mind. The intimacy was staggering, carnal, dissolving her insides until she was awash with liquid heat, dissolving her resolve until she was tempted, oh, so tempted to lower her head that infinitesimal fraction of an inch and press her lips to his.

"Sweet," he muttered again. This time the word was a slurred rendition, trailing off into a sigh. In seconds he was asleep, his arm going limp around her.

Laurel remained where she was, trying to absorb what had just happened, what she had almost allowed to happen. On that imprudent thought, she levered away, far more careful of him than of herself. In a tangle of twisted robe and perplexing emotions, she scrambled off the bed.

*What was I thinking?* Nothing. That was the problem. She hadn't been thinking at all. His move had caught her so unawares that her tired, worried, fool excuse of a mind had ceased to function.

"Well, enough is enough," she declared. She'd be damned if she was going to behave like a simpleton. She had a brain, she was a determined woman. She could, and would, cease this lascivious preoccupation with Brett McKenzie at once.

To that end, she grabbed up her clothes for the day, set her shoulders, and exited for Hope's room.

Brett couldn't remember when he'd ever been in such pain. That was his first lucid thought when he awoke. His second was that he didn't know where in the hell he was. The silent, decidedly feminine room offered no clues.

Shifting on the bed, he grimaced and grunted around a curse. The pain that had dragged him from sleep emanated from his left shoulder. Carefully, he tested the thick bandaging and in so doing, suddenly realized why he was in bed in what he assumed was the middle of the day.

In rapid succession, he remembered the fight in the street, the unruly mob. He had looked up in time to see Laurel Seymore on the brink of being pummeled by a meaty fist. His insides had turned cold with fear and then torrid with rage.

Glowering darkly, he shot his gaze about the room. Where the devil was she? The last he could recall was sending her attacker running, then turning to see that she hadn't been hurt. After that, nothing, at least not in the real sense. Distant hints of dreams teased the corners of his mind.

He could see her hovering over him, her lips a mere whisper from his own, her green eyes wide with wonder and something his memory couldn't grasp. The vague impression of feeling her breasts against his chest brought a narrowing of his eyes. Disjointed memories of feeling her hands stroke his body sent his brows up.

Damn, his dreams of her had been as contradictory as the lady herself.

Purposely, he put off thinking about her and the idiocy

of her actions. It wouldn't do any good to wonder why she had been in the midst of all the mayhem. He'd only fume and he didn't need that now. He had other things to contend with at the moment, most importantly his whereabouts.

From what he could tell, he'd been carefully tended, but by whom? It bothered him not to know whose bed he occupied. It bothered him even more that he was incapacitated. His left arm was bound snugly to his side, his shoulder wrapped tightly to prevent as much movement as possible.

Slowly, he struggled to sit up, gritting his teeth at the agony that lanced his shoulder. By sheer will alone, he staved off the dizziness that threatened, breathing deeply to restore his balance.

Planting his feet firmly on the floor proved to be a major accomplishment. His legs worked sluggishly, taking mental commands seconds after the fact, but success was finally his and he gave into a crooked grin. The lopsided line straightened and thinned, however, when he managed to come to his feet. Weakness pervaded him to a sickening degree, pain planting a perverse nausea in his stomach.

He swayed slightly, waiting for his body to right itself. When it did, he sucked in a much needed dose of air and determined to cross to one of the windows. The feat proved to be trying.

He was as weak as a babe, and his shoulder throbbed. The effort it required to take the few steps away from the bed caused him to break into a sweat. But the window beckoned with the lure of discovery. If he was going to be a virtual cripple, confined, he damn well wanted to know where he was.

The scene below was that of a courtyard, neat and tidy. He recognized it at once. The Seymore residence. Peering to the street visible beyond the wrought-iron gate, he recognized the spot where he had fallen. It would seem that somehow Laurel Seymore had gotten him into her house and up the stairs. Into her room?

He pivoted to stare at the bed and for the first time, noticed the cot. His already raised brows arched further. Had she been the one to care for him? His dreams would attest to that. He couldn't imagine the sister assuming the task and he sensed that it would be out of character for Laurel to turn the responsibility over to the maid.

Carefully, swallowing with difficulty, he made his way to the narrow bed and lifted the silky nightgown he found there. The garment held a touch of floral perfume, a scent he had come to associate with Laurel. Fingering the piece, he easily pictured her wearing the thin bit of nothing.

In defense to the erotic image his mind conjured up, he craned his neck, shoving his chin to one side. He wasn't in any condition to let his thoughts or his body stray in that direction. In fact, his body was rapidly losing the meager store of energy it had and his thoughts were becoming as sharp as oatmeal.

He returned to the bed, irritated by his lack of stamina. His head was swimming and his knees were actually trembling. The injury to his shoulder must have been more serious than he knew. Lying down was suddenly extremely appealing, and necessary.

Silky gown still clenched in his right hand, he wavered on his feet. Dazedly, it crossed his mind that if he were to collapse now, Laurel Seymore would enter to find him on the floor without a stitch of clothing.

He was in the middle of imagining the expression on her face when the door opened, and the lady herself entered.

# Ten

A multitude of impressions assailed Laurel simultaneously. Brett was awake, standing, naked, staring at her . . . and looked to be on the verge of collapse. She ignored all but the last and rushed to his side.

"Major McKenzie, what are you doing?" She circled one arm around his back and the other low across his chest. "Please, lie down."

Brett didn't think he had much choice. His body gave out on him at the same time Laurel's arms offered support. Gratefully, he took it, giving himself up to her gentle ministrations as she went about getting him on his back once more with his legs stretched out beneath the covers.

The relief to his shoulder was immediate and he soaked up the comfort afforded by the bed and the tenderness to be found at Laurel's touch. For such a headstrong, willful woman, her hands were gentle and caring and sensitive.

It was an observation he made at a most gut level. As dull as his head felt, he was rather amazed that he managed to be that discerning. Just lying there required all of his strength.

Eyes slightly narrowed, he watched as she bent over him to arrange the sheet and blanket. Seeing her thus was reminiscent of his dream where her breath had caressed his lips as subtly as her delicate floral perfume permeated her nightgown.

The scent teased him now, piquing his shackled senses with extravagant possibilities. What would she do if he were to hook a hand behind her neck, draw her closer, press his face into her neck . . . or between her breasts . . . and breathe in the scent of her?

"Are you in great pain?" she asked.

"A touch." Damn if his blood wasn't humming with an unexpected fervency.

"You shouldn't have gotten up." Carefully, she loosened the edge of the bandage and checked the wound. "You could have torn the stitches out."

"I assume they're all still intact."

"Yes. Thankfully." Dr. Mathews's handiwork had held. Laurel didn't want to think what might have happened if Brett had injured himself. The wound was greatly improved, but it was far from completely healed. The flesh was swollen and discolored and tender. Any overexertion on the major's part could impair or ruin the progress he'd made thus far.

She sat beside him, securing the layers of soft linen. Through her mind flashed memories of the last several days and nights of harrowing uncertainty. He'd suffered enough already without his having to endure more.

"How are you feeling?"

"Like I was stabbed with a wooden stake."

Hearing the grizzly details made Laurel wince with an inner pain. Wishing to ease his discomfort, she asked, "Are you hungry? I have some broth simmering out in the kitchen."

"Broth?" His voice carried a hint of disgust as one side of his face contorted with blatant misgiving.

"You won't be up to eating anything more solid than that for a while."

Which suddenly made Brett wonder about a few things. Blinking, he corralled pertinent questions that had been wandering uselessly in his head. "How long have I been here?"

"Four days."

He exhaled in disbelief.

"You've been very ill, Major, feverish and unconscious." She didn't have the heart to tell him that he had almost died. "Doctor Mathews took care of you, but I sent for the army surgeon as well. He's been in to check on you every day."

It was a blank void to Brett. Annoyingly, he had no memory of doctors or the days passing one after another. "I don't remember any of it."

"You didn't wake up until this morning, and even then, you were still in a stupor of sorts." In that daze, he had dragged her close and she had nearly kissed him.

She shied from the thought, cautioning herself against the dangers lurking down that particular road. Nothing good could come from such imprudent behavior. "You really should have some broth, Major."

She left the room, not giving him a chance to argue the point, or herself a chance to muse about what his mouth would feel like against hers. Still, like a sly, beguiling serpent, the thought invaded.

Would his mouth be warm and firm? Would he gently coax her lips to mold themselves to his or would he storm her softness with lip and tongue?

"Stars and garters." Her muttered words bounced off the walls and followed her down the stairwell. Hadn't she chastised herself already in regard to her wanton responses to the man? Hadn't she purposely stayed out of her room as much as possible today for that very reason?

"He's your patient, you fool. He's in need of your assistance, not your lust."

Believing herself bolstered by that reminder, she returned to her room with a bowl of chicken broth and a weak cup of tea. He'd most likely balk at the tea, but her mother had always put a great deal of faith in the brew.

Tray in hand, she opened the door and silently sent up a prayer. *Give me strength, Mama.*

"Here you are." She made certain her expression was composed, her voice serene. She'd give him not even the slightest suggestion of the inner turmoil he so easily provoked. A word, a look, the sight of him; all and any had the power to upset her carefully constructed world if she wasn't on her guard.

"I don't suppose there's roasted beef in that bowl," he hinted broadly, eyeing the white crockery with ill-concealed displeasure.

"Not until Captain Jeffers says so."

"Damn," he muttered in a low voice, his brow heavily creased with lines of vexation.

He looked so perturbed, she couldn't suppress the spurt of laughter that tickled her insides. "Don't you like soup?"

"No."

And from that, she garnered he wasn't going to be gracious about it. Oddly enough, it was his disgruntled mien that eased her defenses and reminded her that, everything else aside, he was dependent upon her. When he recovered, he might very well imperil her existence, but for now, he was a man who had risked his life for her, a man who needed her help.

"You'll like this, Major, I promise. It's a recipe my

mother used." Taking up what had become her post by his side, she added, "Your stomach won't be able to tolerate anything more. If it could, I would gladly provide anything that would promote your recovery."

Brett could see that she meant what she said. She was genuinely concerned for his health. Pleased for no accountable reason, he relented and let her feed him the broth.

It wasn't in his nature to be so coddled. His temperament as well as his occupation precluded his being doted on, and yet, he found that after the first initial moments of awkwardness, having Laurel's nurturing attention was remarkably satisfying. Later, when he was in full command of all his senses, he'd most likely chafe at his easy capitulation, but for now, he accepted it. And besides, the broth was damned good.

"You're going to need spectacles if you continue to stare so," Laurel chided with a small smile.

He was staring and he didn't care. There was a softness about Laurel Seymore that was rarely displayed. Gone was the intractable glint in her green eyes, gone was the air of defiance with which she normally blanketed herself. Sitting with her thigh pressed along the outer edge of his chest, her scarlet curls a wild riot framing her face, she emitted a tenderness that he had noted on only one other occasion, and then it had been reserved solely for her sister.

"My sight has never been more clear."

"I'm relieved to hear that." She lifted the spoon. "Open up. I was beginning to think I had grown a second nose."

Brett swallowed. "Nothing that blatant."

"Oh? What exactly do you see, sir?"

"Another Laurel Seymore."

Her gaze snapped to his, her hand halted briefly over

the bowl. Then she relented to an easy smile. "Your infirmity has addled your brain."

"No. Lying down again has helped." So much so that he realized something that up until now had escaped his notice; Laurel's reaction to his nudity when she had first entered the room. She hadn't even blinked—a telling statement for a young, *unwed* woman. "Your soup is doing its job. I'm feeling much improved."

"Good. I would be extremely upset if you were to take a turn for the worse." She'd never spoken truer words. Her heart still ached when she thought of how close he'd come to death. And it was all her fault.

Brett frowned at the sudden paling of her cheeks and the lowering of the corners of her mouth. "Why do you look as if your favorite puppy has just died?"

Laurel dipped the spoon into the bowl, but for the life of her, couldn't finish feeding him. The guilt and shame she'd been carrying inside of her for days churned relentlessly.

Slowly, swallowing past the awful emotions clogging her throat, she lifted her gaze to his. "I haven't thanked you for saving me the way you did. You placed yourself in grave peril for my sake."

Her gratefulness took him by surprise, jarring him out of the comfortable repose that had existed between them. Scrutinizing her features, he saw the contrition she couldn't hide.

"What were you doing out there?" he asked, getting right to the heart of the matter that still had the power to chill his blood.

"Being a fool."

His surprise escalated. He wouldn't have thought she'd admit to having behaved so recklessly. "On that we can agree. I couldn't believe my eyes when I looked up and saw that bastard about to hit you."

"He would have, if you hadn't stopped him."

"What were you thinking to have placed yourself in such a perilous situation?"

She accepted the steely censure underscoring his words. Still, she mentally squirmed and looked down at her lap. "You cannot scold me any more than I have myself, Major. I know that I acted impulsively and far too arrogantly." She lifted her gaze to look him squarely in the eye. "It is a fault with which I have had to struggle all my life. I regret deeply that my shortcomings have resulted in your injury and I can only ask your forgiveness."

It was a while before Brett could take his next breath. Stunned, he glowered for no other reason than he didn't know what to make of her heartfelt repentance. He had cause to be angry with her for her lack of care for her own safety, but he certainly didn't blame her for his wound.

Apparently she did. Making no excuses for herself, she didn't try to evade the issue. She accepted a responsibility she assumed was hers and apologized.

"Laurel, do not berate yourself. I don't hold you accountable for any damage done to my person. Whether I am wounded or not is due entirely to my own skill and competence."

"But you wouldn't have gotten hurt if you hadn't had to come to my rescue."

He scoffed. "I was wounded because I failed to anticipate the man's attack. I admit, I don't allow that to happen often, but it could have occurred anywhere, at any time, with any other combatant."

Laurel wished she could rationalize it as easily as Brett did. What he said was true, but the fact still remained, he *hadn't* been injured defending himself, he'd been injured defending her. And for that, she'd always be indebted.

Danger lurked beneath that sentiment. Brett McKenzie was going to get well. He was going to go back to doing everything he had been doing before, including suspecting her of smuggling. Being grateful to him was going to complicate her life terribly.

Trying for a self-possessed expression, she regarded him with what she hoped was poise, only to discover that he had dropped off to sleep literally between one minute and the next. She sighed. He had pushed himself too hard, first by walking about and then by lying there engaging her in conversation. Somehow it didn't come as a surprise that he would tax himself to his utmost limits. He was a man of rare strength both physically and mentally, a man worth admiring.

The admission cost her dearly. She didn't want to think of him in those terms, but in the weighty silence, the steady rise and fall of his chest an invaluable truth, she couldn't deny that there was much to like about the man.

All the muscles about her stomach braided into an uncomfortable knot and inwardly she groaned. She'd been trying to prevent this very thing from happening. Unfortunately, it was becoming increasingly apparent that all the attributes she longed for in a man were the very same that defined Brett McKenzie.

His valor and sense of purpose were part of his character, not embellishments he donned with his uniform. He was honest, honorable and forthright—perhaps a bit too much so. His unadorned manner more often than not pricked her temper, but in truth, she preferred that to fickleness. That foolish quality was a sign of a weak mind and Lord knew, Brett was anything but simple.

He was one of the most intelligent men she'd ever met. At the root of all his actions was a keen intellect and a practical bend of mind. Combined they made for a sure, steady courage. Twice, he'd given her assistance when he'd made no secret of the fact that he didn't particularly like her.

Her foolish, foolish heart wilted. She might have pretended otherwise, but she didn't. The sense of disappointment she felt was too painful, too real, and in that moment she damned reality. Reality was abhorrent, rife with complications and obstacles. Reality was remembering that she was committed to one course, and the major to another. Reality was knowing that for Brett, a woman was relegated to only one position.

Her foolish heart wanted none of that. It wanted, ached for laughter and love and shared dreams with a man she respected and liked. She'd never longed for a husband before, but in Brett, she could imagine a spouse to hold her through the nights, a husband with whom she'd have children, with whom she'd pass the years, growing old at his side.

She lifted her hand to stroke the hair back off Brett's forehead, but an inch away from threading her fingers through the black strands, she drew back. She had no delusions as to what was real and what wasn't. The yearnings of her heart were feeble wishes and she would do well to remember that all those wonderful attributes she so admired in Brett had, up until now, been exercised at her expense.

He was committed to his duty, and it had been his duty to pry into her affairs. He was dedicated to law and order and in its pursuit, he'd interrogated her with steely resolve. He was proud and arrogant and altogether too powerful.

Time and again he'd wielded that power in her direction. He was a beast. She'd said as much a dozen times.

There was reality, cold and unvarnished. She'd always preferred the truth. At the moment, she found it miserably depressing.

Taking her nightgown from his hand, she crossed to the door, carrying her tray and her regrets from the room.

Tess was waiting at the bottom of the stairs. "Is he dead?"

Appalled, Laurel shook her head. "No! He's very much alive, and awake. His fever broke this morning."

Tess squinted one eye shut. "If he better, then what make you look like you do?"

"My conscience."

"What?"

Laurel waved the matter away. "Never mind. It's something I'm going to have to figure out on my own."

"If you say so." She nodded to the tray in Laurel's hands. "Did he eat?"

"Mmm, a bowl of broth." He'd fallen asleep before he could even think about the tea.

"That a good sign. Before you know it, he'll be on his feet and out of here."

The prospect should have delighted Laurel. It didn't. Imagining Brett gone left her with a hollow sensation inside her.

"Where's Hope?" she inquired, determined to conquer this debilitating weakening on her part.

"Washing up."

"Did all go well at the shop today?"

"Right as can be."

Laurel tried to concentrate on business. Through the course of preparing a light supper, she and Tess discussed the events of their respective days. Hope joined them for the evening meal, but it was only a matter of time before talk of the shop gave way to that of Major McKenzie.

That didn't help Laurel's state of mind. Her common sense was engaged in a full contest with her private desires. That rarely happened to her. She was usually in perfect harmony with herself, her heart and her mind needing and wanting the same things.

But that inner accord was not hers tonight. For the first time ever, she longed for what others would deem the typical life for a woman; wife, mother, lover. What she had instead was a commitment to an ideal that put her in direct opposition to the first man to stir her desire.

The admission was bittersweet. She might very well feel as she did about the man, but he in no way felt the same for her. She vexed him at every turn, provoked his temper and his ire and had even managed to get him stabbed. He had no cause to find her appealing.

By the time she climbed the stairs to check on Brett for the night, she ruthlessly faced herself with an ultimate truth. Even if her circumstances didn't put Brett beyond her reach, he was not a man for love and marriage and happily ever after.

Armed with that logic, she entered her room, every one of her defenses up and primed, only to find that Brett was asleep. Relief and disappointment assailed her in equal parts, but she gave in to neither. Nor did she linger to analyze her feelings. It wouldn't be wise. If she tarried, she would be leaving herself open to all the conflicting thoughts and emotions that had plagued her all evening.

Quickly, as carefully as possible, she pressed the back of her hand to his cheek. His skin was warm and dry. His breathing deep and regular. All were good signs.

She left it at that, then went below to double-check the front door locks. It was an old habit she reverted to upon occasion, in those times when anxiety rode her hard. Reassuring herself that the door was barred was a simple enough task to perform in order to insure a good night's sleep.

And sleep was what she intended. She was tired, her mind in a whirl. Now that Brett was recovering, he didn't need her close at hand. She would share Hope's bed and get the rest she so obviously needed.

The front door proved to be locked. She honestly hadn't expected anything else. Nonetheless, lantern in hand, she peered into the dining room to the right of the foyer and then into the parlor to the left. Expecting everything to be in order, she cast the room a cursory glance . . . then sucked in a frightened gasp.

"Good evening, Laurel love."

She sagged against the door frame, one hand pressed to her chest as if that could still her racing heart. "John St. James!" she whispered furiously. "What are you doing here?"

# Eleven

"I heard that you've got a certain army major upstairs."

Laurel pushed away from the door, ignoring the beguiling smile John gave her. She didn't give a damn how charming he could be or what rumors he may have heard. "How did you get in here?"

Lounging on the settee, his feet propped up on a chair he'd drawn near, he spread his hands wide and repeatedly flicked his brows up. "I have my ways."

"I don't give a fig about your ways. You have no right to intrude into my home this way." This invasion incited her resentment and her anger. They were not friends, they were acquaintances. Theirs was an association for monetary reasons alone. To that end, they always met in the shop's cellar.

Setting her lantern aside, she yanked the armchair out from beneath his booted feet. "You forget yourself, John."

"How?" Straightening, his mouth curled with an innocent-looking smile, his mustache tilting up at one corner.

"By being here." She set the chair in its customary place beside the fireplace. "Our arrangement doesn't allow for this."

"For what? For my paying a call on a business partner?"

"I am not your partner."

"The law might not agree with you."

She wasn't about to enter into a debate with him. "What do you want?"

Coming to his feet, John shook his head. "Ah, Laurel love, so tense, so brusque. You must relax."

"I would like to do that, but your presence makes that impossible. As you say, I have a certain army major upstairs."

"Ah, yes, Major McKenzie. How is the fellow?"

"Recovering."

"A pity."

"No, it isn't. The man saved my life."

John's expression sobered, his dark brows angling downward. "I heard that as well. I suppose, then, that I should be grateful to the man. After all, you have become indispensable to me."

"If that is so, then why did you risk my safety by coming here?" Even worse, he'd placed Hope and Tess in danger as well. "If someone saw you—"

"No one saw me."

"You can't be certain of that."

As was his way, John relented to a smile complete with dimple, his whiskey-hued eyes sparkling. "You forget that I'm Jack Diego. I'm purported to slip in and out of Charleston like a shadow through the night."

"Call yourself whatever you like. Either way, you are the possessor of a monumental self-importance."

"But of course. How do you think I've come to be so successful?"

Thoroughly disgusted with his lack of conscience or repentance, Laurel threw her hands up and spun on her heel. There was no dealing with him when he was in this mood. Normally, she coped quite well, but the worst of her fright had dissipated, leaving her more wearied than ever. "Why are you here, John?"

"To see you."

She peered back over her shoulder. "You've done that, so you can leave."

Annoyingly, he gave a short bark of laughter, its boisterous tones jerking her around to face him.

"Be quiet," she admonished, her gaze darting to the open doorway. "You'll have Tess and Hope down here in a minute."

"That would be interesting." But he did lower his voice and thankfully, broached the reason for his visit. "I came to reassure myself of your welfare."

"You didn't need to sneak into my house in order to do that. You could have sent word around by the normal means."

"There are some things I do not trust to a flunky. I wanted to see with my own eyes that you were unharmed."

"Don't worry," she jeered, "I wouldn't inconvenience you by dying."

"You're a callous little thing tonight."

"Perhaps, but honest." John's interest in her went only as far as her significance to his operation. He wanted her well because it saved him the trouble of having to make other arrangements. And because the present procedure was so perfect.

"Do not think to flatter me with your supposed concern, Mr. St. James, and don't play me for a fool. If I had been dead or injured, word would have been spread all over Charleston by now. You knew I was unharmed before you set foot in this house tonight." She planted her hands on her waist and cocked her head at a challenging angle. "So, I ask again, why are you here?"

The twinkling in John's eyes extinguished in an instant. The convivial air he wore so effortlessly gave way to the streak of viciousness Laurel knew was at the core of John's temperament.

"You always were a shrewd little flower, Laurel love. I think that's why we have always gotten on so well, you and I."

He closed the space between them, stepping near enough for Laurel to see the fine grains of gold in his eyes. Instinct impelled her back, determination held her in place. This wasn't the first time he'd sought to intimidate her with such a ploy.

"We get along," she maintained, "because neither of us has ever overstepped the bounds."

"It works well that way, don't you agree?"

"Yes."

"I know how far to push you and you know what I will and will not tolerate. I keep your secrets and you keep mine." Gently, he trailed his fingertips over her cheek, but there was nothing tender in his face. That handsome visage was marked by a virulent warning. "And you do keep my secrets, don't you, Laurel?"

Laurel jerked her head away from his touch, detesting the feel of his hand as much as she did his innate effrontery. The purpose for his visit was suddenly clear, igniting the embers of her temper.

"If you think I've betrayed you then come right out and say so, otherwise be done with your veiled threats and innuendos."

"You're caring for the enemy."

"He saved my life. What was I supposed to do, leave him for dead?"

"Why not?"

"Unlike you, I have a conscience."

"A weakness, you mean."

"What do you care as long as I hold true to my half of our arrangement?"

"Be sure that you do."

"You don't need to tell me that, John. In case you haven't noticed, I have just as much to lose in this bargain as you. More if we consider that I have a home and a business and family at stake."

John's upper lip quivered before settling into a cruel line. "See that you don't forget that. I would hate to have to remind you of where your loyalties lie."

"Meaning what?"

"Meaning you're part of this bargain until I say otherwise." Reaching up again, he flicked a red curl dangling along her neck. "Or until you've outlived your usefulness."

The unconcealed threat jabbed at Laurel's stomach with a slash of fright. They'd had their disagreements before, but never to such a dangerous flash point.

Doing her best to keep her consternation hidden behind an impassive expression, she returned his stare, but it took a supreme effort on her part. He was deadly serious in his intent. He would see that she remained a loyal member of the "fold" or he would see her dead.

The tremor that raced down both her arms set her fingers to trembling. In defense, she tucked her hands into the folds of her dress and silently cursed John St. James for the bastard that he was, and herself for being so naive. The question of how long they would retain their peculiar association had never arisen. Too late she realized that she had been horribly careless in thinking that she could simply sever their ties whenever she saw fit.

"Do you plan to kill me then?" she demanded, her voice backed by a bravado rooted in as much anger as fear. "To slit my throat or put a pistol to my head if I don't carry on like one of your men?" She wasn't one to live at the whim of others and she'd be damned if she was going to start now. As never before, it was vital that she retain a balance of power between them. It was the only way to ensure her safety.

"Let me tell you, Mr. St. James, I have as much say in this affair as you. I make my own decisions as to what's right or wrong for me. There might come a time when *you* outlive your usefulness."

She let her words sink into the silence, her heart thumping more than she would have liked. There was no help for it. She and John were wading through hazardous waters, each testing the other as never before.

"Brave words, Laurel love." His whisper was a frigid hiss.

"Honest words."

"You really are a little bitch at heart, aren't you?"

"You push me to it."

He didn't say anything more as he scrutinized her with scorching eyes. Finally, he stroked his forefinger over his mustache before nodding ever so slightly. "I think we finally understand each other." With that, he stepped back, then boldly, insolently made his way to the front door and strode off into the night.

He was gone before Laurel fully comprehended his departure. Without conscious thought, she followed behind him to lock the door. Only when she leaned back against the panel to steady her shaking legs did she truly realize that she was alone. Her eyes drifted shut and she placed a hand to her stomach. She couldn't remember an experience that had required so much courage she wasn't certain she possessed.

With a sudden, abhorrent thought, her eyes flew wide. She raced into the parlor and thrust aside the drawn drapes. There she found the answer as to how John had entered. Quickly, she shut the window, secured its latch, then gathered the drapes closed again.

The sense of having been violated made her wrap her arms about her. This was her home, her safe haven, and it had just been invaded. More than ever, she resented John, and more than ever, she realized the precariousness of her position.

Everything had changed between them tonight. Their relationship had shifted from what it had been to something more hostile and infinitely more forbidding to her peace of mind.

She nearly burst into laughter at the thought. It had been so long since true peace had been hers she could hardly remember what it felt like to be completely safe and untroubled. She had few complaints as it was a situation of her own making with the promise of contentment lying ahead for her. Now dread loomed like an appalling weight ready to drag her down into ruin, and she didn't know how to defend herself against it.

"Major McKenzie." Laurel paused just inside her bedroom the next morning. To her surprise, she found the man sitting up on the edge of the bed, sheet draped over his lap. Except for the fierce scowl lining his face, he looked far better than he had the day before. For the first time in days, his skin actually shone with a hint of healthy color and his eyes were clear and bright, the sapphire tinged with that unusual silver. "You, sir, are a most stubborn man."

"You're not the first to accuse me of that," Brett informed her. In a single glance, he took in her slender figure clad in a simple gown of dusty blue. As usual, her hair was atop her head, secured there by several ribbons to match her dress. She was a fetching sight that unfortunately served to point up the harsh irritation that had been building in him since he'd awakened.

His head pounded and his shoulder ached like the devil. The discomfort wasn't any worse than it had been yesterday, but his mind was clearer this morning, more alert. He was more conscious of the pain. Frustratingly, he could do nothing about it. For a man in the habit of taking action, his inability to rectify his physical condition chafed sorely.

To make matters worse, he was unaccustomed to inactivity or confinement. Bandaged as he was, his already limited movements were limited even more. His patience was severely frayed.

"That better not be more soup," he warned, eyeing the tray she carried.

"No, as a matter of fact, it's grits. And toast and tea."

*"Grits?"*

"Cooked in beef stock. It's very good for you." She set the tray on the bedside table before turning her disapproving frown on him. He was in a foul mood. Yesterday, for all of his discomfort, he'd been far more pleasant. "You should be lying down."

He gave her a smug, mocking glare. "I'm not tired."

"Perhaps, but your body has been through an ordeal. You need your rest."

"If anyone looks to be in need of rest, Miss Seymore, it's you."

Under his blatant scrutiny, Laurel dropped her gaze, pretending an interest with the toes of her shoes. She didn't need to be told that her face revealed every sign of her sleepless night. Faint smudges ringed her eyes, her lips were involuntarily drawn and not a bit of color rode her cheeks.

"I'm perfectly fine," she lied. Through the long night, she hadn't been able to rid her mind of the scene with John. The resulting anxiety had kept her tossing until nearly dawn and now vibrated along her nerves. She was very much on edge, her forbearance next to nil. "How does your shoulder feel?"

"Like hell."

The sigh she heaved emerged as an exasperated hiss. Ignoring all common sense, he insisted on pushing himself beyond what was reasonable. "Dr. Jeffers said you should remain in bed."

"Dr. Jeffers is an ass."

"I'm sure he'd be pleased to hear that. He'll be by to see you this morning."

"There's nothing the man can do for me now, except perhaps order you to give me some real food." He punctuated his complaint by thrusting his chin forward, his growth of beard accentuating the contour of his jaw.

Without meaning to, Laurel trailed her gaze from that hard shape to his neck and then downward to the broad expanse of his chest. The dark mat of hair was utterly masculine.

"After you eat," she blurted out too loudly, chagrined by her wayward thoughts, "perhaps you might like to shave." Stepping to the head of the bed, she made a show of fluffing his pillows. "I have one of Papa's old razors you can use. Now, can you lie back by yourself or do you need my help?"

His mouth twisted derisively. "Neither. If I'm going to be incarcerated in this room and forced to eat *pudding,* then I'll do so sitting up." Perversely provoked, he looked from the pillows to the chair across the room by the fireplace. "If you really want to help, you can bring me my pants." He returned his taunting gaze to her. "Or you can stand there and have all of your feminine sensibilities abused when I stand up and let go of this sheet."

Laurel blinked her eyes wide, taken aback by his outburst. She'd almost forgotten how autocratic the man could be. And determined. He was going to get up from that bed, and from the look in his eyes, there would be no stopping him.

Her temper flared, pricked by his high-handed manner and his lack of regard for himself. Didn't he care that he could have a relapse? She certainly did.

"Very well." She relented as graciously as possible, which was to say, she spoke past a rigidly locked jaw. If he was determined to sit in the blasted chair, then she would see to it that he didn't reinjure himself in the process.

Removing his pants from her closet, she mentally berated him. The man was positively unreasonable. Even a child could understand that one's body needed to be pampered after a serious injury.

"I had these cleaned and ironed for you." She handed the pants over, growing increasingly miffed that he should be so cavalier about his condition. It took a great deal of self-control for her to ask, "Can you manage on your own?"

If he had to pull the damned pants on with his teeth,

Brett had resolved to getting dressed without any assistance. Holding the trousers by the waistband, he flicked them out so that they lay flush with his legs, but that was where his efficiency ended. He couldn't bend and twist enough to shove his feet into their proper positions. And he was just angry enough and ill-tempered enough not to look to Laurel for help.

He didn't need to. She could see for herself that he couldn't manage. Stubborn, proud man.

Without saying a word, she snatched the pants away and bunched them up so that each leg formed a short, crumpled tube. Then, ignoring his glare that seared the top of her head, she knelt and slipped the pants over his feet, past his knees and up to his thighs. There, she met with the sheet, but she was so irritated with the man that she didn't let the thought of his nudity stop her.

Feminine sensibilities, indeed. She'd seen him naked, for heaven's sake. What was one more glimpse of what was no secret to her?

In actuality, it was more than she was prepared for. She couldn't ignore the fact that for the most part, any glimpsing she'd done had been while he'd been unconscious. He was wide awake now and so close his heat bathed her skin. That made for an uncomfortable intimacy.

"You need to slide forward a little," she told him, her voice oddly choked.

Through narrowed eyes, Brett watched her every move. Not for the first time, he was struck by her complaisant manner. He knew many a woman who would be blushing to her toes at having to help a man pull on his pants. But not Laurel. She appeared to be more furious than embarrassed. He had half a mind to whip the sheet away and call her bluff. He didn't, though, and in the end, she got his pants under the sheet and over his hips without a fuss.

Once on his feet, trousers fastened, his shoulder protested vehemently. He was grateful and at the same time resentful that Laurel eased an arm around his back to aid in his progress across the room. An intractable, unreasonable reaction, but he wasn't used to needing help. Thankfully, he sank into the chair's cushions and for the time being, at least, could be his usual competent self.

Laurel laid the tray on the table close at hand. "I assume you wish to feed yourself."

"I'm not a baby," he muttered. Picking up the spoon, he jabbed at the grits as if they weren't quite dead. "Hell."

That one curse was all it took to snap Laurel's patience. She jammed her fists onto her waist and glared at him, the green of her eyes practically flashing with heat.

"Major McKenzie, I am doing my best to remember that you are not yourself, that in your pain and discomfort, you are entitled to be out of sorts. But you, sir, are the most cantankerous man I have ever had the misfortune to meet. From the second I entered this room today, I have been your target, when as far as I can tell, I have done nothing to deserve such treatment.

"If I have offended you in some way or if I have treated you unkindly then please tell me so that I may rectify the situation." Her slender figure shook with her ire. "And if not, I suggest you eat your breakfast and save your complaints. I have no desire to listen to them or to tolerate your pigheadedness."

"Pigheaded?" he grated, stressing each syllable in precise tones.

"You define the word."

In a flash, he reached out and took hold of her wrist,

this time forgetting his injury. Pain shot out in every direction and he doubled over, grimacing and cursing as he released Laurel's hand.

She gasped, relinquishing her anger in an instant. Quickly, she wrapped her arms about him, lending him support, whether he wanted it or not.

"Oh, Brett, what have you done?" She could feel the tremors rack his body. With his head pressed into her shoulder, she eased him back against the chair's soft cushion. Sweat dotted his forehead and upper lip. The color that had heralded his recovery had been wiped away.

Remorse threatened to swamp her, but she couldn't afford to give in to the feeling, not when Brett was in such agony. As she had done so often in the past days, she wet a cloth in cool water at the dry sink then returned to his side to bathe his face and neck.

"I'm sorry," she whispered, wishing she had been more understanding, wishing she hadn't let John St. James deplete her of her reserves. She laid the cloth aside and lifted the cup of tea. "Can you take a sip?"

Eyes still clenched shut, Brett battled the pain, willed it away to an incessant throbbing by concentrating on Laurel's gentle touch. The feel of her arms was a balm equaled only by the stroking of her fingers over his brow. He filled his lungs with air and drew in the delicate floral scent of her.

"Brett, can you drink this?"

He opened his eyes to find her standing close, her face tight with worry and fear. Both were out of place, truly out of character for a woman he knew to be the epitome of feminine strength.

She'd called him Brett.

As if that single realization had the power to assuage

the ills of the world, he felt his tension dissipate to a wearied acceptance. Sighing, he let his head fall back against the chair and when she lifted the cup, he drank.

"Better?" Her voice was low, her lips thinned to a narrow contour.

"Yes."

"Forgive me, I shouldn't have provoked your temper."

He studied her expressive features. "The blame is mine, Laurel." He liked being able to speak her name. "I make for a terrible patient."

"And I have a temperament not suited to a good nurse."

A hint of a crooked smile came to his lips. "We are both at fault, we are both regretful." He heaved a sigh and bit back the last of the pain.

"Are you up to eating?"

He was hungry, but his energy was gone, consumed by a body that was wont to betray him. "If you'll stay and help."

The rueful slant to his lips brought a small smile to Laurel's. Pulling the small bench from her dressing table next to his chair, she sat beside him with bowl in hand. He remained as silent as she until he'd eaten half the grits.

"Did you cook this yourself?" he asked.

"Yes." Her forehead puckered ever so slightly. "How did you know?"

"A deduction based on something your maid told me."

"Tess?" Laurel tipped her head to one side in confusion. She hadn't been aware that the two had even spoken.

"Mmm, she and I had a most enlightening conversation the day she brought that bolt of silk around. She told me some very interesting things about you."

She was instantly wary. "Me? I can't imagine what she might have said. Tess is usually close-mouthed."

"Not when it comes to defending you."

"Did she have to?"

"She thought so. She's very loyal to you."

"Tess is special. She hasn't had an easy time of it."

"She said the same of you."

"There is no comparing our situations."

"She said she used to be a slave, but that you took her in a few years ago."

"That's right." She didn't know what to make of their conversation. It was rather unsettling speaking on so personal a level, both awkward and exhilarating. "Here." She handed him half a slice of buttered toast.

He ate slowly, then asked, "You don't believe in slavery, do you?"

The question came out of nowhere, jerking Laurel's stunned gaze to his. "What . . . how . . . ?"

"Don't bother denying it."

Almost suspiciously, she regarded him, trying to fathom why he would mention such a thing. Did he have an ulterior motive, did he know of her activities, or was he merely curious? Logic impelled her to believe that it was the latter. If he were aware of her association with John, she would be sitting in a jail right now. Besides, no one other than Tess knew the true nature of her buying trips.

Still, she proceeded cautiously, but honestly. The subject of slavery itself was prime for confrontation. "No, I can't deny it. I think slavery is an abomination."

Brett's blatant look of speculation turned into one of satisfaction. "That is an unusual attitude for this part of the country."

"In that I have tried to be discrete. Do you have any objections?"

"None." Hearing the defensiveness in her tone, Brett relented to a smile. "Don't assume that I condemn you."

"Others have."

"I have no doubt." In a city and state where slavery was an integral part of life, where the practice of owning and selling human beings had been dragged to new depths, disapproving of the institution was amazing. And it said a great deal about Laurel's inner resolve.

It was easy enough to live true to your beliefs when all around were in accordance with you. But to be so obviously isolated in one's thinking demanded true strength of conviction.

Where had Laurel come by such fortitude? She'd braved fire and personal hazard, withstood censure and suspicions, dared to stand up to him, all the while caring for seemingly all she came in contact with.

"I admire your sense of purpose."

Nothing, *nothing* he said could have shocked her more. Unable to hide her disbelief, she stared at him in open wonder.

He gave into a chiding laugh. "I've surprised you."

"Yes," she scoffed. "We have, you and I, been at crossed purposes more often than not. We can hardly be in the same room for more than a few moments without resorting to an argument."

He remembered a time in the early morning hours when she had been draped in clinging wet muslin and the softness of her curves had beckoned. There had been no thought of argument then.

"Yes, we argue, but that doesn't mean I can't respect you."

Admiration *and* respect from this most demanding of all men. Laurel was truly at a loss.

"Have I embarrassed you?" he asked, knowing he had. Her self-consciousness vibrated between them in living pulses.

"Yes." She released a long, breathy sigh that ended in a miserable chuckle.

"Aren't you used to compliments?"

"Not of this sort." She gripped the bowl in both hands, completely flustered.

"I see. Would you rather I pay homage to your face then? Would that make you more comfortable?"

"No." She set the bowl on the tray with such force that the spoon rattled loudly, then made to stand and leave.

"Don't." He leaned forward, effectively trapping her between himself and the wall at her back. The first impression he'd ever had of her came back tenfold. She was a marvel, possessing virtues and strengths and traits that he had only begun to discover. She was a puzzle of the highest order. He'd thought so from the very start.

"Major—"

And he intended to have some answers to the puzzle of Laurel Seymore. "Who are you, Laurel?" His voice was a low, husky purr. "You rise to any challenge that comes your way, heartened, I'd wager, by more determination than good sense. You have a temper that would make the saints above weep and yet beneath all that fire is a tenderness and a compassion that strikes at the very soul of a man."

He slid his hand up her neck to cup the back of her head. "You care for an injured man, tending his wounds and his body like a practiced woman and yet the simplest praise sets you trembling." His thumb stroked along her jaw line. "Why is that? Why is your heart racing?"

Her heart *was* racing, pounding away in her chest in

painful thuds. An even breath was beyond her, and her mind was adrift, set that way by the seduction of his voice and the lure of his body so close to hers. Escape was the logical course of action, but even if she could manage to slip past him, her mind and body conspired to keep her where she was, hanging on to his every word, absorbing the feel of his hand.

"Look at me," he whispered.

She did, lifting her eyes to his. She saw unnameable emotions shimmering back at her, reaching past defenses and resolve and warnings. Deep inside, near her heart, she felt stroked and enticed until he lowered his head and firmly slanted his mouth over hers.

She sat unmoving, experiencing his flesh on hers with all her senses. His lips were warm and persuasive, taking command of the kiss, of her mouth . . . of her mind, and leaving her wanting more. When his tongue demanded entrance, she parted her lips and gladly accepted him.

The pleasure was staggering. She'd never felt anything even remotely resembling the blazing currents that raced from her mouth to her breasts and then straight to the pit of her. Nothing in her life had prepared her for the wash of warmth that quickly turned into an insistent ache.

Trembling, limbs and body nearly melting, she swayed toward him, not even aware that she did so. To lean into his muscles, to slide her fingers up his chest and savor his muscled strength was an instinct as natural as curling her tongue to meet his in ardent play.

His fingers tangled in her hair, arching her neck back, urging her mouth into closer contact. All too easily, she could picture how she must look, clinging to him, breathless little moans quivering over her lips to be snatched by his.

A little incoherently, she recalled that he'd asked her who she was. At that moment, she didn't know. She didn't care to know and damn the fact that she'd never done anything so wanton. Her body acted on its own as if it had been waiting forever to be claimed by this particular man.

Brett McKenzie. Stars and garters, that she should be kissing him, breathing in his scent, loving the feel of his beard rasping over her delicate skin was amazing. And dangerous.

The thought intruded like some vile serpent, snaking its way first into her consciousness and then, insidiously, into her body. Regret followed swiftly, bitter and somber.

"Brett," she breathed against his lips. There was no doubt that she couldn't let this continue, and yet, she couldn't draw back completely. Her heart had yearned for this, aching through the long empty nights to feel exactly, precisely what Brett was making her feel . . . what no other man had ever made her feel—cared for, feminine, and oddly enough, powerful. She tipped her head so that her forehead caressed his cheek.

"I want you," he muttered, his voice a thick, sensuous growl.

"We can't."

"I know." He brushed his lips along her jaw. "But soon, when I'm healed."

Again, he captured her lips with a dominance that all but shouted that she belonged to him. Repeatedly, his tongue probed deeply, retreated, thrust forward again in a carnal rhythm so blatant that Laurel felt the heat of a blush creep into her face.

With his lips and tongue he was making love to her and her body responded. A wild shudder ripped through her, tearing away common sense and logic and all the reasons she shouldn't be kissing him. She wound her hand around his neck and let herself, for this one glorious moment, relish what they shared.

Breathing raggedly, Brett trailed a line of kisses down the soft flesh of her neck. As if it were the most natural thing for her to do, Laurel tipped her head to one side, shivering as his teeth tenderly nipped, his tongue gently soothed. The sigh she gave was one of pure rapture, but it thinned into a strangled purr when his hand closed over her breast.

"Brett." Instantly, she clamped her fingers around his wrist.

"Sshh."

"No," she moaned, fighting the delicious pleasure his fingers created. She couldn't let him do this, but he was totally engrossed in molding her curves to fit his palm, in stroking his thumb back and forth over her nipple. Fire erupted inside and her whole body clenched.

It was the response that saved her from herself.

Realization came swiftly. Body and mind still drugged with passion, she nonetheless managed to tear herself away. She came to her feet in an unsteady rush, breaths torn from her body, regret and unfulfilled desire darkening her eyes.

A little wildly, she stared at him, seeing in his face the same hunger that she felt in every inch of her. Frantically, she shook her head, denying him, denying herself. Never before had she been tempted to give up her virtue, but she was now—and to the very man she could never have.

"I'm sorry," she choked out.

Brett didn't want to hear apologies any more than he wanted to be refused. She was like fire in his arms and he had barely touched her. Kissing her had been the single most satisfying thing he'd ever done. He'd be damned if he was going to give her up, not after the way she'd responded. In his mind he could still hear her soft whimpers, could still feel her tender flesh.

"Don't play coy, Laurel."

"I'm not."

"The hell you aren't. You can't kiss a man the way you did, let him touch you as I did, and then withdraw."

"I didn't mean for that to happen."

"But it did. And you liked it as much as I."

She twisted her hands together, wishing she could tell him that he was wrong. It would be a lie, though, and they'd both know it. "Regardless of how either of us feels about this, it was a mistake."

"The only mistake you've made is in thinking that I'm finished with you." It was no frivolous warning based on thwarted lust. He wanted Laurel Seymore with an intensity that still had his blood pounding.

He wasn't a man governed by the contents of his pants. Passion was something he controlled, but there was no mastering his body this time. Laurel inspired a desire he'd never experienced before and hell would freeze before he would let her escape him.

Silver-blue eyes glittering, he vowed, "I will have you."

His resolve was intense, unwavering. Laurel swallowed nervously, then rallied all her determination. "No."

A slow, fierce smile curled his lips and in his eyes was bold, relentless conviction. "As soon as I'm able, I'm coming after you. I will catch you and you will be mine."

# Twelve

As far as Brett was concerned, there were two kinds of women, those who were virtuous, and those who were not.

Laurel was neither. Or she was both. He couldn't decide. She exuded the most seductively appealing sensuality he'd ever encountered and at the same time behaved like an untried virgin.

By dusk's violet light, he stood at the bedroom window and silently fumed. He prided himself on judging a character within moments of meeting a person. He had yet to do that with Laurel, for she was one contradiction after another.

What he did know was limited to the obvious. She was independent as all hell and far more intelligent that most women. Beyond that she was more of a mystery now than she had been weeks ago. With insulting ease, she could provoke his ire and his passion in equal measure. She was most definitely a little termagant . . . who had kissed him with honest, gut-wrenching ardor.

He swallowed against the memory, tamping down fires that threatened to burn. Damn it, she ought to be outlawed. Her manner was a rare combination of worldliness and artlessness. While disarming, it was also so seductive that for the first time ever, he was seriously tempted by a woman he couldn't be certain was experienced. That never happened to him, never.

Balling his hand into a fist, he struggled for control, only to have it flit away at the satisfying thought of being the first, the only man to have Laurel. The headiness of that acted on his senses in a wash of rare pleasure that dulled his normal cautions.

Was she a virgin? Damn, he couldn't tell, and in truth, it didn't matter. He wanted to claim her in every way imaginable and the need had only gotten worse since she had run from him. That had been two days ago. He hadn't seen her since.

At the knock that came at the door, he stepped back from the window. "Come in."

Tess entered carrying a tray bearing his evening meal. He smiled grimly. Laurel had relinquished her nursing duties to Tess, her reasons patently obvious. The little termagant actually thought that by avoiding him she could disavow what had happened between them.

The idiocy of that ploy was exceeded only by its unexpectedness. To hide wasn't Laurel's style. He'd seen firsthand that she met life head on whether she was defending her honor or making apologies.

She was as direct as she was self-righteous, but still, she had chosen to evade him. At least physically. He doubted she could have dismissed him from her mind. The passion between them had been too intense, too hot and deep to be easily forgotten. It still had the power to wake him in the middle of the night, his stomach muscles clenched in defense.

Regarding Tess with ill-concealed ire, he longed for the moment when he would have Laurel before him. "Where's

Miss Seymore?" he asked, casting the tray a cursory glance. No soup.

Tess stood straight, her dark face impassive. "Which one?"

He cursed under his breath. "You know damn well which one."

"At the shop."

His brows lowered. "It's awfully late for her to be out alone."

"Miss Laurel she used to that."

"How late will she stay?" He didn't like the idea of Laurel walking through Charleston after dark. The streets weren't safe even at the best of times. After sunset, the threat of danger only increased.

"She stay until she finish her work. That could be in a little while or it could be a few hour."

A few hours? Did the woman have no regard for herself? Did she think she was invincible? Either way, she'd apparently learned nothing from her mishap in the street last week to behave so recklessly.

"Damn." He crossed to the closet, biting back the more savage curses that rose.

"What you doing?" Tess asked in undisguised surprise.

"What does it look like?" He returned to the bed with his boots and shirt. "I'm going after the little fool."

"You not up to that. You get tired walking around this room."

It was the truth. His shoulder was healing well, but his body was a long way from complete recovery. However, he'd be damned if he was going to sit there and do nothing while Laurel blithely put herself in danger. Again.

He managed his boots by himself, but when it came

time to don the shirt, he turned to Tess. "Help me with this bandage."

She thrust her lower lip out, balking at the command. "You going to hurt yourself."

He gave her a punishing glare. "Thank you for your advice, now get over here and get me unwound from this damned thing." He couldn't go out to find Laurel with his left arm secured to his side.

"Miss Laurel don't need your help."

"The hell she doesn't. I've never met a more reckless woman in my life. It's a wonder she's managed to survive this long."

"She manage just fine."

Furious at being forestalled for even this short time, Brett slipped the rein on his ire. "Either help me or get out of the way." The silver in his eyes matched the steel in his voice. "But don't think for one second that you or anyone else is going to keep me from going after her."

Laurel locked the front door to the shop, pocketed the key, then snuggled into her cloak. The air had a distinct chill that penetrated the layer of wool and had her anxious to reach the warmth to be found at home. She amended the wish at once. Brett McKenzie was also to be found at home.

*I will have you. You will be mine.*

His words came to her as they had so often in the last few days, sending delicate ripples of painful pleasure through her. Helplessly, she pressed a hand to her stomach and swallowed the groan that ached to be released.

Giddy trepidation had a firm hold on her, for Brett McKenzie had stated his intent as boldly as any man could.

The arrogance of that should have her furious. Instead, amazingly, she was tantalized by the prospect of his claiming her.

Sighing heavily, she headed for home, bearing no misconceptions about herself. She'd long ago accepted the fact that she didn't think and behave as most women did. Others might look upon passion as a secret to be whispered about or not even acknowledged, but to her it was just part and parcel of the human condition. A most wondrous part, which up until now, she'd never tasted. Brett had changed all of that, making her body feel beautiful, her heart so very, *very* alive.

For that, society would judge her weak of character or lacking in moral fiber, but she wouldn't agree. She was and always had been true to her principles, to others and to herself, while society, for all of its high-blown ethics, saw fit to condone and perpetuate heinous wrongs every day.

No, the passion she felt for Brett was as right and good as it was undeniable. In her heart of hearts, she felt only a wondrous joy in that, and if she could, she would gladly, wholeheartedly give herself to him, despite his scrupulous ideas about marriage.

A telling admission, to be sure. As independent as she was in her thinking about some aspects of life, she nonetheless still adhered to certain precepts. Between men and women, marriage was accepted as a pledge of honor. It was an institution in which she placed great stock.

Yet what she felt for Brett transcended honor and vows. And lust, for that matter. He had somehow managed to reach past her every defense and touch her heart and soul. Now, everything within her ached to share of herself both emotionally and physically.

It wasn't possible. Brett was a man who dominated life. He brooked no half-measures in anything he did. He would demand all of her, completely, without reservation. She would want to do no less.

But she couldn't. Her subterfuge lay between them. She couldn't make love to him, give of her body and soul, and then in the next breath, lie to him about Jack Diego. Nor could she risk the chance of Brett pushing and prodding for the truth he would sense was missing. He was too astute, too discerning; he'd *know* that she was holding something back from him. She shuddered to think what would happen if he discovered what she had been about. At all costs, she couldn't allow that.

Wrapping her arms about her, she turned the corner, saddened by how things must be. There was no help for it, though. To cling to hopes for what couldn't be was a folly. She would have to set her mind to restoring her life to its normal course, before Brett had seized hold of it with his strength of will and astoundingly handsome face.

A little dazedly, she blinked to clear her vision of silver-gilded blue eyes and a wicked smile and took note of her location. She'd been so consumed with her thoughts, she had arrived at that very spot without conscious thought.

Well, thank goodness part of her brain was still functioning. The rest of her was woefully negligent, failing to see the shadows that encompassed the buildings and alleyways, failing to hear the voice calling to her from behind.

Without pausing, she glanced back over her shoulder and her spirits dropped. Daniel Illston. She had no choice but to stop and wait for him to reach her side.

"Good evenin', Miss Seymore," he panted, laying a thin

hand on his equally thin chest. "I was afraid you were goin' to pass right on into the night."

"I must apologize, sir. My mind was elsewhere."

"Hopefully not on any unpleasantness. Surely, you are not plagued by dire plights."

Laurel tucked her chin to hide the spurt of poignant laughter that threatened. In no way would she deem Brett McKenzie a plight, dire or otherwise. He was more like a magnificent dilemma. "No, nothing of that sort. It has been a long day." One crowded with too many thoughts of the man who recuperated in her bed.

"Ah, yes, I see, and now you are on your way home." He yanked his hat from his head and fidgeted with the thing while he shifted from one foot to the other. "You must let me escort you."

It had never failed to annoy her when people told her what she must and must not do, and for a second, she seriously considered telling him so. Thankfully, tolerance and politeness won out. Daniel was trying to be nice in the only way he knew. It wasn't his fault that thanks to Brett, her nerves were particularly threadbare this night.

"Thank you, Mr. Illston."

If she had told him he was the most charming man she'd ever met, he couldn't have looked more delighted. He fell into step beside her, smiling hugely, his legs working in their lanky, disjointed manner.

"You are out and about rather late, this evenin'," he commented.

"Perhaps."

"I find it very commendable that you toil as you do."

"Toil?" She gave him a rather pained look out of the corner of her eyes.

"Of course, Mama doesn't agree with me, though. She's always sayin' a woman's place is at home."

Laurel mentally gave Mrs. Illston a swift kick to her backside. Although Daniel's mother apparently found it necessary to criticize, she also availed herself of Seymore's services on a regular basis.

"How convenient for your mother."

"Beg pardon?"

"Your mother is lucky that her circumstances allow her to remain at home where she obviously believes she belongs."

"Oh, yes, Mama wouldn't ever dream of workin'." Daniel tugged on the lapels of his jacket. "How old are you, Miss Seymore? That is, if you don't mind my askin'."

The unexpected shift in the conversation was to be expected from the man, but Laurel couldn't imagine why he would want to know her age. "I'm twenty."

"New Orleans wasn't even a bustlin' city back then in 1810. I wasn't there, mind you, I only have it on good authority."

To Laurel's dismay, he digressed rapidly, leaving the topic of New Orleans for that of Spanish moss. Italian marble caught his fancy for a moment or two, then William Shakespeare, Franz Schubert, and then of all things, the island of Elba.

Laurel counted herself lucky that there was actually some logic this time to his verbal wanderings. They were all mired in Europe for some reason. Still, she didn't know what point he was trying to make, or if he had one at all.

Unable to help herself, she quickened her pace, her annoyance escalating as rapidly. She had wanted her life restored to normal. Well, here it was and she didn't like it one bit.

". . . turnips being one of my favorite foods."

Turnips?! How had he gone from Elba to turnips? "Mr. Illston." She blurted his name out in sheer desperation, then searched for something to say to him. "That's . . . that's all very interesting."

"What Mama does with turnips is heaven, Miss Seymore, nothin' but heaven."

For Laurel, heaven was the sight of her house. "Here we are." She stopped at the wrought-iron gate and swung it open. "Thank you, sir."

Daniel's face filled with disappointment. "You're goin' in so early?"

"I'm sorry, Mr. Illston, but it is late."

"But . . . but we barely had any time."

"Perhaps another day."

He closed his hand on her arm and asked, "When?"

At this unprecedented show of aggression, Laurel stared wide-eyed at Daniel, momentarily caught by surprise. She'd never known him to be physical in any manner. "I don't really know when."

"I could . . ." His hint of a chin elevated, his mismatched brows lowered. "That is, you could invite me in." He said it as if he were some lordly king issuing an edict.

"I'm afraid not, sir." She tugged at her arm and found it firmly clamped. "I was not planning on company this evening. Please, let go of my arm."

"You're a beautiful woman, Miss Seymore."

Every emotion she'd been feeling up until then gave way to an encompassing wash of astonished disappointment. Never had it entered her mind that Daniel's inclinations had progressed to this point.

"Mr. Illston, please—"

His fingers tightened. "You must know how I feel about you."

"No, I don't."

"For a long time, I've entertained a tender passion in your direction. And I think you return my sentiments."

Again, she tried to free herself. "Mr. Illston, you are mistaken."

"You mustn't say that." He labored for breath, his lower lip trembling, his eyes bulging.

"I'm sorry, but it is the truth. I like you, you are a very pleasant man, but my affections do not go beyond that."

"They could," he insisted. "I know they could." In his mounting agitation, he sputtered and stammered, "You . . . don't know your mind. I am a man. You should . . . you should trust me to know what is best for you." In the next second he showed her what he thought was best for her by tugging her against him and planting his lips over hers.

Laurel gave up being nice the moment he declared she should entrust her brain to his keeping. The feel of his cold, slick lips only added insult to injury.

Shoving with all her might, she thrust herself to arm's length. "How dare you! Let me go at once."

"Oh, Miss Seymore, Laurel—"

She struggled furiously, and brought the heel of her shoe down as hard as she could on his toes. He yelped and danced away, and yet, damnably, did not let her go.

"You lecher," she spat, swinging at his face with her free hand. "How could you!"

"This is your fault," he screeched, dodging the stinging blows. "You cause me to get excited."

His laying the blame on her sent her temper right over the edge. She clenched her fingers into a fist, intent on plunging it into his nose, but he lunged forward and wrapped her in his arms.

"No!" Eyes clenched shut, teeth bared, she arched and squirmed. "Let go of me!"

A terrible stillness met her demand. Then a chillingly dangerous voice commanded, "Do as the lady says."

Brett. Laurel's eyes flew wide in confusion and shock. What was he doing here? He stood just behind her right shoulder, tall, indomitable, his face grim, his eyes icy. And in his hand he held his sword, its tip raised and pressed to the underside of Daniel's jaw.

"Do not make me repeat myself," he whispered to Daniel.

The latter dropped his hands away as if he had been holding burning coals. "Y-y-yes." He made the mistake of trying to nod. Gasping, he jerked his head back, his eyes trained downward to the steel at his throat.

Laurel stepped away, her gaze never leaving Brett. A savage humor lent his face a feral appearance. Barely restrained fury seemed to cling to his every muscle. Startled, she realized he was a hair's breadth from erupting into physical violence.

"Brett, there's no need. Really, I'm unharmed."

He continued to watch Daniel in deadly, menacing silence. Laurel held her breath. Brett was the essence of danger and power. His whole being, his formidable will, his attention, all his energies were concentrated on one matter to the exclusion of all else, and she truly didn't know if he would listen to reason.

"Brett, please." Instinctively, she wanted to reach out, to lay her hand on his arm in restraint and comfort, but she didn't think he'd allow even that small touch.

The deadly blue gaze leveled on Daniel darkened, and

when Brett spoke his voice was so fierce, each word emerged as a concise, separate threat. "For your sake, *sir,* you had best hope Miss Seymore is telling the truth."

"She is, she is," Daniel squeaked, coming to his toes in his effort to avoid the sword's point.

Gradually, Brett lowered the sword, his jaw relaxing, his expression losing its brittle cast. Laurel went limp in relief, barely taking note of Daniel as he scurried down the road. With her gaze caught and held by Brett's, all else was superficial.

He stared back at her, his eyes narrowed in accusation. Laurel felt its force to the marrow of her bones and wondered a bit frantically what she had done to earn that particular look.

"What is it?"

One black brow flicked upward, his mouth thinned. Then in one fluid motion, he grabbed her wrist, turned on his heel, and hauled her after him. By the time Laurel registered the lightning-quick move, her skirts were billowing out behind her.

"What are you doing?"

"Shut up."

The harsh command stung. Bewilderment was instantly replaced by outrage. It was bad enough that he was towing her through the courtyard like a recalcitrant child. She resented the added indignity of being ordered silent.

"You beast," she railed, her temper on the rise once again. "You're as bad as Daniel, pulling me about to suit your own purposes. Who do you think you are?"

He kicked open the door to the kitchen, dragged her in, then slammed the door shut. At the resounding thud, Laurel found herself free.

In a whirl of wool and muslin and feminine fury, she

squared off with him, impervious to the fact that by the dim light emanating from the coals in the fireplace, he looked overwhelmingly menacing. The planes and hollows of his face were etched starkly in red, his shoulders a silhouetted promise that in any physical confrontation, she was woefully outmatched.

None of that mattered. She was so angry with him she didn't even give a damn that he shouldn't be out of bed, holding men at sword point and kicking doors open. Since the moment she had first met him, he had completely disrupted her life, and now his behavior was arrogant and overbearing, and it riled her as nothing else could have.

"What do you think you are doing?" she asked, her voice low and vibrating with all the pent-up emotion he'd inspired.

"I would ask the same of you," he rasped. "I thought you were an intelligent woman, but with each passing minute it becomes increasingly clear that you are a brazen fool." He threw his sword onto the scarred work table. "Have you no sense? Are you completely lacking in reason?"

"Probably, since I'm standing here listening to you."

He growled right over her insult. "You are a woman alone and yet you wait until after dark to walk the streets. It's no wonder I found you at the mercy of that bastard. Do you have any idea what could have happened if I hadn't stopped him?"

"I would have given him a bloody nose."

"He could have raped you."

"Daniel?! He's harmless."

"Harmless? He was doing everything he could to get under your skirts."

She didn't need to be reminded, but that wasn't the issue.

Ignoring the danger that emanated from him in pulsing waves, she spat, "You have no right to tell me what to do. I have been coming and going about this city long before you arrived—"

"That in itself is a miracle."

"—and I'll be doing the same long after you leave. Our paths have crossed. You have been injured in my defense and I will always be grateful, but you make assumptions you're not entitled to."

"Any assumptions I have made have been at your hand. You behave like a rash fool."

"I do no such thing."

"Madam, you have done nothing else!"

"What concern is that of yours? True, you kissed me, I kissed you back. That does not make you my keeper or give you any say in what I can do. If I wish or want or need to come home after dark, I will."

She was shaking so hard she had to grip handfuls of her cloak to keep her arms steady. There was no help for her knees, though, or her lips. They trembled uncontrollably, but she would not relent to the need to sink into a chair. She'd see this through, standing on her own two feet, looking him dead in the eye.

She watched him in open defiance, waiting for him to say something, do something. He didn't move. The seconds sped past and he remained ominously still. She sucked in what was supposed to be a calming breath, but his stillness unnerved her to the point that the inhalation rasped down her dry throat.

She squinted for a better look at him and it hit her then, the true, full force of his will. She'd been too caught up in her own emotions to note it before, but she did now. Pure masculine power, uncompromising authority, and an intense energy buffeted her until she felt the urge to take a step back.

"Oh, it concerns me," he vowed softly, his mouth curling in an ominous smile. "As an officer of the army, I'm sworn to protect you." The silver in his gaze took on an unholy light and his voice dropped to an indecent growl. "As the man who intends to make you his own, I won't tolerate another man touching you."

He moved then, with a speed that belied his injury. Laurel choked out a startled cry, only to have it smothered beneath the pressure of his mouth.

Her world spun, tilted on its edge by the staggering heat and dominance of him. His tongue surged past her lips as one arm banded across her back and the other lowered. Fingers open, he curved his hand over her buttocks and pressed her into greater intimacy with him.

Mentally, she felt suspended, unprepared for the sudden shift from anger to passion. She struggled to find her bearings and found instead a heady temptation to give in. For days she'd been suppressing a deep, deep desire for this man, and with this single kiss, it blossomed anew when she knew that was the worst thing that could happen.

She had to stop this, now. He was already hard, his flesh pressing insistently against the softness of her belly. Incoherently, she thought that she shouldn't be able to feel the intimate proof of his arousal though the layers of clothing between them, but she could. He rose up bold and demanding, silently proclaiming that the yearning she felt was well met within him.

"You little termagant," he growled, burying his face in the wild disorder of her curls. They were in the kitchen with only a hard table at their disposal, his shoulder was aching clear down to his legs; he wasn't going to make love to her here. Neither could he turn her loose.

He kissed her again, drinking in the sweetness of her mouth. She was the most luscious woman he'd ever encountered, and he couldn't get enough of her. Sweeping her cloak aside, he unerringly found the delicate perfection of her breast.

Against his lips, she moaned. He swallowed the sound, taking it into him, committing it to memory, letting it assuage the awful pain of seeing her in the arms of another man. The feeling had stunned him, intensifying into a blinding white fury when he'd realized that Laurel hadn't been a willing participant.

His arms tightened with the need to hold her as close as he could. Their clothing conspired against him. Impatiently, he tugged her skirt and petticoats up out of his way and slid his hand past her frilly garter, over the cool contour of her outer thigh. Everything male within him surged hotly.

"Brett." The touch of his hand was foreign, almost alarming, searing her like a brand, making heat coil low in her belly, between her thighs, and around her heart. She wanted that heat to consume her. "Brett, no."

"You've said that before," he breathed, kissing the hollow of her throat.

"And I've meant it. We can't. I . . . I don't want this." But she did, so badly that she was trembling and her insides were burning. She had only herself to blame. She should have fought him as insistently as she had Daniel.

"Please, Brett, this has to stop." They couldn't continue to torment each other with what they couldn't have. Drawing into herself was a pain of the heart and spirit.

The stiffening of her body reached him as her words

never could have. He jerked his head up, saw her refusal, and swore viciously. "Why? Give me one good reason."

Laurel gazed up at him for as long as she could, aching to tell him the truth, but it was destined to be unspoken forever. Slowly, she shut her eyes and relented to the excuse that would suffice, excuses that were acceptable and reasonable.

"Despite my actions, I am not a woman of loose morals."

"I never said you were."

"But you have made clear your ideas of marriage. By your own words, you are pledged to the military, not to any one woman. What you expect of me would be demeaning." At one time, she may have felt that way, but no longer. The lie was bitter and she hated herself for using it.

Understanding hit Brett hard and he swore again. He thrust her away, his face scored with fury. "Then you're nothing but a vulgar little tease, content to alleviate a carnal urge and then dance away."

His words slashed at her, wounding her until she wanted to shrivel up with the pain. She wouldn't have thought that he could hurt her that way, that she had given him the power to do so. Somehow, she had. She had come to care for him and that had made her vulnerable.

"The same could be said for you. Only in this man's world, your actions are to be applauded, while mine are to be condemned. For your desire, you are a man exercising his masculinity, while I am reduced to a vulgar tease. The hypocrisy of that is unfair, you're being unfair."

"Welcome to life as we know it." He shook his head, issuing a laugh that was completely without humor. "You have definitely answered some questions this night."

"Questions about what?"

"About you."

He thought the worst of her. Pride demanded that she tell him the truth, that she make him understand that she hadn't been playing some heartless, wanton game with him. Common sense dictated otherwise. He was ready to despise her. It was for the best.

It broke her heart.

"I never meant for this to happen."

Eyes narrowed to virulent slits, he retrieved his sword. "I know what you intended: a few stolen kisses, a safe grope in the dark, just enough to mess your hair and gain you a wedding band in the bargain."

"No, it wasn't like that at all. You make me feel things I can't control."

"You admit that you want me?"

"Yes, but it's not that simple." *I want to give you all, and I can't.*

By the last trace of light in the room, Brett remained unmoving, jaw rigid. Again and again, he asked himself what it was about this woman that could make him forget his personal beliefs. What was it about her that could confound his logic and test his convictions?

He hated her for doing that to him and he hated himself for allowing her to do so.

Squaring his shoulders, he gave her a last look, then pivoted and strode into the night. Any further recuperating he did would be at the post. There he would see Laurel Seymore relegated to a name. Nothing more.

# *Thirteen*

"What can you tell me about Jack Diego?" Brett posed the question in a hushed voice, his head dipped low to conceal as much of his face as possible. He didn't expect anyone in the crowded tavern to recognize him, but he preferred not to take any chances. To that end, he was wearing what he thought of as civilian clothing, all of a quality that left a great deal to be desired.

Stretching his shoulders to ease the slight strain left over from his month-old injury, he eyed his companion thoughtfully. The man was a squat, stout fellow, not prone to personal cleanliness. Even with the smoke of pipes and cigars clouding the room and the stale odors of whiskey and rum hanging thick in the air, Brett could smell the man from across the table between them. In the shadowy darkness of the corner where they sat, the rank odor seemed intensified.

Somehow that seemed in keeping with the man's bearing. A ragged gray beard and equally coarse hair of the same color put his age at somewhere near fifty. Lines of excessive drink and dissipation gave him the appearance of someone far older, while his clothes marked him as routinely being at the mercy of the elements. All in all, the man looked to be the disreputable sort to lurk on the fringes of earshot, the very kind who just might know something about Jack Diego.

Brett smiled inwardly. Weeks ago, he had let it be known that the army would pay good money for any information leading to the capture of Jack Diego. It had all been done discretely; a word to a certain barkeep, a hint to one of the shoremen. The last thing Brett wanted was for everyone in the city to know exactly how actively he was seeking the pirate. That news would have reached Diego and sent him into hiding for certain.

Three people had come forward so far, none offering the kind of information Brett sought. There was the usual hearsay and rumor. One woman, a prostitute, had claimed to have bedded Diego, but when pushed for more pertinent disclosures, couldn't even give an accurate description of the bastard.

Brett was hoping for more than that from the man opposite him. "You said you might have some information about this Diego."

"I might," the man drawled, his lips parting to reveal teeth stained the color of dirt. "It'll cost ya."

"Only if what you tell me proves to be true."

"What I got to tell is the truth."

"That remains to be seen. So far, you haven't told me anything worth hearing."

The man twisted his face, the heavy shadows surrounding him giving him an unnatural appearance. "You ain't paid me nothin' yet."

Brett narrowed his eyes, reached for the bottle close at hand, and poured the smelly little bastard a shot of whiskey. "That'll do until you say something of value."

The man stewed openly, gulping his drink and mumbling at the same time. In the end, he wiped his chin on his jacket sleeve and sniffed in a noseful of mucus. "Friggin' bastard. Shoulda never gotten word to ya, shoulda kept my mouth shut."

"But you didn't," Brett shot back, drilling his gaze into the whining man. "You're the one who talked to the barkeep, you're the one who agreed to meet me, so either talk or go to hell."

Brett gave him to the count of five to make up his mind. When six seconds had elapsed, he came to his feet, disgusted that he had wasted his time on yet another false lead.

The man grabbed hold of Brett's arm. "Where ya goin'?"

Brett's response was to shake the man's hand away.

"All right, all right," the man relented desperately. He cast a cautious glance first to his left and then to his right, sinking into his shoulders as if to protect himself from prying eyes. "Just . . . just sit down." Quickly, he looked around again, his unease obvious.

Brett sat, his silvery gaze never once wavering. "Talk."

The man hesitated, but this time within five seconds, he muttered, "I've seen him once or twice."

"Diego."

"Yeah."

"How do you know it was him?"

"I heard some of his men talkin', callin' him by name."

"Where was this?"

"Over by the marsh that comes up to Bay Street."

"When?"

The man exhaled and shook his head. "The first time, maybe six months ago. Just stumbled on the whole lot by chance, unloadin' bundles and crates from a dinghy in the middle of the night."

"What were you doing there?"

A careless smile pulled at the man's face. "The night was hot. I was tryin' to find some place to keep cool. The river's always good for that. I heard some noise and snuck up to see what was doin'. That's when I saw 'em."

"Diego."

"And his men."

"How many?"

"Eleven, that I counted. Mighta been more, but can't say for sure."

"And they didn't see you?"

"Hell no. When I figured out who I was watchin', I laid right down in that swampy muck like I was dead, reeds coverin' me up. Didn't want no trouble with the likes o' Jack Diego."

"Yet you're willing to risk his wrath by talking to me."

"That's 'cause you're gonna pay me. Once I got that money, I'm leavin' town. I ain't no idiot."

"What about the next time?" Brett asked.

"What?"

"You said the *first* time you saw Diego was six months ago. Have you seen him since?"

His question met with a resurgence of the man's caution. The informant licked his lips before rolling them inward. "Yeah. A few days ago."

Brett started, his every sense alert. "What?"

"I seen 'em two nights past."

"Where?"

"Down by the swamp again, only closer to Smith's wharf."

"What were they doing?"

"What they was doin' the last time I seen 'em: loadin' crates and barrels onto a wagon."

"Did you see where they took it?"

The man hesitated for a moment, then poured himself another shot of liquor. Once downed, he sucked in a bracing breath. "I followed at a distance."

"To where?"

"Up Meetin' Street. I was a safe ways behind, and not out for no trouble, but I seen em' turn down Broad Street and then into one of them drives that come up behind them shops."

"Any shop in particular?"

"Can't say for certain, not the way those buildings is crowded next to one another. But it was over behind that bookseller and that hat place and that dress shop."

"Seymore's?"

"Coulda been. I didn't hang around. Figured at that point, I didn't want to know no more. Wouldn't be healthy for a body, if you know what I mean."

Brett ignored this last bit, his mind focused on Broad Street. Randall's Book Emporium and a milliner's were located next to Seymore's. Diego's presence there could have been a coincidence, or Brett's worst suspicions could be confirmed.

Disregarding his surroundings completely, he dissected the situation. What in the hell was Diego doing taking his booty into town? The safe, prudent thing to do would be to dispose of whatever wares he had in some out of the way place, divide it up, and sell it off a piece at a time. It didn't make sense to cart it all off into the center of town . . . unless he had good reason to . . . unless he had a safe storage place.

*"Sonofabitch."*

"Look mister, I can't tell ya more 'n that. I told ya what I seen. Now you owe me."

Without acknowledging the man in any way, Brett reached into a pocket for two gold pieces and handed them over. The man snatched them up and ran from the building, never once looking back.

Brett continued to sit, unconsciously rubbing at his left shoulder. It didn't pain him, the ache had long ago been reduced to an occasional twinge, but he kneaded the scarred tissue beneath his jacket as if to assuage an inner hurt. All the while, his mind raced with a multitude of possibilities, settling finally on only one.

Laurel.

In an instant, his businesslike attitude dissipated to be replaced by a churning of emotions he had believed were conquered. For weeks, he had fought to banish her from his mind and yet at the first reminder of her, he was ridden by a seething fury and an unwelcome disquietude.

Damn her, *damn her!* It was imperative that he be emotionless, that he feel nothing for her. He couldn't. The all too real likelihood that she was associated with Diego made him angry. Angry that she might have lied to him, angry that she might be breaking the law. And damnably, it worried him to imagine her embroiled in such a dangerous undertaking, plotting with criminals, risking her safety and her welfare.

He told himself that it could all be speculation, that his concern for Laurel was completely unfounded, but even if he could overlook his earlier suspicions, he couldn't overlook this latest piece to the puzzle. If the informant had been telling the truth, and Brett suspected that he had, then Diego's secret storage was in the vicinity of Laurel's shop.

She could very well be Diego's accomplice, as he had suspected all along. She could be up to her pretty little neck in danger, and whether he liked it or not, he could not be impassive to that.

He shoved himself to his feet and strode from the smoky confines of the room, needing the chill night air to clear his head. With every step, he mentally kicked himself to hell and back for having been so stupid as to have allowed himself to feel anything for Laurel.

His job demanded that he remain impartial. How in the hell was he going to do that if he had to arrest her, interrogate her, lock her up? This was the same woman he wanted to the ends of the earth and back, the same woman whose kisses had stolen into his body and whose spirit had the power to dance around his heart.

Goddamn it, he hated to admit that. Nothing like this had ever happened to him; he had never allowed it. His life was a neat package with everything and everyone in their respective places. His honor and integrity, his duty and commitment, his personal and his professional relationships were all neatly defined. Women didn't have a place in that. They couldn't. Laurel included.

Sucking in deep breaths of damp cold air, he ground his eyes shut for the few seconds it took to restore his normal self-control. When he at last gazed about the Cimmerian night, his eyes were flinty with resolve, his mouth drawn with a virulence rooted in bitterness.

"Laurel, are you unwell?"

Laurel looked up from the dress in her lap, surprise raising the twin arches of her brows. "Of course not. Why?"

Shrugging, Hope said, "You're pale. And, you haven't been yourself lately."

"I'm fine." At Hope's skeptical grimace, she added,

"Honestly. There's nothing wrong." Even if her smile was a bit forced, Laurel congratulated herself. Smiles did not come easily these days. Heavy sighs were more a common and she longed to give in to one now. For Hope's sake, she didn't, having to content herself with a quick glance about the shop.

From where she sat in the work room, she could peer into the front room and out the windows. Sun shone weakly through the glass panes, barely casting any shadows at all. The morning was rather gray, matching Laurel's mood exactly. She'd been possessed of that mood for nearly a month and she knew why.

The dress in her lap held little inspiration, but she forced her mind to attend to the garment. Experience had taught her that it helped to keep busy, and in so doing, not to dwell on the past. On Brett. By day, she succeeded to some extent, but the nights. . . . Oh, at night, where enveloping darkness and silence were a fertile ground for memories, she was helpless, quite, quite helpless to the urgings of her heart.

The sigh she had been suppressing slipped past now, a mournful sound. She glanced up quickly to see if Hope had heard. She had.

"Laurel?" The beauty of Hope's face was only increased by the concern she couldn't hide.

Laurel gave up trying to take tiny stitches and confessed, "I haven't been sleeping well."

"You do look tired. Are you sure you're not sick?"

"Positive."

"Then is something bothering you?"

"No." Even to Laurel, her response sounded false. "No," she repeated more slowly. "Why would you even think that?"

"Because you've been tense ever since Major McKenzie left."

For several seconds, Laurel simply stared, stunned and chagrined that she might have been so negligent in hiding her feelings. She thought she had been doing a credible job of pretending that Brett's parting words hadn't left her feeling as if there was a hole where her heart should be, that his absence hadn't left her feeling adrift.

Apparently, she had been so transparent that any further prevarication on her part would be useless. Still, it was difficult to speak of the man. He had come to be a part of her even though she wished it wasn't so, despite the fact that she had repeatedly told herself that it was better this way. Better to have him hating her.

"I . . . he has come to mean something to me."

Hope tilted her head ever so slightly to one side. "Are you in love with him?"

"No!" That was the one question she had not let herself ponder. The risk of the heartache involved was too great.

"I thought perhaps you might be," Hope hinted badly. "That is, I wondered if while you nursed him back to health you didn't form a tender affection for him."

Laurel tried to scoff away the assumption and failed miserably. "I don't . . . I don't know." She tucked a curl behind her ear, fidgeted with her needle and thread, sent her gaze to the ceiling. "He is arrogant and annoying and all together too opinionated."

"But he is handsome and strong and protective of you."

*Not to mention in lust with me.* "None of it matters though."

"Whyever not?"

"He isn't a man for marriage. He made that very plain."

"Oh." Hope considered that with a full pout. "Oh."

Her sister's disappointment was so pronounced, it struck a humorous chord within Laurel. "These things happen, Hope."

"I suppose, but I had been hoping."

"For me and the major?"

Shrugging, Hope rolled her eyes. "You don't have to sound so dubious. He's a . . . a very handsome man and you're so very pretty."

Laurel did laugh at this. "He's a very determined man, set in his ways, and I'm an independent woman who riles him at every turn. Nothing can come of that."

Giving voice to the sentiment was a timely reminder which Laurel used to strengthen her resolve. She adjusted the dress she'd been sewing. "How did we ever come to this point? I swear, we'll never get these dresses made."

They worked in silence for a while, Laurel oddly relieved to have shared her anxieties with Hope. It was something she'd never been able to do before now.

"Do you think you'll ever marry?" Hope asked.

The unexpected query brought Laurel's head up. "What kind of a question is that?"

"I don't know, but do you ever think you will?"

Laurel had no idea what had prompted the inquiry. "I couldn't say."

"I think you should. At least you might think about it."

"Why?"

"You'd make a wonderful wife."

"I should think I'd drive a man to distraction. I'm not what men consider malleable enough to be a wife."

"But you are compassionate and caring and capable.

And you have so much love to give. A man would be very lucky to have you as his wife."

Hope's opinions were as startling as they were rare. Laurel didn't know what to make of them. "What has prompted this discussion?"

Looking at nothing in particular, Hope toyed with the lace of her collar. "I'm not sure. I had never considered any of this before, but recently, it seems my mind has been occupied with more thoughts than normal. Especially while I was here in the shop by myself."

"You mean weeks ago, when I was home nursing the major?"

"Yes. I found I was suddenly thinking of things that until now had escaped my notice."

"Things like my marrying?"

"And how much we all depend on you, and how sad Tess can be at times." Warming to her subject, Hope scooted forward in her chair. "And it didn't stop there, Laurel. I actually considered this shop."

"In what way?"

"Oh, little things, like why we have the bolts of fabric where they are and the color of the swags over the windows, and . . . and how it might be nice if we had a small rug on the floor back here. Little things."

Which, Laurel knew, were not so very little for Hope. She wasn't prone to creative thinking. Until now, she'd relied on others to do that for her. This new side of Hope was remarkable and Laurel couldn't have been happier.

Regarding her sister with a soft smile, Laurel realized that Hope had matured in the past weeks. Whether it was because circumstances had forced to grow or if it was simply nature finally coming to the fore, Laurel didn't know. Either way, the results were wonderful.

"We can do anything with the shop that you like."

Hope's chocolate-hued eyes lit with enthusiasm. "Truly? You wouldn't mind if we made some changes?"

"Heavens no. This is just as much your shop as it is mine."

The smile Hope gave was wide and infectious. Laurel responded in kind, grinning even as the front door opened. A heartbeat later, her smile dropped away.

"Laurel, what is it?"

She swallowed with difficulty, her blood seemingly frozen in her limbs while her heart thudded in a painful cadence. Slowly, she came to her feet.

"Brett." She whispered his name without conscious thought, her mind stopping, incapable of getting past his presence. Then just as quickly, her brain started up again, making observations so rapidly they tumbled one on top of the other.

He looked well . . . fully recovered . . . as handsome as ever. He moved with ease and assurance, exuding an air of strength and authority that was only enhanced by the blue and gray of his uniform. Eyes glinting with silver lights on a field of blue—she'd forgotten how fascinating that gaze could be. And looking at his mouth made her insides twist in remembered desire.

He crossed the room with strides long and purposeful, not stopping until he was within arm's length.

"Miss Seymore."

The dead formality of his tone was disconcerting. The last time he had spoken to her, his voice had been teeming with emotion. In her dreams, she had remembered him that way.

"Major."

"You're under arrest."

# *Fourteen*

"*Under arrest?!*" No sooner did the words leave her mouth than two soldiers came through the front door, muskets shouldered. Stunned, she noted two more soldiers stationed outside, three others in the courtyard behind. "I'm under arrest?"

"If we find what I suspect, then yes, you'll have to come with us."

Hope sidled close to slip her hand through Laurel's. "What's happening? I don't understand."

The look Brett leveled at Laurel contained not even a flicker of emotion. "Why don't you explain, Miss Seymore."

She couldn't. Dread had seized her, turning her insides as cold as the ice in Brett's eyes.

Dear Lord in heaven, this was her worst nightmare come to life. How many times had she woken in the blackest part of the night, frightened that this very thing would happen . . . a cellar full of goods she couldn't explain and soldiers looming over her. Only it hadn't been Brett's face in her dreams. That it should be *him,* of all people, to execute this horror was a hideous blow.

The wintry fingers of panic scratched up her spine, but she willed them away, brutally reminding herself that this exact likelihood had always been possible. It was the single reason she'd let Brett walk away, taking with him the promise of happiness and passion. She'd known, but she wasn't prepared for the pain of realization. It was consuming in its intensity, nearly sending her to her knees.

"Laurel?" Hope whispered, her voice a near nothing.

Hearing her sister's terror, Laurel jerked her gaze from Brett's. Hope stared back at her in alarm and fright so profound that Laurel half-expected her sister to collapse on the spot. She sobered to the urgency of the moment at once, and somehow scraped together her abused sensibilities. For Hope's sake, she forced herself to think.

"It's all right, Hope."

"But he says he's going to arrest you."

Laurel lifted her gaze to Brett's. "Are you? Why?" As if she didn't know. As if she weren't guilty of so many things, all in the name of decency and moral righteousness. But both would be meaningless. She'd never harbored any delusions to the contrary. The best she could ask for now was that she alone suffer. Hope had to remain safe.

"For conspiring with Jack Diego," Brett answered.

"You have no proof of that, Major."

With a quick tip of his head, Brett gave a silent signal to his men, then followed it up with a brisk command. "You two men come with me." To Laurel, he ordered "The keys to the basement, Miss Seymore."

The chill in his eyes was unnerving, piercing Laurel when she was her most vulnerable. Into her mind flashed the image of those silvery orbs heated with passion and the air locked in her lungs.

"This has nothing to do with Hope," she choked out. It was imperative that he know that she alone was guilty. Hope could not be made to suffer in any of this. "Do you understand?"

He didn't reply, not by so much as a flick of his brow or a move of a muscle. To Laurel, he was sealed off, completely and utterly beyond reach.

Hope looked from Laurel to Brett and back again. "Laurel?"

Moves marked with a visible trembling, Laurel patted her sister's arm. "Stay here." Then she collected the ring of keys from a nearby table and handed them over.

"If you'll come with me," Brett dictated.

She heard his words, she understood them, but it was as if some part of her mind had clouded over with a numbing veil. Her vision as she followed Brett out the back door appeared slightly skewed. The sounds of the key being fitted into the cellar door, of that door swinging wide, were strangely muted. Physically, time seemed to have sped up; mentally it dragged as though weighted. The duality of awareness was disorienting.

The lantern held high by the soldier ahead lit the way, beckoning and condemning in the same instant. Slightly dizzy, she made her way down the stairs, concentrating on the most simple of things: breathing normally, swallowing the nausea born of dread, wishing she could feel warm again.

All the while, she could feel Brett's remote gaze slicing into her from behind. Even through the curious lassitude that swathed her, the ruthlessness of his power and condemnation had the strength to touch her, to wound her.

*I could have loved you.*

The thought came to her out of nowhere. Almost hysterically, she likened it to the final wish of a dying man. Desperation did have a way of making one face all of life's truths.

Out of respect for those lost hopes and dreams, she began to tuck her chin, realizing belatedly, disbelievingly, that the cellar was empty.

Empty . . . blessedly, amazingly empty . . . *empty.*

Her heart jumped in her chest, her brain struggled to function. How? Sweet Mary, *how?* The supplies had been there yesterday, they weren't supposed to be moved until tomorrow night. For whatever reason, John had moved them early.

The cellar was empty . . . dear God, empty. . . . She could almost bless John St. James!

Slowly, carefully, she looked up at Brett. She was instantly sorry. Fury was etched into every line of his face, rage radiated from his body in shimmering waves. Not only had he not caught her redhanded, he'd been made to look the fool.

"There's nothing here, sir," a soldier made the mistake of remarking.

"Get out," Brett snarled. "All of you."

Laurel didn't need to be told that the dictate was not for her. Even if it had been, it would have been a struggle for her to move. Her legs had begun to feel the effects of her relief and her knees literally knocked together. The condition only increased as Brett made a thorough, scrutinizing search of the basement floor. By the dim light of the lantern, she wondered what he saw that captured his attention.

"Do you ever use the cellar, Miss Seymore?" he muttered, going down on his haunches to study the compressed dirt beneath his boots.

"No, rarely." She wished he would look at her, or at least acknowledge her in some way that would make him seem human. She knew that mortal individual. This cold, distant denouncer was a stranger to her.

"Then how do you explain these marks?"

"What . . . marks?"

In a fluid play of controlled strength and muscle, he came to his feet, took hold of her arm and yanked her forward. "These," he snarled over her startled gasp. "And these." He pointed to an array of indentures in the dirt, fresh footprints and marks of heavy objects having been dragged across the room.

Too late, she realized her mistake. "I . . . I . . ." Words failed her. The need to protect herself was real, impelling her to deny any knowledge of the evidence, but she couldn't lie again. Her life of late had become rife with falsehoods and denials. She couldn't force out another, especially to Brett.

"Nothing to say?" he sneered.

She winced as his fingers bit into her arm.

"If you don't use this cellar, Miss Seymore, then who does?" Her silence lengthened, until he finally grabbed her up by both arms, lifting her to her toes as he drilled his gaze into hers. "What's the matter, at a rare loss for words, or are you suddenly possessed of a conscience?" He didn't give her a chance to say anything, but charged on ominously, darkly, succinctly. "I know what's going on, Laurel. I know Diego is hiding his supplies here. I may not have found his stash, but I've seen enough to know I'm right. Aren't I?" He shook her roughly. "Aren't I?"

She couldn't tolerate his manhandling her. It was enough to goad her into action, tapping into reserves that were already severely depleted by the strain of it all. On bravado alone, she cried, "Let me go."

"Answer me."

"Go to hell!"

"You might have everyone else in this city fooled, but I've found you out."

She struggled furiously and gained her release, but only because he allowed it. It didn't matter. She was momentarily free of him and she put the width of the cellar between them.

Back pressed to the chilly stone wall, she dragged in ragged gulps of air, feeling battered from the inside out. By luck alone, she'd been spared discovery and punishment. Brett truly had no evidence that could hurt her. Now, she needed to be as strong as she'd ever been, cautious, alert, close-mouthed. She watched him in much the same way he did her, unflinchingly.

"Why?" he asked, the line of his lips parting only enough to issue the single word.

Intuitively, she understood what he was asking. If she though he might understand, she might have explained. It wasn't possible. No matter how just or humane her reasons, at the core of her actions lay a need for money, and she had broken the law to get that money. Brett would find no justification in that.

"I asked you a question," he grated.

"I have nothing to say."

"No? Not five minutes ago you were practically confessing."

"To what?"

"Smuggling."

"I did no such thing."

" 'This has nothing to do with Hope.' Those were your words, Laurel. What exactly is Hope not involved with?"

"Nothing. I didn't want her upset is all."

"You should have thought about that before you got involved with Diego."

Even in the dim light, Laurel could see the blue of his eyes take on a flinty cast. When he spoke again, his voice was a harsh vibration. "What a pretty little liar you are, pretending to be generous and charitable. All the while you've been consorting with a known killer." He took a step closer, a travesty of a smile marring his face. "Is that why you wouldn't bed down with me, because you're already spreading your legs for Diego?"

"No."

"I wouldn't have thought you'd have bothered with being selective. After all, what's one more man to a woman like you? Tell me how it works. Does he service you or do you service him?" He took another step. "Is that it? Do you bare your breasts and use your mouth like some high priced whore?"

His words slashed at her, drawing pain so fierce she ached to cry out. Mutely, she shook her head in silent denial, but he continued, cruel and bitter.

"What do you get in exchange? Expensive fabrics, money, the pleasure of feeling a man's hands slide up between your thighs?" A third step brought his body flush to hers. "Is that your price, Laurel? The filling of your body?"

She shut her eyes, jerking her head away, but there was no escaping the feel of his thighs pinning hers to the wall and his chest flattening her breasts. He was as indomitable and solid as the polished buttons of his uniform digging into her flesh.

"Stop," she choked out.

"Only when I have your confession."

The heat of him seared her, reminding her of other times when she would have gladly bathed in the warmth to be found at his touch. Her traitorous heart twisted with longing.

"Brett, stop . . . please." It was a pitiful plea, laden with tears she could not suppress a minute longer. Face studiously averted, she kept her eyes clenched shut. If she dared to look at him, she'd break into a million tiny teardrops.

A few seconds could have passed, or it might have been more lengthy minutes. She had no idea how long he continued to crush his sinew into her softness, stripping her down to levels of heartache and hopelessness she didn't know how to combat. When he finally did step back, relief assailed her in a huge encompassing wave.

Her senses reeled and she flattened her hands against the wall to steady herself. A little incoherently, she wondered where her self-confidence had gone to. She'd stood up to the worst John had ever offered and never once been reduced to tears. She'd matched him ire for ire to emerge unscathed because she'd never let her emotions get involved. It was too late for her to wish for the same with Brett. Her emotions were fully engaged and that put her in a very precarious position.

Opening her eyes required all of her resolve. Brett towered over her. His black brows lowered over eyes glazed with the need for retribution.

"I'm not finished with you," he swore. With that, he ascended the stairs.

The promise speared into her, vicious in the awful solitude his absence created. She couldn't handle his departure any more than she could his vow.

Shaken to the core, she sank onto the lowest step, hands in her lap, head lowered in exhaustion. That was how Hope found her.

"Laurel?"

Summoning the strength to reply was difficult. "I'm . . . down here."

"Oh, Laurel, what happened?"

It would have been so easy to excuse the incident away with "it's nothing to worry about." It was what she would have done in the past. But nothing this serious had happened in the past, and as Hope sat beside her, she thought of how best to explain. In her own way, Hope made the telling easier.

"I don't understand what Major McKenzie wanted with you, Laurel. Why did he accuse you of conspiring with Jack Diego?"

Laurel hesitated, not because she was at a loss for words, but because she weighed them carefully. Given today's events, Hope had a right to know what had been going on. Laurel's instincts were to protect her sister as much as possible. Perhaps it was a bit trite, but what Hope didn't know truly could not hurt her. She was innocent in any wrongdoing, including guilt by association.

"I can't tell you everything, Hope. I will not have you held accountable for my actions."

"What does that mean?" Hope demanded to know, her smooth brow lined with equal parts confusion and fright. "Are you in league with this smuggler, this Jack Diego?"

Gently, Laurel took her sister's hands between her own. "In a way."

"Which way?"

"Please, don't ask that. It would be best if you didn't know."

"Know *what?*" Hope exhaled in rare vexation, clearly upset. "You're talking in circles, telling me nothing."

"Only because I do not want you to suffer for choices I have made."

That didn't placate Hope as it once might have. She pursed her lips, openly debating the issue in her head. "Are you a smuggler?" she asked at length.

"No."

"Have you helped Jack Diego in some way?"

Laurel looked down at her lap. "Yes."

"Why?"

This was exactly what Laurel wished to avoid. "Hope, this isn't a good conversation for us to have."

"Why have you been helping this man?"

Hope's persistence pricked Laurel's temper and forced the truth. "For the money."

"Money?" Surprise widened Hope's eyes and parted her lips. "Are we in need of money? Is the shop failing?"

Laurel rubbed at her temples, resigned now to the inevitable. "No, to both."

"Then what did you need the money for?" Hope's guileless query was completed with an innocent gaze and an ingenuous candor.

"I used the money to buy slaves their freedom."

Her words fell into the hush of the cellar with all the impact of a weighty stone crashing down from above. The resulting silence only served to eat at Laurel's raw nerves. Slavery, like so many issues, was something they had never discussed. She didn't know what reaction to expect from Hope. Unable to sit in suspense, Laurel came to her feet, wrapping her arms about her waist. "Well, say something. Tell me what you think, that I'm a fool or absurd or even crazed."

Hope simply continued to gaze up at her, her expression mute. Then gradually, ever so slightly and by infinitesimal degrees, a soft smile graced her features.

"I think what you've done is quite lovely."

Censure and condemnation would not have been beyond the realm, Laurel realized. In Hope's case, mystification and even fear would have been more in keeping. Surprisingly, she had responded with none of those and instead, was genuinely pleased by the entire matter.

"You don't think badly of me?"

"No. I think you're noble and fine."

For as long as she could remember, Laurel had acted on her own merits, to suit her own sense of decency. People's opinions of her rarely mattered, but hearing Hope's compliment touched her heart deeply.

Sitting again, she gave Hope a fierce little hug, loving her sister as never before. "Thank you for feeling the way you do, but I didn't want you to know about this. I didn't want you involved in any way at all."

"Why not?"

Laurel raised her hands to indicate the obvious. "You have to ask that after today? *I* chose this course. If there is a price to pay, I'll pay it. I don't want you hurt by my actions."

"You're in trouble, aren't you?"

"Almost."

Hope nibbled on the inside of her lip. "Major McKenzie was in a fury when he left."

"I know."

"Does he know you're smuggling?"

"He thinks he does. Only I'm not smuggling, not exactly."

"What *have* you been doing?"

Laurel had kept her silence on this for so long, it was difficult to talk about it. Rubbing at the nape of her neck, she explained, "I've been letting John use the cellar to hide his goods. In turn, he pays me the money I need to buy the slaves."

"John who?"

"John St. James."

"What does he have to do with this?"

"John St. James is Jack Diego."

*"Stars and garters!"* Hope exclaimed.

Hearing her own expletive come from Hope struck Laurel with unexpected humor. She burst into laughter, welcoming the break from the tension. "It is rather amazing."

"I never knew."

"Neither does anyone else."

"But Mr. St. James, of all people. He's flirtatious and carefree, not the least like the type who'd be embroiled in something so nefarious as smuggling."

"There is another side to the man."

"There must be. Doesn't it frighten you to be . . . well, to be connected with him the way you are?"

"Until now there has been nothing to warrant my being afraid." That was a stretching of the truth. John had proven what a threat he could be by breaking into her house the way he had. "Beyond that, I've concentrated on the end results."

"How do you go about doing what you do?"

Laurel explained the real purposes of her frequent travels to different cities.

"I never guessed," Hope admitted. "You always returned with some kind of fabric." As if a sudden thought hit her, she looked about. "How many slaves have you . . . have you set free?"

"Sixteen, over the past two years."

"That many? How thrilling."

"For them. I've only been doing what I believe is right."

"What are you going to do now that Major McKenzie is suspicious of you?"

Laurel had known the answer ever since she had locked her door and widows against John. Brett's suspicions and her near arrest reaffirmed her convictions. Her reply came easily. "I'm going to put a stop to this. I can't afford to continue any longer."

"That would be wise," Hope agreed. "I don't know what I would do if you were jailed."

"If I'm lucky, we won't have to worry about that." If she was lucky, John would listen to reason and see that the present arrangement had become implausible. If she was lucky, Brett would have no further cause to arrest her. "As soon as I make one last trip, I'll put an end to the arrangement."

"Where are you going?" Panic tinged Hope's voice.

"Savannah."

"Why?"

"Because John has paid me already for his use of the cellar. That money was never intended for me."

"Will you buy another slave?" At Laurel's nod, Hope inquired, "Why can't you just give the money back? Wouldn't that be simpler?"

"It would be," Laurel conceded, disturbed by her sister's rising alarm. "But I doubt John would take the money." That would upend the balance of order between them. He would be indebted to her, something he would never allow. "Besides, I don't even know where he is right now."

"But Major McKenzie already suspects you."

"He can't arrest me for leaving the state. And buying a slave isn't against the law." She slipped her arm about Hope. "Don't fret about this. Please, don't."

"But I do. I'm frightened for you."

"I'll make this one last trip and then put an end to all of this once and for all."

Laying her head on Laurel's shoulder, Hope gave a heavy sigh. "When will you go?"

"Soon. At the end of the week, probably."

"You will be careful, won't you?"

"As careful as I know how." More, given the circumstances. She'd exercise every bit of caution she possessed, and then make a clean start for herself. Beginning with trying to forget that Brett McKenzie had stormed into her life and broken her heart.

# *Fifteen*

"Nine hundred and fifty, ladies and gentlemen, do I hear nine hundred and fifty for item number 629?"

Laurel raised her hand, indicating to the auctioneer that she would bid the asked amount. Careful to keep her feelings from showing, she silently admitted that for the things she was thinking about the man, she would have to spend the entire next week in church to even get close to being absolved.

"We have nine hundred and fifty. Do I hear one thousand?"

A mumble of voices rose from the group that crowded into the dark, close quarters of Cradock Auction and Commission Depot. The wide planked floor below and the heavy wood beams above absorbed some of the sound, giving Laurel the odd impression that the voices emanated from another room rather than from the area surrounding her.

"The Widow Seymore's last bid was nine hundred and fifty," the auctioneer cajoled. "Do I have one thousand dollars, ladies and gentlemen?"

Laurel held her breath, praying that no one would answer. She had just under seventeen hundred dollars in her reticule, some of which she needed to pay her hotel bill and passage for sailing home. If the bidding escalated much more, she would have to drop out of this particular auction, something she did not want to do.

Eyes narrowed, she stared at the young woman on the raised platform, "item number 629." She was young, slender, neatly dressed in a blue and white striped muslin dress, well-groomed, seemingly poised . . . and very, very pretty. Her obvious appeal to most of the men in the room had had a marked effect on the auction.

The bidding had been fast and furious at first, several men doing little to disguise the true nature of their interest in the young woman. The prospect of having such a lovely female "so readily available for one's personal needs," as one planter phrased it, had resulted in a spate of bids that had the auctioneer grinning like the greedy monger he was.

No one had counted on Laurel's interest, or her consistent participation that drove the price up beyond what most in the room were willing or able to afford. The bidding had tapered off and now only she and a couple of others were actively engaged in the auction.

Tension gripped Laurel hard. With all her heart, she did not want this young woman to be reduced to some man's personal whore. To be a slave was bad enough. To be further denigrated was more than Laurel could bear.

A woman should have the choice of who she welcomed into her bed, into her body. If the young woman on the platform went to one of the men in the room, she would not be given that choice. Laurel would bid every penny she could to spare the woman that fate. She would pay the absolute limit of her finances to gain the woman's freedom and in the process, the right to choose.

"One thousand," a man called from the back of the room.

"One thousand dollars, thank you, Mr. Oliver," the auctioneer stated. "Do I have eleven hundred, eleven hundred?"

"Eleven hundred," Laurel said.

"The Widow Seymore bids one thousand, one hundred."

"Eleven fifty," someone chimed in.

"Eleven seventy-five," Laurel bid.

The auctioneer could not contain his glee. "Do I hear twelve hundred, anyone, twelve hundred for this prime specimen, ladies and gentlemen."

For a moment, no one said anything, and Laurel dared to hope that she had ended the bidding. Then in a flurry, the bidding resumed in earnest. The price rose rapidly to thirteen hundred dollars and then fourteen. At fourteen hundred and fifty, she quickly reassessed her budget, eliminating new clothing for the young woman entirely.

Trusting that she would put an end to this for good, Laurel cast out what she knew could be her last bid. "Sixteen hundred dollars," she announced, mentally damning any man lascivious enough to top that.

The mumble of voices in the room increased, and people swiveled about to stare in wonder and speculation. Laurel ignored them all, concentrating on tamping down her apprehension. In growing anxiety, she waited as the auctioneer tried to spur the price up once again.

"The price is sixteen hundred dollars, folks, do I have a bid for sixteen fifty?"

Silence.

"Sixteen fifty?"

Silence.

"Then the price stands at sixteen hundred. Sold to the Widow Seymore."

To Laurel's chagrin, the people gave a small round of applause. She had inadvertently provided them with an afternoon of entertainment. The perversity of that was enough to rouse her resentment and her temper.

Heaping silent curses on their heads, she composed her features into a dignified mask and made her way to the billing officer's table in the next room. By the time she laid out her coin, the young woman had joined her. The transaction was completed quickly, and within minutes, Laurel and the young woman took their leave.

Only then did Laurel take in an unfettered breath. The past half hour had been riddled with too much tension, first with the intensity of the auction itself and then with the amount of attention it had focused on her. She had always tried to be as unobtrusive as possible. Today she'd failed miserably in that.

With a skill that would have made a thespian proud, she surreptitiously glanced around, turning the movement into nothing more than the attempt to adjust the fall of her cloak. Secure that no one was paying her any heed, she settled the brim of her black bonnet. To the passersby, she was simply a widow with a slave in tow. She did nothing to destroy that image as she made her way toward the nearby park.

"What's your name?" she asked of the woman who up until now had been "item number 629."

"Cassie."

"Hello, Cassie, I'm Laurel Seymore."

Shyly, Cassie smiled. "Yes'm, I know. I heard the man call you the 'Widow Seymore.' "

"Yes, well, he got the Seymore right."

"Ma'am?"

Laurel waved the matter aside. Once they were in the

relative privacy of the park, she'd have the time to explain all and to adjust her plans. Given her own expenses and those for Cassie, she was on the fringes of being desperately short of funds. But she wouldn't have changed the outcome for any amount of money. No woman deserved the fate that had awaited Cassie.

Bolstered by that certainty, she found an isolated bench situated along one of the park's less traversed pathways. "I want to start right off by saying that I have no intentions of keeping you."

"Ma'am?" Cassie's expression pursed with trepidation. "Are you going to sell me off to someone else?"

"No, I'm setting you free."

Cassie sat unmoving, clearly stunned. Her lips parted several times, but no sound came forth. After three false starts, she managed to put voice to her words. "You're going to let me go?"

"Yes."

Without warning, Cassie burst into tears, doubling over at the waist, burying her face in her hands and her hands in her lap. Laurel blinked in surprise, never having encountered such an extreme reaction from anyone.

"Cassie, please don't cry so. I know it's a shock, but—"

"Oh, Miz Seymore," Cassie exclaimed, straightening in a rush of tears and smiles. "You've answered my prayers."

Laurel pulled a hanky from her purse and handed it over. "I'm glad I could help."

"Every night, I've prayed to the good Lord above, but I never thought I'd see this day. You're a saint, an angel."

"No, I'm not," Laurel protested adamantly. "I'm not good at all." Her temper alone was enough to condemn her, and there was the matter of her lying to Brett and breaking the law. "I'm a woman who merely wants to do the right thing." One who had gone about doing so in a way that had nearly landed her in prison.

"No, no, you've saved me." Cassie dissolved into tears again, shaking with the force of her emotions.

Laurel did the only thing she could. She slipped her arm about the young woman and simply let her cry.

"Better?" she asked, when all that remained of Cassie's tears was a stray sniffle.

"Yes'm."

"Good, because we have some planning to do."

"Ma'am?"

"We have to get you settled." Laurel knew that she was responsible for Cassie's present circumstances. Auspicious as they were, they were also riddled with unexpected complications.

"I have enough money to see you on your way, if you like." In her mind, she was already writing a letter to Hope, asking her to send money. She decided on an amount and then doubled it. By the time she heard back from Hope, her stay in the city would be extended greatly. "It's not much, but I think we can manage passage on one of the ships headed north. Or if you like, we can find you a family to travel with. There are convoys of wagons leaving the city every day."

Cassie dabbed at her nose. "I suppose, if you think it's best, but what would I do when I get north? I've been a house maid in this town most of my life. I don't know anyone outside of Savannah."

This was one of those complications Laurel hadn't counted on. Cassie couldn't be expected to make her way in life in a strange city as a man might have. "I suppose you could come home with me and we could find a solution there."

"Where's that?"

"Charleston."

Cassie looked to her lap, twisting the fabric of her dress. "I could stay here." She gaze up in earnest. "I don't mean no disrespect, and I'm beholden to you for what you've done, but do I have to go with you?"

"Stars and garters, no. You can do almost anything you like. That's what being free is all about. If you want to stay here, then by all means, stay. We'll do what we can to get you a position."

"If it's all right with you, Miz Seymore, I think I'd like to find my husband first."

Laurel exhaled in disbelief. "Your husband?"

"Yes'm, Tyrus. He bought his freedom two years ago. He's a blacksmith now; has his own shop on the east side of town."

"Good heavens, here I've been going on about arranging a new life for you and you've already got one waiting." It occurred to her to ask Cassie why she hadn't spoken up at once, but thought better of it. Thinking and acting like a free woman was something Cassie was going to have to get used to. "Did Tyrus know that you were being sold?"

"No, ma'am. I tried to get word to him, but I don't think he got it, otherwise he would have been there at the sale."

"I should think so." Elated, Laurel came to her feet. "Let's go find your husband."

Within the hour, Cassie was reunited with Tyrus. More tears flowed, but they were tears of happiness, tears from the heart. To Laurel, they were ever so sweet. She left the couple standing in the middle of Tyrus's smithy, buoyed by the love the couple shared, strengthened by their joy.

She stepped out of the dimly lit shop and into the bright light of afternoon's slanting sun. Half a dozen paces to the left, and her arm was seized from behind. Gasping, she spun and came face to face with Brett.

Fear washed up through her, gripping her as relentlessly as the hand at her elbow. A moment of pure panic made a chaos of her thoughts, draining all the color from her face and the breath from her lungs.

What was he doing here? The answer was ridiculously simple, giving her impetus to think, to rationalize. He was spying on her, trying to catch her at some illegal act, only she'd done nothing wrong here. Quite the contrary. She'd done one of the most right things of her life.

"Major," she intoned coolly, the green of her eyes beneath the brim of her hat calm and direct. "Aren't you a little bit far from your post?" She flicked his uniform with a taunting glance.

"I would ask the same of you, Miss Seymore." His mouth thinned into a line as taunting as the look she'd given him. "Or should I say, 'Widow' Seymore."

The full extent of his spying took her aback. Obviously, he had been watching her for the better part of the day, certainly during her attendance at the slave auction. "I wasn't aware that melting into the shadows was one of your talents."

"I have many talents that you aren't aware of, one of which is ferreting out criminals."

"Do you see any in the vicinity?"

"Perhaps."

She lifted her free hand to indicate the innocence of her presence there on the tree-lined street. "I've done nothing wrong."

"No, I'll grant you that. In fact, both morally and ethically you're the saint Cassie professed you to be."

His eavesdropping was galling. "You are abominable."

"I'm curious." His fingers tightened. "And I want some answers."

"I suppose you're going to haul me off again, drag me with you whether I wish to go or not."

From his superior height, he smiled briefly. "Phrase it however you like, Laurel, but you are coming with me."

"Where?"

"Back to the hotel where I'm staying."

She wouldn't have expected that. He was there in an official capacity. If he were to take her anywhere, she assumed it would have been to a sheriff's office, or some place equally intimidating. But either way, he wasn't going to give her any more of a choice now than he ever had, and he had the physical strength to ensure that.

"Very well," she conceded as graciously as possible, as calmly as her heart allowed. Memories of the vile things he'd accused her of assailed her. She told herself that his opinion didn't matter, but that was a lie. It hurt to the marrow of her bones to know he believed her not just a vulgar tease, but a lowly whore.

Her indignation grew apace with her sorrow. Both kept her silent as she rode beside Brett in his carriage. She did her best not to dwell on everything that had passed between them, and determinedly, she studied the passing scenes. Still, it was impossible to ignore him the way she wished to. His sheer male presence stroked, and lured, and tempted all that was female within her.

Being closeted in the sitting room just off his bedroom did not help the situation, she decided moments later. The limited dimensions of the room only served to enhance his power and her own susceptibility to it.

Disconcertedly nervous, she distracted herself by removing her cloak and then her bonnet, taking extraordinary pains in arranging its delicate netting before setting it aside. All the while, she wished he would get on with whatever he intended. Accusations that pitted them against each other were what she needed, arguments that would make her wayward heart forget its dreams.

"All right, Major, I'm here. What did you want to discuss?" He'd removed his tall leather shako; she wished he would do the same with his sword. Both were military accoutrement that accentuated the gulf between them.

"I came to discuss your purposes in Savannah."

"You already know why I'm here."

"You buy slaves and set them free."

"That's right."

From his place beside the fireplace, Brett took up a relaxed stance. "That's a very expensive hobby you have."

"It's not a hobby."

"But it is expensive."

"I'm not one to put a price on human life, Major."

"Neither am I. And that's not the point I'm trying to make." He sauntered forward with a deceptively casual stride. "I'm more interested in where you've come by such exorbitant amounts of money. Seymore's must be making a pretty profit these days for you to be so benevolent."

"If it is, I hardly see how that concerns you."

"Haven't you learned yet, Laurel, that everything you do concerns me?" That was why he had had her followed back in Charleston ever since that day in the shop's basement. She hadn't denied his accusations, but rather, talked around them.

He studied her now with more interest than he would have liked. She was definitely a cool one, with her chin elevated primly, her expression telling him nothing. Dressed entirely in black as she was, he could almost mistake her for the piteous little widow she portrayed . . . if he didn't know her to be a scheming liar.

Every time he thought about the failed raid on Seymore's his blood boiled. The stolen goods had been there, of that he had no doubt. It rankled to the ends of the earth and back that he had been too late to discover Diego's "warehouse." It angered him even more to discover that Laurel truly was in league with the bastard.

The exact nature and extent of their association was a question rife with detestable possibilities. *Was* she Diego's lover as well as his partner?

He swallowed the sensation of pure loathing at the thought of Laurel giving herself to the smuggler, or to any man. Two months ago, he wouldn't have cared, but through the weeks, that detachment had been ravaged by the allure of her. Her winsome smiles and impudent breasts were a temptation as potent as her fresh, audacious manner. A stupid reaction on his part, since the reason for her presence in Savannah had him more confused than ever.

When he'd followed her from Charleston, booking passage on the same ship, he'd assumed she'd made the journey for the most illicit of reasons. He had fully expected to catch her conspiring with Diego, both in bed and out. Instead, he had trailed her about Savannah's charming streets to find her delivering a woman from slavery.

Damn, it didn't make sense. Nothing about Laurel ever had. She was so guilty of aiding a criminal he could almost feel her culpability across the room. And yet, she was so genuinely kind and humane that he was stirred in spite of himself.

Picking up her bonnet, he asked, "Why the disguise?"

"It makes life so much simpler," she said, unnerved by his close proximity. She moved away, putting a comfortable distance between them. "As a widow, I can come and go as I please."

"And coming and going is essential in what you do?" He tested the strength of the netting between his thumb and forefinger.

"You know the laws in South Carolina as well as I do, Major."

"Better."

She shrugged with her brows. "Then you should know that I can't set a slave free there. I have to leave the state."

"That's very noble of you, but why bother?" It wasn't a casual query. More than ever, he needed to understand this woman, if for no other reason than that the tenderness of her healing touch and the pure sweetness of her kisses had become fixed in his mind.

Laurel gave an indelicate scoff and crossed to stand before the settee. "Your question is insulting."

"Humor me."

"I told you once before that I don't believe in slavery."

"Many people don't, myself included, but you won't find us going to the lengths you do."

"Are you hinting at something?"

He tossed the bonnet aside and pinned her with his gaze. "You feed the hungry, doctor the wounded, emancipate the slaves. I'd like to know to what lengths you take your charity." And exactly how she defined that charity. Did that include gifting Diego with her body? He'd accused her of such, but damn her, he didn't want to believe it.

"Answer me," he commanded, his voice thickened by resentment and puzzlements and a scorching hunger for this one sole woman who had somehow danced her way into his life, and made a shambles of his normal self-control. "Do you take your *charity* to a personal level?"

His insinuation hit her hard and all the abhorrent slurs he'd hurled at her the week before knifed her anew. *Do you bare your breasts and use your mouth like some high priced whore? Is that your price . . . the filling of your body?*

Pain wrapped itself about her heart and no amount of internal chastisement alleviated the anguish. She'd told herself a hundred times over that she couldn't let his opinion matter to her, but in the end, it did. He thought the worst of her and that was a wound to her heart.

"Is that why you really came here?" she asked, keeping her emotions in check by will alone. "To take up where you left off, to call me a slut and a hussy?"

Brett stared at her with his own emotions hanging by a thread. He knew exactly why he had come to Savannah, but his suspicions had played him false. Once again, Laurel had tripped him up, clouding his normal logic and foresight just as she always had. Worse, she fascinated him, enticed him and tempted each and every one of his resolves, provoking emotions dangerous to his convictions. Damn it all, she was like a constant burning ache within him that craved to be assuaged.

Suddenly, he wasn't sure what he was doing there. He hadn't caught her with Diego, or discovered her in the midst of some wrongdoing. All he had done so far was to insult her, to hurt her, and in so doing, himself.

He scrutinized the pale loveliness of her features and damned her again. She was to be condemned for much, and applauded for far more.

"I must apologize for the things I said to you last week." But he'd been eaten up with rage at the game they played and with the things she made him feel—emotions he had no business feeling about her, of all people.

Across the ten feet separating them, she whispered, "Thank you for that. I may be guilty of many things in my life, but whoring is not one of them."

"What are you guilty of?"

*Loving you.* "You know most of my faults."

"And your strengths." He could sense his command of the moment slipping from his grasp, and yet it couldn't be helped. From the first moment he'd met Laurel, his professional duties and his personal life, normally in such perfect harmony, had been headed for a collision of monumental proportions. The need to preserve his control was as strong as ever, but there didn't seem to be any stopping what they had begun weeks ago when he had first stepped into her shop. "You're a remarkable woman."

"Not so terribly so."

"Enough that you confound me at every turn."

"Is that so horrible?"

"I'd like to understand you."

"Why?"

"I think you know."

She sucked in a trembling breath, shaken by the tension sizzling between them, a tension that impelled the release of a bone-deep honesty. "All I know is that you touch me when you will, kiss me at your pleasure, and then vilify my character with hideous insults."

"You've kissed me in return."

"I shouldn't have. It's caused a terrible strain between us."

"The 'strain' between us was there long before I kissed you, or touched you."

He was right. They had been aware of each other on myriad levels—private, intimate levels—from the very start. From that moment on, their lives had become a tangle of half-truths and longing, lies and passion, accusations and thwarted passion. The pain in all of that was so pitifully, horribly sad.

"How did we let this happen?" she asked, her eyes filling with the very real grief of regret, of dreams lost forever. "How did we come to this end, hurting each other the way we do?"

"I never wanted that."

"Nor I, but that is the truth of it." And after all the lies and subterfuge, she needed the truth and the exquisite catharsis it provided. If they could share nothing else, if all their chances were ruined, at least they could have that.

"We kiss," she offered wistfully, "we argue, and then yearn, we cling to each other in comfort, and then lash out in distrust and suspicion. And still, the desire doesn't go away. It remains, caged by principles and pride, until we say and do things that bring each other pain." Tilting her head to an angle that was intrinsically somber, she added, "With all my heart, I wish things could have been different for us."

He stared at her with silver-blue eyes glittering fiercely. "Would you have given yourself to me?"

"Yes. I could have."

"And now?"

"Now?" She dragged in a shaky breath and shut her eyes. "There's nothing left between us but your commitment to your duty."

Her word seared straight into him, striking at the heart of tenets on which he had based his life, damning him to realms where lifelong beliefs were suddenly accursed.

He wanted her. God help him, regardless of the consequences, he wanted to know this woman. For one night—just this one—he had to hold her in his arms, to take the essence of her into his keeping and make it his for all the years to come.

Breathing deeply, he lifted his chin. The significance of his decision was momentous. He'd never allowed any woman to push him to this point where his feelings for her superseded all else in his life. Tomorrow and the day after, he would face the repercussions of that with no regrets or excuses, but for tonight, for the chance to embrace Laurel through the sweet hours of bliss, he would cast everything aside.

The major would not exist. Neither would the smuggler's accomplice. They would be a man and a woman whose lives had been headed for this very end.

Slowly, he crossed to stand before her. "Look at me."

She opened her eyes, her gaze caught instantly by his.

"How much courage do you have?"

Courage? There were times when she lacked it entirely. "I don't know."

Tenderly, he trailed his fingers up her neck to seek out the delicate line of her jaw. "Are you strong enough, courageous enough to share yourself with me for one night? Can you forget the worst of the past weeks for a few hours, and then face what has to be faced?"

Deep inside, her pulse began a slow, steady pounding. Could she, would she dare do as he asked? "I don't see how."

"Don't say no." His fingers curled around to her nape, persuasive in their gentleness, alarming in their ability to strip away reason. "Give us this one night together."

Dread assailed her. "And tomorrow?"

"Tomorrow we go on as if nothing happened."

Her eyes rounded. "Would you be able to do that?"

"I'd have to. We would both have to."

Hence his question about courage. To do what he asked would require the kind of inner fortitude she wasn't certain she possessed.

Feeling as if the energy necessary to sustain her had been suddenly ripped away, she sank to the settee. He followed her down, sitting on his haunches before her, piercing her with the intensity of his gaze.

His suggestion was tempting and frightening. She wanted him, loved him, but until now, her conscience had prevented her from acting on that love. And, too, common sense had precluded her going to his bed. He had his duty, the very nature of which pitted them against each other.

Insult crept into everything else she was feeling. "How easy this must be for you. How convenient."

"Easy?"

"You've never made any secret of the fact that you desire me. I must admit, this is a rather unique attempt to entice me into your bed."

Brett's eyes narrowed to flinty slits. "You think that's all this is for me, a seductive ploy?"

"Isn't it?"

*"No."* He cupped her face in his hands, his features drawn by an anguish that squeezed at Laurel's heart. "I'm willing to sacrifice all I hold dear for you."

She blinked at that.

"Don't you see? You make me want you past reason and honor and commitment. Those are my life, the basis of my existence, yet I'd disregard them all to have you. Just this one night."

A wild trembling seized her insides when she considered his words. She needed no reminder of just how bound by loyalty and duty he was. He'd made that painfully clear to her on more than one occasion. His every action and intent and purpose had been marked by an unwavering dedication she'd assumed were part of his chosen profession, but she'd been only partly right.

By his own words, the army was his life . . . because he was at heart an honorable man. One was a natural extension of the other. And yet, convinced of her guilt, knowing where his duty lay, he would turn a blind eye to all to have her.

"Oh, Brett," she sighed, touching her fingertips to his jaw.

"Say yes, Laurel. Give us this time together."

Tears she never shed rose to turn the green of her eyes as brilliant as emeralds. "Lord give me the strength to face what I must tomorrow, but yes, tonight I'm yours."

# Sixteen

Brett leaned forward the few inches separating them and kissed her, opening his mouth on hers with a commanding insistence. Laurel sucked in her breath, struck as she always was by the heat and pleasure he evoked, and she died a little inside. This one night was all she had. Its memories would have to carry her through a lifetime.

Impatient to create those memories, she also wanted to linger in their creation, to stretch each one out and in so doing, sate herself on the subtle as well as the bold. In the end, she surrendered to her instincts and leaned her body into Brett's, slipping her arms about his neck.

One of his hands was already unfastening the few buttons between her shoulder. His other was at her waist, holding her as though daring the fates to dispute his possession of her. As if that could be possible. Fate had brought them into each other's lives, delivered them to this point.

Clinging fiercely, she met his kisses with her own. When he shifted to his feet and settled on the settee, she gladly, willingly, flowed along his body until she found herself straddling his lap, her breasts snuggled to his chest, his tongue caressing the column of her throat.

"I have dreamt of you like this," he muttered.

Her own dreams had traveled the route closer to nightmares; of his forcing her into a cell, of that steel door shutting out light and freedom and the sight of Brett's face.

His beloved, beautiful face. She cupped it between her palms and memorized the slant of his brow, the exact color of his eyes, the hint of his beard just below the surface of his skin. But it was his mouth that ultimately caught her gaze and then her lips.

His tongue twined with hers, thrust forward, withdrew, thrust forward again. Against her spread thighs, his hips did the same, seeking her intimate softness with his hard, straining flesh.

"I want you," he growled. He slipped her dress down her shoulders and arms, leaving the fabric draped at her waist. Her chemise quickly followed, baring her to his view, but only for a moment. He covered her breasts with his hands, caressing their lush fullness before bending low to capture a rosy nipple with his lips.

She cried out, wild tremors racking her, piercing heat inundating her chest, her belly, and between her legs. The most desperate sense of urgency urged her hips forward.

"Oh, Brett, please," she whispered. She wanted him as much as she loved him, to the ends of the earth and beyond.

Gasping for breath, she pressed her face into his neck, and dimly thought to have him as naked as she. Blindly, she sought the buttons on his jacket, but her fingers fumbled in their haste.

Brett came to her aid. Holding her gaze with his own, he had the coatee off in mere seconds while she sat in mesmerized fascination. With her hair on the verge of tumbling loose, her lips swollen and red from his kisses, the milky perfection of her breasts rising and falling rapidly with her breathing, she was woman personified. Beauty and strength combined, innocence and lust incarnate.

His hunger for her intensified painfully, to that level of desire where his body took command and his mind ceased to function. Quickly, he unbuttoned his pants even as he delved beneath the layers of her dress and petticoats. Unerringly he found her most delicate flesh, moist and ready. With his last semblance of thought, he waged a battle with his body for control.

It was a losing battle. Even though he wanted to stretch this first time out to its most delicious limits, he couldn't wait another second. His moves deft and sure, he lifted her slightly, brought her chest flush to his, and thrust upward into her waiting softness.

His low cry of exultation joined Laurel's breathless gasp as he absorbed the arching of her body. Dimly he realized that she was a virgin, but he was unable to check his movements. On a primal male level, he had no wish to. He was glad, *fiercely* glad, that he was the first, the only. He stared deep into her eyes, relishing the moment of complete and utter satisfaction.

Laurel felt enveloped by that same sense of pleasure. The pain had been nothing while the joy of being united with Brett was all and more than she ever could have begun to imagine. She'd known what to expect, but nothing could have prepared her for the sensation of being filled, of being whole.

How could anyone have made her understand this astonishing feeling of oneness? It was all-encompassing, taking her beyond the realm of a simple joining of two bodies to a place where her heart and her mind joined in freely, jubilantly.

Slowly, she opened her eyes and saw in his silvery gaze both surprise and pleasure. Still, she needed to ask, "Are you glad?"

"That you've never known another man?" He rotated her hips ever so slightly. "Exceedingly."

Her words choked off at the quivering of her insides. "I want to please you."

"You do." More than any woman ever had. Or ever would. She pleased him so much that he doubted this first time would last much longer.

Helpless against the desperate need to make her his, he drove into her repeatedly, his hands on her hips to guide her movements, his mouth crushed against hers, drinking in her throaty whimpers.

The sensations engulfing him were staggering in their intensity. Eyes clenched shut, breathing raggedly, he absorbed the feel and taste of her, silkiness and heat and the hint of flowers. He gripped her more securely, desperately, and in his mind, claimed her for all eternity. She was his, his mind decreed it. In the next second, his body echoed the sentiment, erupting into a climax rooted in the soul of him. Again and again, he called her name until the last of the tremors abated.

Face pressed into the hollow of her neck, he remained serenely spent, incapable of doing anything more than holding her while he slowly regained some sense of the present.

"If I had known this was your first time, I would have made things more comfortable for you," he muttered, running his hands up over the soft curves of her buttocks. But he hadn't known, not for certain. As in all things with Laurel, nothing was ever simple or obvious. "By the time I found out, I was beyond moving us to my bed."

Slightly dazed, Laurel tipped her head against his. She was rarely at a loss for words, but she was now. The physicality of the act was stunning. A little whimsically, she likened it to a well-guarded castle having been stormed by a mighty, unstoppable force. Once she let down her defenses, the force had boldly, fiercely, made a place for himself within her castle walls.

She enjoyed the idea, wishing she could spend the rest of her days just as she was now. The closeness was to be treasured, even if she did ache unbearably. It wasn't a residual pain of penetration, but rather a need that had arisen with Brett's every move.

"Did I hurt you?" he asked, levering away to study her closely.

"No." She studied him as carefully. He looked disreputable with his hair mussed, his skin damp with sweat, and his shirt half-unbuttoned and askew. And then of course, there was their present position. Modesty was nowhere to be found between them.

A rueful smile curled about his face. "I am sorry."

*For what?* her expression asked.

Threading his fingers through the riot of curls framing her face, he cupped the back of her head and eased her forward. "For leaving you unsatisfied," he whispered against her lips. "I'll take better care of you this time."

True to his word, he had her in his arms and in the bedroom almost instantly. There he slowly undressed her, removing each garment with a tenderness that belied the soldier in the man. He was, after all, military at heart. Fighting and warfare by nature were not given to tenderness.

And yet, his hands unlaced with almost erotic gentleness, his fingers trailing over her skin, touching, lingering, increasing the yearning inside her. With equal care, he placed her on the bed before quickly divesting himself of his own clothes.

His body was not a secret to her, but when he lowered himself over her, she felt as though his body held secrets that had been kept from her. As never before she was aware of the differences between them and she was enchanted.

The smoothness of her breasts was a complete opposite to the hair and steel of his chest. The breadth and strength of his shoulders were wholly dissimilar to hers. He was a source of raging heat to her tame warmth, a contrast that was, oddly enough, heightened by the weight of him. To be so solidly pressed into the bed was a unique pleasure, to have his thighs urge hers to part, a special delight.

Still, he didn't slip into her at once. He kissed her hungrily, as if his desire hadn't been assuaged only moments ago. Her senses, already heightened and expectant, whirled anew with passion's flame.

Lifting her hips to his seeking fingers, she nearly curled into herself at the delicious sensations that spiraled through her. It came to her vaguely, unwillingly, that he knew a woman's body; his touch was that skilled, that scintillating.

She could have been jealous, she could have hated all the other women before her, but the sentiment would have been a waste of time she didn't have and energy she would not expend. Their moments together were so few and so short. And they had promised; tonight they were simply a man and a woman with no past and no future.

Unable to help herself, she kissed him fervently, committing every nuance to memory. If the kiss was desperate, she didn't care—if her embrace was a bit frantic, so be it. She loved him and while he was hers, she would revel in the intimacy of that love.

This time, the pace of their passion was slower. He thrust into her with measured strokes, inching forward and then retreating, filling her only gradually, deliberately leaving her to want more. And she did want more. Every muscle and nerve clenched and gripped in anticipation, needing the release that Brett alone could give her.

She whispered his name, drawing the sound out on a plea.

Brett's answer was to increase the driving tempo of his lower body, to wrap her in his arms, to kiss her with unbridled passion. The combination was more than she could bear. Ecstasy swept through her, racking her body with an unparalleled joy that cast all else aside and narrowed the realm of her world to her and Brett. Above her, he ground his hips to hers in a final surge and then joined her in sweet oblivion.

A languor such as she had never felt pervaded her entire being. Physically and mentally, she was sated and more in love with Brett than she had been moments before. More in love with him than was wise.

She wouldn't allow the heartache that threatened. In silent defense, she clung to him with arms surprisingly determined given the precious lassitude still enveloping her.

He rose to his elbows and regarded her with eyes highlighted with silvery glints of peace and triumph. The former she could understand, the latter was cause for inquiry.

"What are you thinking?" she asked.

Trailing his fingers over her forehead, he smiled. "What I have always thought of you."

"What is that?"

"That you're a marvel."

"Truly? There have been times when your opinion of me has been more temperate, less complimentary."

"Shh." He silenced her by placing his fingertips over her lips. "Remember."

She did at once. "I'm sorry." She pressed a kiss to his shoulder. "I'll try to do better."

Brett gave vent to an indulgent laugh, deliberately misinterpreting her words. "I don't think I could stand it if you did any better."

"No?"

"At least not for a little while." He shifted away and to his side, taking her into the crook of his arm as he went. "As I said, you are a marvel."

With her head resting on his shoulder, she snuggled closer to his side. "Is that wrong?"

"That you're enthusiastic?"

"I wouldn't have phrased it that way," she sputtered, "but yes."

"No, there's nothing wrong with that. In fact, I wouldn't want it any other way."

She was pleased by his pleasure. Contentment, even if it was doomed to be short-lived, was hers. "How is your shoulder?" She lifted her head to scrutinize his scarred flesh. "Does it pain you?"

"Hardly ever."

For that she was relieved and happy. She didn't want him suffering, she never had, even when the discord between them had been at its worst. Resting once more, she sighed, letting her fingers toy with the hair on his chest.

The thick curls were such a manly peculiarity, as was the density of his muscles. She scanned the length of him and not for the first time, was taken aback by the physical beauty of him. Their differences aside, it was rather amazing to think that they should be together. She wasn't a stunning beauty and most men did not find her personality inviting, while he was what most women longed for.

"Now it's my turn to ask, what are you thinking?" Brett breathed against her forehead.

"Something you'd find excessively female."

"I should hope so." Shrugging the shoulder beneath her head, he urged her to answer. "Tell me."

"I was thinking that of all the women you could be with, you're with me."

His brows lowered at the vulnerability underlying the statement. She was the most dauntless women he'd ever met. To hear even a hint of uncertainty in her was astonishing. Giving her no warning, he rolled over and pinned her body with his.

"I'm here with you because I don't wish to be with any other woman." He linked his fingers with hers and pressed her hands back to the pillows on either side of her head. "I'm here because you're one of the most special women I've ever met, and I desire you more that I have any other woman."

In the region around her heart, Laurel felt her love for him expand and grow. "Still, it amazes me. There are others who are truly beautiful."

"Facially, perhaps. Bodily . . . " He shrugged, "But in regard to character and disposition, you are far more than beautiful."

"You call me a termagant."

"Only because you're stubborn and foolhardy. But you're also caring and compassionate and selfless. Those are what make up true beauty. The rest is an accident of birth, a meaningless collection of features passed on to us from our parents. They signify nothing."

He thought she was beautiful, in ways that were richer and more meaningful than appearance. Lying beneath him, seeing the admiration in his eyes, she felt beautiful. "Oh,

Brett." Lifting her mouth to his, she kissed him with aching tenderness.

They made love again, and yet again, and once rested, again. They slept, but only for brief snatches at a time. Laurel was too aware of the diminishing hours to give in to rest. She'd reach out if for no other reason than to touch him, to feel his heat, to find his heartbeat.

Brett was no less needy. When he wasn't buried deep within her silken heat, he wished to be. The craving was like an addiction; the more Laurel gave of herself, the more he wanted. So he took and gave in return, his own pleasure secondary to Laurel's.

It was only as dawn crept near that she lay still and silent in his arms. She was no more asleep than Brett was. The prelude to morning brought with it an inescapable reality that made sleep impossible. Sighing, she thought back over their hours together.

They had touched and teased and laughed and loved. The conversations between them had been limited to the immediate.

*Are you ticklish?*

*I love the feel of you.*

*Keep me warm.*

They hadn't given a thought to food. She hadn't been hungry, she still wasn't. Her body was replete. Her mind, however, was not. There was so much that hadn't been said, so much she wished to know.

"Brett," she began, and then stopped, wondering how best to proceed. Even if he agreed to talk to her, she was leaving herself open to an awful hurt. But if she didn't ask now, another chance would likely never be hers.

Hearing her whispered voice, Brett tucked his chin to peer into her face. She lay with her thigh cradled over both of his, her head on his shoulder, her arm draped across his chest. He tightened his arms about her. "What is it, love?"

With that single endearment, he gave her the means to broach the subject most on her mind. "Am I your love?" She smiled sadly. "Could I have been?" Shifting, she came to rest on his chest, arms folded beneath her chin, eyes raised to his. "I know we agreed not to think beyond the night, but it's morning now, and I'd like to know . . . I need to know . . . if circumstances had been different between us, if you hadn't been a soldier and I. . . . Could you have loved me? Could you have married me?"

The queries speared straight into Brett, striking basic fundamentals of his life. Instinct impelled him to turn away from the matter, but the bald yearning on Laurel's face stayed him.

Threading his fingers back through her hair, he considered the seriousness of all she'd asked. The night just past had given him a glimpse of what his life could have been in another time, in those other circumstances she referred to. The glimpse had been sublime.

"Perhaps," he murmured. "It would be easy to love you." If he allowed himself to. It was out of the question.

"And marriage?"

His answer was a long time in coming, preceded by a weighty sigh. "I try not to think about marriage."

"Why?"

She was as direct as ever, probing as most women, most people never did. It was one of the things he liked best in Laurel. He liked *her.* Because of that he would tell her.

He'd never made any secret of his disinclination toward marriage, but neither had he brazenly announced his opinion to the world. That would have entailed explanations, and they were personal, known only to a very select few. Still, he felt a remarkable ease in confiding in Laurel.

The night just past had brought him to that end. Her honesty and generosity inspired the same from him.

"I've seen what my profession can do to a marriage." His fingers made another pass through her hair. "It can suck the joy and life right out of a union."

"Are all husband soldiers unhappy?"

"No. The shortcoming would be within me."

"You?" She couldn't believe him lacking in any way. "You are the most true and committed man I've ever met. What fault could you bring to a marriage?"

He smiled at her defense of him. "The very same virtues that make me such a good soldier would make me the worst husband."

She didn't understand and her expression said as much.

"Laurel, you have it right in saying I am true and honest and faithful. I live by a code of honor that binds me to my duty. One hundred percent. Were I to take a wife, I would want to be as committed to her. I can't do both. One would suffer."

Frowning, she said, "You sound so positive."

"I am. My father was a soldier, given over to his duty. I saw what that did to my mother."

He'd never spoken of his parents. That he did so now was in some ways far more intimate than anything they'd shared thus far. "Did she love him?"

"Blindly."

"And your father? Did he love her?"

"He professed to."

"But you don't think so?"

"It's hard to say. His priority was never to his wife or his children."

"And you wanted it to be."

"What child doesn't?" The resentment he carried with him from his youth churned inside. "At four or six or even eight, a child doesn't understand the intricacies of neglect. He simply reacts." He punctuated the declaration with a narrow-eyed gaze and a twisting of his mouth.

Against her, Laurel felt his tension, and her heart broke for the child he'd been and the man he'd become. Both had been denied a much-needed love: that of a parent. "Is that how it was for you?"

He nodded. "It wasn't until I was going on ten that I was able to look at my parents, at our family, and see what was happening." His mother's longing and heartache. His sisters' disappointments, and his own. "The love my mother bestowed so freely on my father was never returned, not the way she deserved. Oh, he'd make the occasional attempt, but he was forever wishing to return to his post, to be surrounded by the sights and sounds of army life."

"Did he love any of you?" she demanded to know, incensed that Brett had been hurt by someone who should have provided love.

"I don't think he was capable of loving—not as my mother did. She needed to be loved. Father needed the adulation of hero-worship." He paused, his sights turned to the past. "He would come home from wherever, gallant and victorious, sweep into our lives like some conquering hero. We would all crowd around with our praise and our cheers and hugs, happy to have him back. He thrived on that, lived for it, if you want the truth. But it wasn't a natural state. We couldn't live our lives feeding his need to be adored. Everyday life went on with all its mundane problems. That's when he would begin to get restless."

"How long before that would happen?"

"Sometimes a week, sometimes a month. It varied, depending on how long he'd been gone. But it was always the same. We could see in his manner a certain distractedness that would eventually become irritability. I learned to read the signs and knew he would leave soon." And that was when his mother's tears would flow. And when his own resentment would swell.

"Your father sounds like a selfish person," Laurel observed, her voice carrying a healthy dose of her own resentment. "Excuse me for saying so, but I don't like him."

The sound of her pique brought a crooked smile to Brett's face. "Loyal little termagant."

"Where is he now?"

"With my mother, in Philadelphia."

"That surprises me. I would have thought he'd be out trying to find another war."

Fingers splayed over her ribs, he hugged her close. "He would if he could, but he lost his sight several years ago."

Laurel couldn't say she was sorry, and she wasn't going to seek absolution for the uncharitable thought, either. "How does he manage? After so many years of running off, staying home must be difficult."

"It was at first. He's had to adjust."

Which, Laurel vowed with another defiant jab at repentance, was the man's just rewards. "How on earth did you ever become a soldier, then?"

"By choice. History has proven time and again that no country can exist without a national militia. I believe very strongly in that."

"You don't have any beliefs that aren't strong."

"True. Which brings me back to my original thoughts

on marriage. For the sake of a family alone, I wouldn't subject them to my profession."

"Are you so much like your father?" she asked in genuine, innocent curiosity.

"No," he declared, insulted that she would think such a thing. He'd gone out of his way to ensure he wasn't his father's son. Only in their chosen profession could he say they shared anything in common.

"Then why do you assume that you will bring to a marriage what he did? If you are so different than he, how do you know you would neglect a wife and family?" Before he could answer, she inched upward until her face was directly over his.

They had no future together. She knew that with every painful beat of her heart. This loving interlude would end the minute she left this room. She would return to her shop and try to pick up her life, heartened for their time together and saddened that it couldn't last a lifetime.

Leaving him would be the most difficult thing she would ever have to do. But if that was to be her fate, then she would leave him a wish for his happiness. He deserved as much.

"You would make a wonderful husband. And an even better father."

"Laurel," he stared to object.

"You would think to dispute that, but I have been on the receiving end of all your better instincts. You are loyal and honorable and protective." Regret and longing spiraled upward from the pit of her. "A woman would be blessed to have you for her spouse."

"If it's marriage you're after—"

"No." She shook her head slightly, the move as forlorn as the narrow curve of her smile. "I don't ask this for myself, Brett. I have no delusions where you and I are concerned. I'm speaking on your behalf. You sell yourself short and disallow the possibility of so much in your life."

"You can't know that for certain."

"Yes, I can," she vowed a little fiercely. "The very fact that you are so conscious of hurting a woman, of betraying her, says it all. You would never take her for granted, not any more than you would your duty to your country. It isn't in you to do either. You are strong enough to have both, if you want them."

Wishing with all her heart that that future could include her, she pressed her lips to his, and knew with a sudden instinct that this was their final moment together. "I can think of no one who deserves to be loved as much as you. Don't deny yourself that, Brett. Find someone to love." *Someone who loves you as much as I do.*

She slipped from his arms, blinking to keep her tears from showing.

"Laurel?" He reached out to draw her back, but she spun, stepped away, and offered him a brave smile. He needed to hold her, needed her to put the last few wildly improbable moments into perspective. "Let me love you one last time."

"No. It's better this way." She gathered up her clothes and donned them with commendable calm. To his credit, Brett didn't try to stop her. He knew as well as she that it was time to part. Standing at one of the windows in nothing but his pants, he seemed to wrestle with the idea, damning her with glittering eyes, accepting with the rigid stance of his body.

Only when every bow was fastened and every button secured did she allow herself a last, lingering look. "I wish you all the good things in life, Brett."

"Laurel, don't."

She smiled into the stormy scowl darkening his features. "I wish you happiness and love." Tilting her head to one side, she dropped her gaze to the floor, bit her lower lip, and searched deep for composure. All would be changed the next time she saw him. The next time they met, he would see her as the enemy.

Shoulders slumped, she took her leave.

# *Seventeen*

Brett couldn't remember the last time he'd been so angry—with the idiocy of those around him, with the pettiness of polite society, with the world, *with himself.* His rage was all inclusive, and tonight, made itself known in the sheen in his eyes and the acidic bite of his tongue.

Peering around the crowded salon of the Planters' Hotel, he cursed the couples dancing, damned the musicians and their instruments, and consigned to everlasting hell the matron who had whined and wheedled her way into having every officer in the city present for her asinine little gala. Her insistence had resulted in a direct order.

Tossing back the last of his brandy, he set the glass aside then made his exit from the ground floor salon. An assortment of vapidly excited faces smiled his way as he wended a path through the throng of people gathered in the foyer. For the first time ever, he was going to blatantly, knowingly, disobey an order. And he didn't give a good goddamn what anyone, including his commanding officer, had to say about it. There was only so much a man could take, and Brett knew he could take no more.

Outside, he sucked in a bracing dose of night air, paced a few short steps in one direction only to pivot sharply and pace back the way he had come. An inner tension had him as tightly coiled as a newly wound clock. He had been so ever since he'd returned from Savannah over a week ago.

The memories assailed from within, music and laughter buffeted him from behind. To either side, the darkened length of Church Street seemed to close in on him. The space he needed just then was absent, and that alone increased his anger tenfold. Remembering that he'd left his shako inside set his blood boiling.

Determined to retrieve the damn hat and be gone with all haste, he turned for the door and nearly tripped over a woman whose face was vaguely familiar.

His hands came out to steady her. "I beg your pardon," he excused himself, forcing as much civility into his voice as he could muster.

"That's quite all right, Colonel."

"Major," he corrected automatically, setting her away.

Her hands lingered on the lapels of his dress coatee. "How silly of me," she laughed.

"Not at all." He made to step away, but she sidled herself into a spot in front of him. "Madam?"

"Oh, please don't say you don't remember me, Major."

"Then I won't." If she wanted to hear a lie, that was her business. "If you'll excuse me."

"No, I don't think I will."

The curse that came to mind would have blistered the hide she so obviously prided. He was sorely tempted to deliver it. God alone knew why he didn't. Perhaps because he wasn't a mean person, or maybe because he was basically an honest person. That honest, fair character prodded him into admitting that she'd done nothing to warrant his censure.

With the confession came a resigned lessening of his

ire. "Forgive me, madam, but you have me at a disadvantage."

"Do I? How absolutely charmin'," she cooed in a voice as honeyed as her smile. "We met some time ago, your first night here in the city, to be exact." She extended her hand in an overstated show of grace. "Anna Lee Prescot."

Brett recognized the name at once, not because of any special allure he could attribute to Anna Lee herself, but rather because of the dress she'd been wearing when he'd first seen her. The soft pink gown had been embroidered on its hem with a delicate laurel blossom.

*Find someone to love.*

Laurel's words came back to him now as they had countless times since she'd left him. Deep inside, his muscles gripped in self-defense.

"Major McKenzie?"

Find someone to love, she'd told him. His eyes scoured Anna Lee's face. Her? Loving her would be impossible. Bedding her was even out of the question, a most telling consideration given the fact that Miss Prescot was presently on the verge of popping out of her bodice. The sultry look in her eyes as well as the coy movements of her bare shoulders announced that she was ripe for the taking.

He had only to reach out, but he didn't. After Laurel, not a woman in the city held any appeal for him, least of all this pampered miss who had, even weeks before, neither attracted nor fascinated him in any way.

And still, he couldn't get Laurel's words out of his head. *Find someone to love.* It was unthinkable. He wouldn't allow it.

"Is something wrong, Major?"

There was definitely something wrong, Brett knew, as he focused on Anna Lee. His well-laid plan of spending a single night with Laurel had gone awry. He was supposed to have returned to Charleston with her purged from his mind. Instead, he was consumed by the essence of her.

The image of her face plagued his days. The memory of her laughter filled his mind while the feel and taste of her had his body in a constant state of near-arousal. If he thought seeing her again would alleviate the situation, he would have been at her door his first night back. But he knew the folly in that. Seeing her again would only increase his desire for her and he couldn't allow that to happen.

"I am needed inside, Miss Prescot," he remembered to say. Then, just short of rudeness, he offered a sketch of a bow and retrieved his hat. Moments later, he was mounted on his horse and headed no place in particular. Only as he recognized a row of buildings did he realize he was less than a block from Laurel's house.

Swearing, he abruptly directed his mount toward water's edge. In the shadows of the grand mansions of East Bay, he finally stopped and sought distraction in the sights and sounds of the Cooper River.

The night breeze hit him full in the face, bringing with it pungent odors of brackish water and sluggish mud. He detected hints of smoke and ocean air, irate voices in the distance, a dog barking. Night in the city as usual, composed of the ordinary, the habitual, and the mundane. Above all else, he wanted those for himself, yet damnably, they were, and had been, beyond his reach.

In the past week, he'd gone about his duties with a single-minded purpose, hoping to rid himself of Laurel's hold as much as he hoped to catch Diego. His hopes had met with frustration. His informants had come to him with nothing pertaining to Jack Diego. If the smuggler was in the city, he was being extremely careful, for he was nowhere to be seen. And as long as Diego remained at large, Laurel's fate remained in question. Again and again, Brett was forced to ponder her when he least wanted to.

The dispassionate composure he so needed had been sorely lacking, his self-restraint dubious. He had not been a model soldier.

With a grating laugh he imagined what his father would think of that. Nothing good. But then, his father's opinions were often critical.

He had to give in to a rueful smile when he remembered Laurel's dislike of his father. She'd been remarkably accurate in calling Samuel McKenzie selfish. Brett had realized that years ago. It had taken Laurel mere minutes to reach the same conclusion. Smart woman. Of course, Laurel was, if nothing else, extraordinarily discerning.

And loyal. She truly believed in him and his capacity as a man—not just as a soldier, but as—a husband and a father, as well. Given the tempestuous nature of their association, he was extremely gratified by her faith in him. Given her keen, honest nature, he was deeply moved . . . and goaded into weighty and uncomfortable speculation.

Although Laurel *was* dangerously rash and stubborn, he could not dispute her ideals or her intelligence. Her sense of logic was sound. Why then, did he have such trouble accepting her rationale on his suitability to marriage? Was it out of habit, or was he more affected by his father's' behavior than he would have liked?

The idea did not sit well. Brett prided himself on having survived his childhood intact, a blunt resentment toward his father the only consequence. But if he were to believe Laurel's reasoning, that he was incapable of neglecting a woman, then he had been deluding himself for a long while.

He was not his father incarnate. Then why did he cling to the conviction that a wife and family did not fit into the scheme of his life? The too obvious answer was because a family had not fit into Samuel's life, and that was a lesson Brett had unconsciously carried with him.

He shifted in his saddle, jerking his head to one side as if to escape the thoughts rifling his tolerance. Whether he liked it or not, he had been more greatly influence by his father than he had suspected, and that riled him to no end.

Swearing liberally, he damned his father for his greedy self-indulgence, and then himself for relenting to this mental inquisition. When he was finished, he damned Laurel for provoking him to such scrutiny to begin with. Until recently, he had been content. Now she had him questioning the basis for his own life.

He needed to focus himself once more. The order and reason to be found in the army afforded him a certain measure of control over his life. He was comfortable with that. He liked that.

Then why in the devil did he feel so infuriated?

"Are you just about finished, Laurel?"

At Hope's query, Laurel swept the last of the scraps of fabric into a tidy pile. "Just about." She could have left the chore until the morning, but she'd gotten in the habit of leaving the shop clean before going home. She went through the ritual now, grateful for the little bit of serenity to be found in the routine. Serenity had been sorely lacking in her days of late.

Storing the broom in its corner, she passed a weary hand

along the nape of her neck. It was barely nine o'clock and she was tired down to her bones.

From behind, Hope commented, "You've been doing that all day."

Laurel turned, brows raised, to find Hope standing amidst the chaos that had become the shop that day. It seemed that everyone and her sister had either needed a fitting or an alteration. "Doing what?"

"Rubbing the back of your neck. Are you feeling the ague coming on?"

"No."

"You haven't been yourself lately. Should you call for the doctor? Maybe there's something wrong."

There was nothing wrong with Laurel that seeing Brett wouldn't cure.

A tiny hurt blossomed in her heart, spreading with insidious accuracy throughout the whole of her. It took a concerted effort for her to keep her feelings from showing. However, there was no controlling the need.

When would it end? When would the hurt go away? When would she be able to endure a day free of the awful longing?

"A good night's sleep is what I need," she said. And it was the truth. Her nights had been a series of memories too sweet to forget, too tormenting to withstand. She yearned for peace of mind. What she had was a love that would go unfulfilled.

"Then why don't we leave the last of this for tomorrow?" Hope suggested, gesturing to the array of dresses that had yet to be stored on their hangers. "We could do that." Her delicate lips pursed in blatant worry. "I mean, if you wanted to, if you thought it best."

Dear, dear Hope, Laurel thought. She'd made such progress. Still, there was a bit of the old insecurity that lingered in her manner which Laurel wasn't sure would ever dissipate completely. There were times when Hope sought direction, and Laurel gladly gave it, only tonight, she wasn't up to giving it.

"We'll do whatever you wish, Hope."

Forced into making a decision, Hope scanned the room with doubt threading across her features. "Do you think it would take very long to set things to rights?"

Whether it did or not didn't make any difference to Laurel. She wanted to ignore it all and be home. She wanted also to spend as much time as possible with her mind directed toward something other than Brett.

Dear Lord, he was a rare man. She would love him to her dying breath, for all the good that would do her. She didn't regret her actions in Savannah; they were the stuff of magic, but she had grossly mistaken her fortitude. She didn't have the strength to carry on as if nothing had happened.

Not a day went by when she didn't search for the sight of him. She told herself that was all she needed to survive her days, a single lovely glimpse. That was a lie, though. She needed him, his smile and his laughter, his temper and his strength, his arrogance and his sense of honor.

And too, she needed his body moving within hers. It had been too long since she'd basked in the gleam of his silvery-blue eyes and felt bathed by his heat. In the wanting, she had become less than whole.

She yanked away from her musings, reining in hard on her wayward emotions. What had Hope asked? *Do you think it would take very long to set things to rights?* For Laurel, the answer was a lifetime.

"I think if we put our minds to it, we can at least have

everything in its proper place. No one will know the difference, unless they make a point of looking closely. And no one is likely to do that."

"All right," Hope beamed. "I'll start in the front room, unless you want some help back here."

"No, I'll be fine." She wouldn't be, but Hope didn't have to know that.

Determined to spare herself the heartache brought on by yet another resurgence of memories, she concentrated all her energies on tidying the room, and then had to laugh. It was amazing how inspiring the *un*inspiring could be. Fabrics and spools awaited her with a singular expectation to match that of emptying the bucket of fireplace ashes out back. Even the water she drew from the well and poured onto the dead coals was a sufficient distraction.

Studiously avoiding condemning a future of more of the same, she set the bucket aside the well and headed for the shop's back door. She never heard the figure approach from behind, never saw the arms reach out and yank her back into the shadows.

Reflexively, she fought against the fingers clamped over her mouth and the arm imprisoning her against a solid male form. Fear came fast after that, more potent for its split second delay. The undiluted alarm and dread provoked the most gut level of instincts to flee for safety. Silently, she cried out for Brett.

"Be still," John ordered.

Laurel sagged in relief, her breath leaving her in a single, deep rush. Yet her ease was fleeting. Anger rose up in a hot surge that primed her limbs anew.

Yanking her head to the side, she squirmed her way to freedom. "What do you think you're doing?" she hissed, hands clenched into fists at her sides. "Was that absolutely necessary?"

"Perhaps," Jack asserted, his eyes roving over her with insulting exactitude.

She didn't try to fathom his meaning, but instead cast wary glances about. "Why are you here?" she whispered. The last time he'd changed the normal routine, he'd broken into her house, and nothing good had come of that. "Is something wrong?"

With seeming nonchalance, he leaned against the side of the shop, stretching his legs out before him. In the darkness of the surrounding alley, he was hardly more than an additional shadow. There was barely enough light for Laurel to see the impression of his mustache above his smiling mouth.

"Something might be wrong," he drawled.

"What?"

"You tell me."

He was in one of his moods, she realized in mounting pique. "John, you aren't making any sense, and I'm too tired to wade through the intricacies of your thoughts. Just tell me why you're here."

"Ah, Laurel love," he laughed. "You always were a spirited one. Always so direct, so candid. That's what I've liked best about you." Shoving away from the wall, he reached out to toy with a curl behind her left ear. "That and all this hair."

She slapped his hand away. "*Why* are you here?"

"Why must there be a reason?"

"Because every move you make is calculated."

"You are no different."

"Only out of necessity, not because it's in my nature to do so."

"And how well you've handled 'necessity.' It's kept you alive through all those little jaunts to Georgia. Tell me, how was this last trip?"

There was something about the way he posed the query that gave her a moment's pause. "Fine."

"Made another of your peculiar purchases, did you?"

"Yes." She squinted for a better view of his face, but saw nothing in the darkness that would tell her what he was thinking, or still the onset of a small fear within her.

"And all went well?"

"Yes. Why wouldn't it have?"

"Oh, I don't know." He stepped closer. "You've been lucky up until now. I would have thought it would only be a matter of time before someone discovered what you've been up to."

The small spark of fear that had flickered to life seconds ago burst into a flame. With absolute certainty, she knew where John was headed with his questioning, and every one of her defenses came up. She knew why he was there. It didn't matter that what she did with Brett was none of John's concern. *He* obviously thought it concerned him enough to bring him out of hiding.

And he was angry. His nonchalance didn't fool her for a second.

"Are you waiting for me to make some sort of a confession?" She went right on the offensive. "I have a private life and it is exactly what the term implies, *private.* I don't appreciate your spying on me."

"Oh, not me personally." His voice emerged as a murmured threat. "That's what I have my men for."

"To take care of all the sordid little tasks that you can't be bothered with."

"Exactly."

Hearing that, she exhaled sharply. "John . . . " She shook her head, squeezed her eyes shut for a brief instant, and hoped for the best. She'd been anticipating this moment ever since she'd made her decision to sever their alliance. This wasn't the way in which she would have done it, though. She would have preferred that Brett not be an issue. "It's time for this to end. There's no sense in our continuing if we don't trust each other."

"Interesting," was all John said.

"No, inevitable. The arrangement we have has worked, but things have changed."

"What about the money? How are you going to carry on with your 'buying trips' without the money I give you?"

"I earned that money. But this was my last trip to Savannah, or anywhere else for that matter. I can't go on taking the risks I've been taking. It's become too dangerous. The authorities are looking for you."

"They've always been looking for me."

"Not the way they are now. If they find you . . ." *If Brett finds you* ". . . they'll make the connection to me, and I can't, I won't do that to Hope."

She finished on an adamant note, waiting for his flare of rage she knew was never far from erupting. In silence, she watched him stride a short distance into the courtyard, his posture that of a man deep in thought.

Surprisingly, he turned with a hearty chuckle, planting his hands on his waist. "You should have been a man, Laurel love. All that bravado of yours is wasted on a woman."

Without warning, a man emerged from the alleyway behind her, another from the darkest recesses of the doorway in the next building. She turned in time to see a third and a fourth materialize out of the shadows.

"John?" His name was still on her lips when she heard Hope's muted cry. She started for the door only to find John blocking her way. "What have you done?" Her efforts to evade him proved worthless. Desperately, she sucked air into her lungs and searched the shop for some sign of her sister.

"Hope!" she called out.

Instantly, she was seized from behind, a calloused hand shoving her cries down her throat. Over those brutal fingers she stared wildly at the scene that developed like an eerie aberration. Two men crowded into the shop's open doorway. Between them, they held a struggling, frantic Hope, her face ashen, her beautiful eyes terrified.

"Laurel!"

At her sister's cry, Laurel bit into the hand over her mouth and tried to lunge away. All she got for her efforts was a tightening of the arms that held her, and the sound of livid cursing filling her ears. The guttural voice joined Hope's entreaties for help.

"Shut her up," John ordered, nodding to Hope. That was all the attention he spared her. Every trace of humor wiped from his face, he stood before Laurel, his mouth curled into a cruel line.

"You had it right, Laurel. We don't trust each other. It's time for our partnership to end, but not before you pay for betraying me."

She shook her head as best she could, trying to make him understand that she hadn't betrayed him. But he didn't listen. He strode away, leaving her and Hope to be bound and gagged and carried off into the night.

# Eighteen

It was the stench of the room that Laurel noticed more than anything else. Like some putrid essence of vomit and the cloying smell of decaying fish, the odor made her want to gag. Oddly enough, it was the overwhelming fear for Hope and herself that kept her stomach in place.

With her arm wrapped securely about Hope's shoulder, she took in the sight of their jail. The room in which they had been locked could be called nothing else. The few pieces of furniture were as crude as the splintered flooring. The low pallet on which they sat offered no comfort. A single window had been boarded up and the door locked and barred.

On the other side of the door was another room in a miserable little hovel somewhere on the northwest side of town. Laurel had rarely ventured into this part of the city so near the Ashley River, so she wasn't completely certain where they were. Then again, night . . . and the anticipation of death . . . had a way of distorting one's perceptions.

"What do you think they're going to do?" Hope asked, her voice thinned by fright, her lovely features drawn by shock.

"I don't know," Laurel lied, hating herself for bringing Hope to this end. Still, she didn't waste time in berating herself, in recounting her many faults. Nothing would be gained by decrying her idealism and her arrogance all in the name of good intention. Hope's life was what mattered now. To think on anything else was meaningless.

Scanning the room again, she sought a possible weapon. The only thing that even came close was the rusted lantern set on a table beneath the window. The light it provided was a blessing. The flame and oil, however, could be hell on earth if Laurel could manage to use both to their advantage. She wouldn't hesitate to set the place afire if it meant Hope's escape.

"I'm sorry, Hope," she murmured.

Through her alarm, Hope frowned. "Why?"

Laurel had to scoff in disbelief. "For putting you in this position." She took Hope's hands between her own, her gaze steady and intense. "I want you to promise me that if the chance arrives, you'll run as fast as you can."

"Oh, Laurel, you're scaring me."

"I don't mean to, but we have to be prepared for any chance that comes our way. I may not be right beside you, so you'll have to be brave and get away. No stopping or looking back."

"But what about you? Where will you be? Where will I find you later?"

There would be no later for Laurel. She knew that with utter certainty. John had brought her here to kill her. And Hope, too, although why he hadn't done so already was a mystery.

"Don't worry about finding me. Just get yourself to Major McKenzie." She hugged Hope close, and prayed for her safety. All the while, her mind conjured up an image of dousing herself with the lamp's oil, setting her skirts on fire, and running from one man to the next. As distractions went, it would be effective. Instinct would impel the men to flee, chaos would break out. Hope would stand a good chance of slipping away unnoticed.

Of course, the timing would have to be right. And the door would have to be open.

Into that thought came the sound of the door being unlocked. Her heart leapt into her throat even as she slipped her arm about her sister's shoulders again.

John entered, dark eyes virulent, mouth reduced to a nasty slash. "Ladies." He tipped his head to one side, the gesture both mocking and ruthless.

Laurel swallowed hard, her blood still frozen in her limbs despite the frantic beating of her heart. Part of her dearly wanted to plead for mercy, or at the very least, ask what he intended. Another part of her kept her silent, watchful, alert.

"What, nothing to say?" John goaded, sauntering forward with brows raised. He stopped directly before them, his boots brushing the hem of Laurel's dress. "I would have thought you'd have an opinion or two, Laurel love."

How she hated that name. Her gaze said as much.

John laughed. "You always could say more with your eyes than most could with an entire vocabulary." Turning his attention to Hope, a smile came to his face. "She's quite a woman, wouldn't you say so, Hope? Unfortunately, she's gotten the two of you into a wee bit of trouble."

"She hasn't done anything wrong," Hope offered, her tearful eyes beseeching.

"But she has, Hope, she has."

"How?" Laurel asked, infuriated that he would bait her sister.

John feigned an obvious regret. "By telling Major McKenzie all about me."

"I didn't tell him anything."

"You slept with him, Laurel love. You can't expect me to believe you didn't let any secrets slip in a, shall we say, passionate moment."

"That's exactly what I'm telling you. I didn't invite him to join me in Savannah. He showed up there, ready to arrest me."

"And instead, you ended up in his bed. You bought your way out of trouble with your body and the use of my name."

"If I had betrayed you, your name would be posted from one end of the city to the other."

"I think not. McKenzie is too keen for such obvious tricks. He's planning a trap or two, I'd wager. And you'll get off without even a scolding."

"He's not stupid, John, and neither am I. If I had told him about you, I would have implicated myself as well. And he's not about to let me off at all. He's already proven that. He and his men raided the shop before I even left for Georgia. He was expecting to find your supplies and take me to prison."

"It's true," Hope confirmed. "His soldiers surrounded the shop."

John merely shrugged. "That very well may be, but the damage is done. You've consorted with the enemy."

"John, I swear, I didn't tell Major McKenzie who you are. I never even admitted to knowing you or helping you."

From one second to the next, John's counterfeit affability vanished. "Spare me." Reaching down, he yanked Hope to her feet.

Laurel followed her up, her hands reaching out in instinctive protection. "Let her go," she insisted over Hope's choked cry.

With careless brutality, John planted a hand square in her chest and shoved her into a tumbling sprawl. At the same time, he hauled Hope to the far side of the room.

"No!" Laurel scrambled to her feet, ready to grab the lantern. "Leave her alone."

Hope struggled like a trapped bird, her hands fluttering uselessly. "Laurel!"

"Shut up, the both of you," John snarled.

"What are you going to do?" Laurel demanded to know, her breath heaving in and out of her chest.

"Set my own trap. You're my bait." He gave Hope a shake. "And here's my messenger."

Everything inside Laurel stopped, only to speed right up with dizzying intensity. "Trap who?" But she knew. God above, she knew. "No."

"Rather clever of me, don't you think? Once McKenzie knows I've got you, he'll come. Honorable bastard that he is, he would never leave a woman in my hands, especially a woman he's bedded."

She shook her head in a slightly disjointed manner. "He doesn't know, John. I didn't tell him!"

"I can't take that chance."

He gave Hope another shake and for one horrifying second, Laurel thought he was going to drag Hope from the room right then. Instead, he shoved her away and headed for the door. Once again, he locked it behind him.

As if a strange lethargy gripped her, Laurel moved slowly to gather Hope in her arms. Against the length of her, she could feel Hope's violent trembling. For the first time that night, tears came to Laurel's eyes.

"I'm so sorry." She couldn't bring herself to ask Hope to forgive her. "I'm so sorry."

Face pressed to Laurel's shoulder, Hope tired to regain

her composure. "He's going to kill Major McKenzie, isn't he?"

"He'll try."

"And you."

Laurel rolled her lips inward to keep from blurting out the truth. Her fate was sealed. The same could not be said for Brett or Hope. John had inadvertently provided them with a chance, and suddenly, with brilliant clarity, Laurel knew what had to be done. "You can save Brett and yourself."

Hope's head came up, her eyes rounding enormously. "How?"

"Go to Brett. He'll keep you safe. Tell him everything that's happened, about John, about the smuggling, and about my involvement. Tell him what John plans, but you mustn't tell him anything else."

"But I have to." Hope's trembling increased. "He'll need to know where you are."

"Say you don't know. Tell him you were miles from home and you were wandering around lost, that you found your way back only by accident."

"What about you?"

Laurel ignored the question. "Promise me you'll do this."

"I can't. I can't leave you here."

"You have to, Hope. It's your only chance." *And none of this would be happening if it weren't for me.*

"No, John will kill you."

He was going to do that anyway. "We don't know that, but this way, you'll be safe, Brett will be safe. He'll be warned. He can come after John in his own way, not because he's been blackmailed or tricked into doing so."

"No." Hope shut her eyes as though to retreat from reality.

"Listen to me, Hope." She gripped her sister's arms fiercely, ruthless in her desperation to protect those she loved best. "If you won't think about yourself, then think about Brett. He's devoted to his duty, to a code of honor that is the very makeup of his life. I won't have him compromising that sense of honor or his principles for me."

"He won't do that. He'll come to arrest John."

"No, he'll come because he won't have any other choice. You heard John. He's setting a trap. How much of a chance do you think Brett will have?"

She gentled her touch and her voice, her eyes filling with a poignant heartache. "Let him catch John in his own way. Give Brett all the help you can, but don't put him in the position of sacrificing everything he holds dear. That would be worse than anything John could do to him."

The door to the room swung open unexpectedly. Before Laurel's eyes, one of John's men grabbed hold of Hope and pulled her away.

"Laurel!"

"Promise me, Hope!" she cried, reaching out and finding nothing.

"Oh, God . . . Laurel."

*"Please, Hope, promise me!"*

The door was shut and locked.

Ever so slowly, Laurel sank to her knees, tears trailing over her cheeks. Silently, she wept and prayed, for Hope and for Brett.

She never had a chance to tell him she loved him.

* * *

Brett rolled over in bed and cursed the knocking that came at his door. Irritably, he swore that Ransom had better have a damn good reason for waking him.

"What . . . Come in."

Corporal Ransom stood as a silhouette in the doorway. "Excuse me, Major, but there's trouble."

Coming to his elbow, Brett was instantly alert. "What kind of trouble?"

"Miss Seymore is below, sir, demanding to see you."

Just hearing the name was like a jab to Brett's stomach. He came to his feet in a fluid play of muscle, all his senses trained on the thought of Laurel waiting for him. "Put her in my office, Corporal."

"Yes, sir, but I think you should know, it's not the younger one." His face took on an expression of smitten amazement. "It's the other one, the beautiful one, sir, Miss Hope."

"Hope Seymore?"

"Yes, sir. She's going on about her sister and Jack Diego."

All the fury and frustration rifling through Brett coalesced into a jolting energy, and with the upsurge of that energy came a clear and alarming foresight. Dressing with all haste, he practically threw his uniform on. All the while, common sense and instinct warned him that Hope's presence boded more than trouble, a very real danger.

He muttered every curse he could think of, damning Diego, damning Laurel, and finally himself. To even imagine Laurel in danger at Diego's hands was enough to chill his blood.

Still shrugging into his coatee, he stalked into his office to find Hope sitting in front of his desk, her face absolutely white. At his entrance, she pulled her glazed eyes from the nearby hovering Ransom. Brett saw all and more of her wild panic.

"Hope?"

"Major, oh, Major, you have to help," she exclaimed weakly, jumping to her feet. "He's going to kill her . . . he came to the shop and now she's locked up . . . she made me promise, but . . . he's going to kill her, I know he is!"

Brett took hold of her flailing hands and bent low to peer into her eyes. "Slow down, Hope. Calm yourself."

"I can't." But she did. Closing her eyes, she seemed to gather herself, at least to the point that she was no longer breathing quite so raggedly.

To Ransom, Brett ordered, "Corporal, see if you can find Miss Seymore a cup of tea."

"Yes, sir," Ransom replied. He made his way to the door by rote alone, his eyes never once leaving Hope's beautiful if distraught face.

"Now, Hope, sit down and tell me what's happened."

Again, she followed his orders, as though the commands gave focus to her world. Nonetheless, he kept a wary eye on her, waiting for her to fall apart once more without warning.

"What's this all about, Hope? Who's going to kill Laurel?"

"John." In the remnants of her panic, she said the name as if everyone on earth should know who that was.

"John who?"

"John St. James, but he isn't really. He's really Jack Diego and he's got Laurel locked up while I'm supposed to come back here for you—"

She was rambling again. "Hope, start at the beginning," he coaxed with a gentleness that belied the rage he felt.

For frustratingly long seconds, she could only look at

him and blink repeatedly. At length, she finally dragged in a shaky breath, glanced about a bit bewilderedly, and began.

"We were working late at the shop when these men broke in."

"What men?"

"Friends of John's, I suppose. I don't know their names, but they were with him."

"Did they hurt you or Laurel?"

"No, but they scared me. I was in the front room and Laurel was in the back. They broke open the front door, grabbed me, and took me out back. That's where I found Laurel. A man was holding her so she couldn't scream or move."

All too clearly, Brett pictured the scene, and it was all he could do to stand there and listen.

"John was going on about Laurel betraying him, and Laurel was doing her best to escape, but nothing worked. We were tied up and gagged and taken to a filthy, foul shack and locked in a room."

"Is Laurel still there?"

"Yes."

"Where?"

The ease and rush of her words ceased as her expression became guarded, doubtful.

"Hope, can you tell me where this shack is?"

Twisting her fingers together, she opened her mouth, clamped it shut, opened it again, and finally blurted out, "She doesn't want me to tell you! John is setting a trap for you. He means to kill you and then Laurel."

"Why?"

At that, her face filled with the ruby stain of embarrassment. Her gaze slid away. "He knows that you and Laurel,

I mean, that the two of you . . . were in Savannah. Together. Alone. He thinks she told you all about him, but she swears she didn't."

"She's telling the truth. She never said a word."

"I didn't think so. Laurel is very circumspect that way. I didn't even know about John or the smuggling until the day you came to arrest her. She'd kept her activities from me because she was afraid I'd get hurt. That's the way Laurel is. She wouldn't betray anyone, not even John, but he won't believe her. That's why he sent me here to you."

"How did you get here?"

"One of his men brought me on the back of his horse. He's waiting for you at the end of the block, but . . ." She hesitated again, her indecision painfully obvious. "But Laurel doesn't want me to tell you this part."

"Tell me what?"

"About John's plan to trick you. I'm supposed to tell you that if you want to see Laurel alive again, you'll go with the man who brought me here. You're not supposed to tell anyone and you're supposed to come alone. If not, John will set the whole city on fire, but it's a trap, Major McKenzie. John plans to kill you because you know who he really is."

He shoved a hand back through his hair. "Why the devil didn't she want you to tell me any of this?"

Hope's face softened to reveal every measure of its considerable beauty. "Because she loves you."

The words stunned him, halting his mind and his senses at a time when he needed both to be at their prime. And yet, all he could do was silently indulge in the most wondrous sensation of well-being. Laurel loved him.

"She does, Major. She didn't say as much, but I know Laurel. I know how she is with those she loves. She puts their welfare above her own even if it means a hardship for herself. She gives with all her heart and soul, never asking anything for herself."

It was something to which Brett could attest. Laurel had given herself to him for a single night of passion, but it had been so much more than the mere exchange of pleasure. That would have never been enough for Laurel. Her ethics were too intact, her principles too fine for her to engage in something as insensate as meaningless desire.

She had gifted him with her body, true, but the giving had been selfless, complete, and unconditional. And the more she had given him, the more he had taken while he'd never once considered why she would do so.

The answer was there for him to see now. She loved him, and in true Laurel fashion, she would sacrifice herself for that love.

"I don't care what she told you to do, Hope, I have to know where she is."

A sad smile graced Hope's lips. "I'm glad. You have to save her." Tears welled and glistened in her deep brown eyes. "Her only concern was for you and me. She wanted me safely away, where you could protect me. But more than that, she didn't want you sacrificing your sense of duty or your honor for her. She's willing to die to ensure that, Major. That's how much she loves you."

# Nineteen

Dread ate at Laurel like a treacherous plague. Sitting on the pallet with her arms wrapped about her drawn-up knees, she shook with an inner chill and prayed with all her being that Hope was safe . . . and that she had done as Laurel had asked. The worst fear of Laurel's life was that Brett would risk his life and come for her.

For years, she had wanted Hope to be more self-assured, to be able to think more independently. Ironically, now that she was finally capable of both, Laurel wished for the opposite. If there was ever a time for Hope to blindly do as she was told, it was now. For her own sake as well as Brett's

The image of his face filled her mind, and she was swamped by love and grief. In rapid succession, she thought of every moment they had had together, and a host of impressions brought a trembling smile to her lips. The arrogant lift of his brows. The insolent nod of his head. The heated rage in his eyes when he argued with her. Those very same eyes darkening with desire when he joined his body with hers.

The memories came more quickly, an unrestrained melange that had her, for several blessedly dear seconds, aware of nothing except the sound of his voice, the masterful air of his disposition, the feel of his hands slipping over her curves. Bliss saturated her being. When she lifted her head and opened her eyes, she half-expected to be in Brett's arms.

Instead, she was hit with an appalling reality that stripped her down to a miserable, pathetic fright. She didn't want to die. For her alliance with John, she deserved to be punished, but not with death. Surely some of the good she had done in her life should count for something. Surely, Brett and Hope should not be made to suffer because of her mistakes.

She surged to her feet, suddenly impatient with John's game. Why didn't he just kill her now and be done with it instead of making her wait? Either way she was going to die. But then, John was innately cruel, and she didn't doubt for a second that he was enjoying her fear.

If she could control the fear, she would. There was no help for it, though. Anxiety and dread had long ago sapped the heat from her body. Every little noise that came to her scraped her senses raw. The urge to imagine all manner of things was so strong, it took a conscious effort on her part not to give in to panic.

She took comfort in her sister's safety. Once John was finished here, he wouldn't hesitate to go after Hope, but Brett wouldn't allow that to happen. He would protect Hope, and Tess, until John was caught.

Reminding herself of this was a balm to her soul. She clung to that small reassurance until the door was unlocked and John filled the crooked portal. Then her fears trembled anew, threatening to overwhelm her. It was difficult to retain any composure, especially under John's lengthy perusal and a chorus of raucous voices sounding from the other room.

"You're awfully quite this evening, Laurel love," he teased.

"I have nothing more to say to you," she averred with a touch of haughtiness to belie the pounding of her heart.

"Did ya hear that, Jack?" someone called out. "She ain't got nothing to say to ya."

Harsh laughter resounded, beating mercilessly against Laurel's nerves. Pride and plain old-fashioned stubbornness strengthened her resolve. Shoulders back, hands resting at her sides in a show of calm, she tried to give John—all of them—every impression that she was far from afraid. At the same time, her mind instinctively sought a means of escape.

John leaned against the door frame and laughed. "You never were one for pleading and crying, but I would have thought that in this case you'd have at least tried."

"You're going to do whatever you please, regardless of what I say."

"It's about time you realized that."

"I realized that from the start."

"True, but back then you and I were in agreement on most things."

"Only on one thing, John. We were never in accord on more than that." Despite her best efforts, her hands began to shake and she tucked them behind her.

"Nervous?" he speculated, one side of his face creasing with a nasty smile at her gesture.

"I'm angry."

In a gregarious show of mock injury, he shoved away from the door and laid a hand over his heart. "You wound me, Laurel love."

His enjoyment of the situation was more than Laurel

could bear. "Why don't you just kill me and get it over with?"

"Why?" he jeered. "Why don't I kill you right out?" Shaking his head, he advanced on her. "And miss what I have planned for you? I think not."

To the hoots and hollers of the men listening, Laurel stepped back, feeling her skin crawl. Into this nightmare that had become her immediate existence came the threat of rape. She could see it in his eyes, sense it with a purely feminine instinct.

Her move brought her up against a spindly wooden chair, nearly tumbling her backwards. Quickly, she skirted to the other side of the piece, knowing it provided no real protection at all. Still, the impulse to survive was too strong to be rejected. She gripped the chair with both hands and shoved it out before her like a feeble barrier. He might very well rape her, but she would be damned if she would peacefully acquiesce.

Eyes filled with scorching rage and a soul-blanching fear, she stared at John, careful to keep the chair between them, trying not to think that she was woefully over-matched in this contest.

Before she could fall victim to that last thought, she darted to one side and swung the chair at the same time. The impact reverberated clear up to her elbows, but she had the great satisfaction of hearing his grunt of pain as the chair caught him on the shoulder and sent him staggering for an instant.

That was all she wanted, more, more than she had hoped for. She dashed away, and managed to gain the door before he was on her, grabbing her from behind and spinning her about.

"No!" she cried out, struggling wildly. Twisting about,

she beat furiously at his head, his chest, trying to inflict as much damage as she could.

Behind her the men cheered, calling out obscene suggestions. In front of her, John's face smiled down at her. She wanted to block it all out: the sight of animal lust, the sounds of promised violence, the smell of sweat and fear. Incensed and crazed, she raked her nails down his face.

John bellowed in agony, yanking his head to one side. Furious, he thrust her away and sent her sprawling into the other room.

She landed on her right hip and shoulder, momentarily stunned. Pain shot up her arm, and she began to curl into herself, wounded and defeated. Instantly, she checked the impulse, acting on innate reflexes to endure, to strike back.

Struggling to breathe, she ignored the discomfort in her shoulder, and righted herself, for the first time seeing the men who surrounded her. Cold, piercing panic seized her. She was no match for John. Against five more men, she was as good as dead.

She stilled entirely. Was this how he planned to kill her, to turn her over to these brutes who glowered at her with savage lust distorting their faces?

Without warning, she was grabbed from behind, yanked to her feet, and held immobile against a beefy expanse of chest. The strain to her shoulder brought a cry to her lips and forced her eyes shut in pain. When she looked up again, it was to find John looming before her, blood trickling down his cheek, a feral gleam deadening his eyes.

Ever so slowly, he lifted a hand to trail his fingers up her neck to her chin. "You little bitch," he whispered. Inch by inch, he lowered his fingers until he wrapped his hand around her throat, his other hand finding the softness of her breast. And then he squeezed.

Laurel reared back against the body behind her, fighting the hands imprisoning her arms, struggling against the ever increasing pressure at her throat and the agony in her chest. The air necessary to scream was choked away, reducing her to strangled sobs. Helplessly, she gave way to tears of pain and fright as she clutched at John's hands. With all her might she tried to pry his fingers loose, but her efforts were useless.

She prayed for instant death: a pistol shot to the head. She couldn't die this way, her flesh cruelly tortured, her life choked away by infinitesimal degrees. Not even realizing what she did, she lunged forward and sank her teeth into John's arm.

"Aargh!" he cried out. "Get her off me," he screamed.

The words were a jumble to Laurel. She was beyond real comprehension. Some primal part of her brain was in control and all she knew was that John's hands had dropped away from her, and that it was imperative that she retain her bite.

She breathed in desperate gulps of air, the taste of blood making her want to gag. Grunts and raised voices bounced off the walls, while coarse and punishing hands forced her to their will. In no short amount of time, John was standing free and she was thrust into the arms of one of his men.

"Leave her to me, Jack-O," the burly man laughed, shoving his groin into her belly. "I'll take the spit out of her."

Someone chortled, "You're nothin' but wind in the sails," and his comrades erupted into gales of laughter.

Amidst the laughter, Laurel drew in ragged, aching breaths. Despite her flagging strength, she was determined not to give in. She would fight to the very end, but her arms and legs didn't seem to want to work. Weak sobs tore from her throat, weaker tears streamed down her face.

"You're welcome to her," John declared. "Do whatever you want with the bitch."

It was a declaration straight from hell, acting on the last reserves of Laurel's will. She put her head back and screamed out in fury and frustration and horror, the scream dying when she was yanked against another, and still another.

Hands tore at her clothes and mauled her flesh. Again came the urge to curl into a protective ball.

"Get that friggin' dress off her," a burly brute ordered.

The only thought Laurel had was *over my dead body.*

How she managed to think, from where she got the strength, she had no idea. But suddenly, her mind seemed to separate itself from her body and view the room and her predicament like some curious bystander. She was so close to the door she had only to reach out and place her hand on the rusted latch.

In the next instant, she jerked her knee up and slammed it straight into the groin of the man holding her. He clutched himself in agony and doubled over, sparing her seconds of precious freedom, seconds during which all around her stared rather stupidly at their mate writhing about on the floor, seconds enough for her to spin for the door and fling it wide.

Four steps into the graveled clearing and she was caught from behind. Dismally, she realized that she had accomplished nothing. She had simply moved the arena from inside to out.

Her defeat was crushing. The futility of continuing was obvious and bitter. Helplessly, she went limp, and with all her heart, prayed to faint, to fall into a stupor, for death to take her now.

As ordered, Brett dismounted and tied his horse to a low, scrubby bush. Automatically, his hand came to rest on the hilt of his sword, but it wasn't there at his hip. Like his pistol, it had been left at the post.

"This way," his escort muttered, coming down off his own horse. He jutted his bony chin in the general direction of the Ashley River.

Again, Brett did as he was told, and not because the bastard had him at gunpoint. There was only one way to find Laurel and that was to do what this man said.

He stepped along a narrow path, shrouded on both sides by shoulder-height marsh grasses and thickets of underbrush. The light of a half moon was bright enough to illuminate the way and to give him an unobstructed view of where he was in relation to the river, and to landmarks.

The path curved to the right, away from the river and into a thicket of trees. Here the light was nearly snuffed out.

"Hurry it up," he was told, the dictate punctuated with a jab of a pistol barrel into the center of his back.

Brett swallowed the grunt of discomfort, and fed off of the icy rage that crackled though his body. He could disarm the slimy little bastard and have him unconscious in less than ten seconds. He was half-tempted to do so. Common sense and Hope's information told him that Laurel had to be nearby. He should be able to find where she was being held, but he couldn't be absolutely certain of that. So he held on to his patience by a tenuous thread, cautioning himself for Laurel's sake.

Directing his attention back to the path, he observed all around him, and walked on until the trees gave way and marsh claimed the land once more. In a slight clearing in the distance stood a crude dwelling, its dilapidated lines and angles accented by the moon's light.

Voices raised in crude laughter echoed through the night air, the sound touching off every one of Brett's defenses. Knowing that Laurel was surrounded by that coarse, boisterous hilarity escalated his rage another degree. He would kill anyone who dared to harm her.

On that thought came Laurel's scream, and everything inside him exploded into a scorching fury. He swung around and slammed his fist into the man's face, at the same time wrenching the pistol out of his hand. Before the unconscious weasel even hit the ground, Brett was running for the shack, for Laurel, careful to keep to the concealing curtain of stunted trees and underbrush.

Time seemed to slow, his mind raced ahead. And then, the door to the shack was flung wide and Laurel stumbled out, choking on whimpered sobs, her dress hanging in tatters from her shoulders. Behind her, men followed, spewing out their vicious threats and promises.

Brett saw it all in a kind of bizarre haze . . . Laurel's attempt to flee, a man grabbing hold of her, her body going limp. Fear such as he had never experienced in his life struck at his heart and it was all he could do not to race headlong into the clearing and snatch her into his arms.

A decade of military training came to his rescue, tempering his wild needs with cold, hard reasoning. Steeling himself to caution, he circled to the far side of the cabin, crouched low, every sense alert.

To his left, he spied the shadowed figure of a look-out, and then a second closer to the rear of the building. Both were obviously supposed to be standing guard, both were preoccupied trying to catch glimpses of Laurel. In different circumstances, Brett would have laughed at the ease of dispatching them both.

He snuck up on the first, felling him with a single blow to the back of his head with the pistol. The second guard went the way of the first. With little fuss, Brett raced to the shack and made his way around to the front just as Laurel gave a high, piercing shriek.

The sound was beyond Brett's bearing. He came out from behind the shed, taking in the scene and its participants. In a split second, his mind examined all, analyzed, reacted, and urged him on toward the one man he knew had to be Diego.

In all of that, he studiously avoided looking at Laurel's prone figure, her body stripped down to a single petticoat. Some part of his mind wouldn't let him think about that. Some part of his mind knew that if he actually considered the fact that she was trying to shield her nakedness from all around her he would go crazy.

His insides filled with a frigid iciness, he charged the circle of men. Pistol primed, he raised it to Diego's head, caught the bastard around the neck with his arm, and hauled back.

"Let her go," he ordered.

His voice cracked into the revelry, penetrating the lecherous blood lust that had them oblivious to all else. Men scrambled to their feet, cursing and shouting, eyes bulging in shock and hatred. Diego struggled for a count of five, until he obviously realized that there was a gun jammed against the base of his skull.

"Tell them to back off," Brett snarled.

Diego issued a string of curses. "You son of a bitch."

Brett increased the pressure of his arm, choking Diego in the process. "I'll kill you right here if I have to, Diego. Nothing would give me greater pleasure." He cocked the pistol's hammer.

Diego went rigidly still. Except for his frantic gasping, he didn't even move his head. "Do as he says!"

Left with little choice, the men backed away. Brett tipped his head toward the shack. "All of you, get in the there."

Mumbling and muttering threats of retribution, the group tramped into the shack. Brett spared them only enough notice to make certain they were out of his way before he shoved Diego into their wake.

The pirate lurched forward, going down on one knee. Gulping for air, he clawed at his throat, desperate to draw in an unfettered breath.

"Get up," Brett sneered, half-wishing Diego wouldn't. Brett's need to exact revenge was so fierce, he was looking for any excuse to beat Diego into a bloody pulp.

Fortunately, Diego staggered to an upright stance. Still, Brett didn't, couldn't look at Laurel. He could hear her behind him, her soft cries piteous and anguished, tearing at his heart.

"You'll pay for this, Diego." He raised the pistol an inch higher. "Beyond your crimes of smuggling, I'll see you pay for this."

Diego shifted his chin to one side, his eyes narrowing. "And how are you going to do that without landing her in jail beside me?" He gave a jeering laugh. "You arrest me and she's as good as dead. I'll tell everyone between here and kingdom come that Laurel was part of the whole operation."

"She was your victim."

A deadly light came into Diego's eyes. In a dangerously silky voice he taunted, "Perhaps, but you're forgetting my threat to burn down the city. I've got men posted, they've got their orders. When they hear I've been taken, they'll torch every building they can."

Brett had forgotten nothing. "When they hear you've been taken, that there's no escape for you, they'll make their own escape. They won't risk their necks for a lost cause, and that's what you've become, Diego—a lost cause." He flicked a glance to the shed. "Now, get in there with the rest of your scum."

"I don't think so."

Without hesitation, Brett aimed his pistol straight at Diego's forehead.

"You won't do it, McKenzie."

Out from the side of the shed stepped Corporal Ransom, fully armed. "If he doesn't, I will."

More soldiers joined him, muskets poised and aimed. They took up a defensive position behind Brett.

"It's about time you got here," Brett told Ransom, his gaze never once leaving Diego.

"Sorry sir, but you said to keep a good distance back. Almost lost track of you for a while there."

"You did fine, Corporal."

"Thank you, sir."

"Put him in there with the rest of his men, post a guard. Then tie them up and get them out of here."

"Yes, sir."

It was the last thought Brett gave the matter. Not bothering to see if his orders were being carried out, he rushed to Laurel.

She lay on her side, knees drawn up to her chest, one

arm curled over her torso, the other wrapped about her head. Tremors shook her frame with her silent weeping.

Going to his knees, Brett gathered her into his arms, clenching his eyes shut against the rage that strained his sanity.

"Hush, love, hush," he murmured, trying to hold her as close as he could, wanting her to feel safe and comforted. "I won't let them harm you. It's all over."

# Twenty

Laurel tried not to think. Propped up against a brace of pillows in her bed, she forced herself to contemplate the angle of the afternoon sun shining through her windows or the way the lace of her nightgown's sleeve fell over her hand. With absolute conviction, she ignored the aches that riddled her body. They were too ready a reminder of her ordeal last night.

It was simpler to let her mind go numb. Simpler and safer. Dignity, courage, and serenity had been stripped from her. In that, a horrid danger lay, ready to turn her into a cowering, weeping child.

In truth, she felt very much like a child just then, helpless, directionless, dependent. Tess and Hope had been fussing over her ever since Brett had carried her home.

The image of his face filled her mind. Quite against her will, memories of last night crowded forward. She couldn't think of Brett without thinking of what he had rescued her from.

Tears bathed her eyes, horror clenched her stomach. Not for the first time, she was overcome by the insatiable need to bathe, to wash herself clean. She felt violated and dirty. A little frantically, she sent her gaze to the tub that had been brought up hours ago.

Her hair was scrubbed, her skin washed, her bruises

tended. Logically, she understood and accepted that she was as clean as anyone could be. However, logic was a paltry thing compared to the abuse her emotions and body had endured. Her only solace was in the fact that she had escaped rape by a hair's breadth. Until her dying day, she would be grateful to Brett for sparing her that end.

"Are you awake?" Hope asked as she peeked her head into the room.

Laurel nodded, relieved and gladdened by her sister's appearance. "I slept for a little bit."

"How are you feeling?" Perching herself beside Laurel on the bed, she searched for signs of the awful distress and misery that had marked her sister's features last night. "You look better," she claimed, ignoring the hint of tears in the green eyes.

"I'm feeling better."

"Does your head still ache?"

"Not nearly as much as it did."

Hope gave a sigh. "I wish you had let me send for Doctor Mathews."

"No." Laurel's response was curt and instantaneous. The fewer people who knew what had happened the better. It would be difficult enough to regain her sense of being without a near stranger being privy to the facts. "I'm just sore and bruised. I'll be fine in a few days."

That, of course, was just as much speculation as it was wishful thinking. Her body would heal, and no doubt in time, so would her mind. But her future was a dismal prospect. With the capture of Jack Diego, her own fate was bleak.

It was no more than she deserved. She could not dispute her guilt, and for that, she would accept her punishment.

But the thought of never seeing Brett again precluded her ever being well or whole or "fine" again.

Awkward and unsettled, she whispered, "I'm sorry, I didn't mean to snap at you."

"It doesn't matter."

"Yes, it does. You were so utterly blameless in all that had happened. You shouldn't have to abide my petulance."

Tipping her head to one side, Hope's face softened with an abiding love. "You've suffered greatly, Laurel. It's only natural for you to be easily irritated."

"I've suffered by my own doing. No one else is to blame, and I will not have you or Tess or even Major McKenzie hurt because of me."

"None of us has suffered, least of all the major."

Laurel's unease intensified. "Have you . . . have you heard anything from him?" she asked, studying the scrapes on the back of her hands.

"No."

"I-it's rather amazing the way he rescued me."

"He was horribly upset when he brought you home."

"Was he?" She couldn't remember. After he had pulled her into his arms and wrapped her in his jacket, she had given herself up to a bewildered daze.

"I've never seen him look as he did when he carried you up the stairs. I don't think I've ever seen *any* man look the way he did."

"How was that?"

Hope considered how best to describe it. "Like he was going to break apart. Like there was a terrible energy hurting him inside. I wasn't sure we'd ever persuade him to turn you loose. Tess finally had to raise her voice and actually move him aside so we could tend to you."

A trace of a smile played at Laurel's lips. "He's a man

accustomed to being in charge. I presume he didn't take well to Tess ordering him about."

"He was furious, especially when I insisted that . . . that he, uh, he leave the room so we could . . . uh, remove your clothes. But it was more than being ordered about that enraged him. It was as if he couldn't stand to be separated from you."

Joy suffused Laurel, only to die entirely. She wanted to believe that Hope was right, but she couldn't imagine Brett feeling so inclined about her. She was, after all, a criminal. Her half-truths of the past had been exposed for the lies they were.

"What's wrong?" Hope asked. "Are you angry I told him where you were?"

"No. Everything turned out as it should. John and most of his men are being held, you're safe, Brett is uninjured. The city is still standing."

"I couldn't leave you there to die, Laurel. Neither could the major, especially after I told him . . ." Hope's words trailed off to an uncertain murmur.

"Especially after you told him what?"

Hope fidgeted with the ribbons at her waist, studiously avoiding looking at her sister.

"Hope, what did you tell him?"

On a heaved sigh, Hope scrubbed at her forehead. "The truth."

"About what?"

"About you. And . . . and your feelings."

Even as Laurel blinked in confusion, a horrible suspicion took root. "My feelings about what?"

Chin lowered, Hope flicked a glance upward. "About him."

Laurel's eyes snapped wide. *"What?"*

"I'm sorry, Laurel," Hope got out in a rush. "I didn't mean to say anything untoward, but I had already told him that you wanted me to keep your whereabouts a secret and he asked why the devil you would want to do that. I told him it was because you love him."

A new mortification joined all the other humiliations Laurel was feeling. "Hope, how could have said anything like that? More importantly, *why* did you say it?"

"Because it's the truth, and I thought he deserved to hear it."

"I never told you how I felt about him."

"You didn't need to. I could tell."

Laurel buried her face in her hands. "Oh, Hope."

"I don't see what's so terrible. You love him, otherwise you wouldn't have . . ." She waved her hand in a vague gesture. "You know, you wouldn't have . . . have . . ."

Dropping her hands away, Laurel continued, "Have gone to his bed?"

"Yes, that. You went to his bed because you love him."

"You're right, I do love him, but *he doesn't love me."*

Hope's face lined with consternation and dismay. "How do you know? Did he say as much?"

"He didn't have to because it wasn't relevant. Love has no place in his life."

"Perhaps you're mistaken."

"I wish I were. The man has his life planned out and it does not include a woman, marriage, or love."

"Oh, dear."

"Exactly."

"Oh, dear." Hope was looking more and more forlorn. "I have made a mess of things."

Laurel heaved a tired sigh, drained of the brief burst of energy that had fueled her chagrin. Pressing her fingers into her throbbing temple, she breathed, "No, not really. Whether he loves me or not doesn't matter. In the end, I'll be in prison and he'll be about his duties."

All the color drained from Hope's face, leaving her eyes to shine like wounded orbs. "Prison? Y-you're going to prison?"

Laurel hadn't meant to be so blunt. Disgusted yet again with herself, she reached for Hope's hand, careful to keep her voice as gentle as her touch. "I would think so. Now that John has been captured, he'll waste no time in implicating me. Brett won't have any choice but to execute the law."

With every word she heard, Hope shook her head, openly denying reality. "But he can't. You . . . you helped him find Jack Diego. If it weren't for you, the army would still be looking for him."

"If it weren't for me, Jack Diego wouldn't have been operating out of Charleston."

"But you weren't doing anything truly bad. You didn't use the money for yourself."

Hope's defense was interrupted by Tess's knock at the door. "What you going on about, Hope?"

"Laurel says she's going to prison."

Tess scrunched up her face, her disgust with the suggestion apparent. "Good Lord above going to hear from me if He let that happen." She peered quickly up at the ceiling. "But we going to know real soon. The major downstairs." She paused, straightened her features into a solemn mask. "He's asking to speak to you."

Laurel's heart slammed against her ribs. Apprehension gripped her relentlessly. Her initial reaction was to send word down that she wasn't up to seeing anyone, but she wouldn't let herself be the coward. If she was to know her fate, she might as well find out now.

"Very well." She smoothed her hands over the bed coverings. "Send him up."

To Laurel's surprise, Hope jumped to her feet and declared, "Laurel! You don't have to see him if you don't want to."

"I don't have a choice."

"He's only going to upset you."

Dispiritedly, Laurel thought one more upset wasn't going to matter. "Given the circumstances, I'm sure he'll be very considerate."

Frantically, Hope looked to Tess for support. "Can he do this? Can't we stop him? What if he wants to arrest her? She isn't in any condition to go anywhere."

Tess planted her hands on her hips. "She going nowhere."

"Please," Laurel beseeched. "Nothing will be gained by the two of you working yourselves into a stew. In fact, you're making me feel worse. I'd just as soon get this over with." Frowning deeply, she whispered, "Please."

Tess and Hope would have gone on debating and defending forever. That much was obvious. With ill grace, they left, but not before they made her promise to call for one or both of them if need be. Laurel had to smile. She'd bet her very last penny that they would be hovering nearby, at the end of the hall or at the bottom of the stairs, ready to protect her against Brett.

He opened the door without bothering to knock. The panel swung wide and there he stood, resplendent in his uniform, the blue of his coatee and the steel of his sword catching the glints in his eyes.

An overwhelming urge to cry attacked her. She loved

him with all her heart and yet it was difficult to see him. Even though their history was complex, they had shared so much: laughter, anger, philosophies, confidences. And their bodies. For one glorious night, they had given of themselves in a way that transcended their pasts or their futures.

Unnerved, she tugged the bed clothes a bit higher, unable to withstand the intensity of his gaze.

Shutting the door, he advanced to the side of the bed, his face set, his shoulders straight. "How are you?"

She took in a steadying breath before responding, but found she couldn't find the words. What was she supposed to say? I hurt, I'm frightened, please tell me you love me? Finally, she resorted to a nod, her gaze still fastened on the lace on her cuff.

"Do you mind if I sit?" he asked, lowering himself to the bed with his question.

"No, please." Strange as it was, his closeness startled her. Through the sheet and blanket, she could feel the iron hardness of his thigh against her hip.

"You're looking better."

"I feel better."

"Then why won't you look at me?"

Her gaze jerked up to meet his, and everything inside her seemed to twist in on itself. Silently, she admitted she'd been afraid to look at him, afraid she'd see condemnation, frightened that his beautiful face would have the power to make her feel more vulnerable than she'd ever been before.

Tears rose up, that vulnerability encompassed her, and all the terror and the horror came back in a wave that broke her restraint and reduced her to shaking sobs.

Brett swept her up against him, crushing her body

against his, trying to absorb her tremors and give her his strength. Pressing his face into her hair, he ground his eyes shut and breathed in the scent of her.

"Oh, Brett," she cried, clutching him as if her life depended on it. "I was so scared."

"I know, love."

"And stupid."

"That, too."

"They were going to kill us. All of us—"

In his remembered fury, he talked right over her words. "I wouldn't let that happen."

"You shouldn't have risked your life."

"I thought I was going to lose my sanity when I heard your screams."

"I was so frightened—"

"And then those men pawing at you . . ." To his dying day, he would never be able to wipe away the image of her tender body at the mercy of those bastards.

Her sobs became hoarse rasps, torn from the depths of her. "I feel . . . dirty."

"Oh, God, Laurel." Her terror and shame ripped at him, making him once again want to kill Diego, violently. "I'm so sorry."

Her tears went on. He did nothing to stop them. She needed the release, and he needed to hold her, to reassure her and himself that she was safe. She hadn't been, and in that he had failed her.

It was a long time before her weeping dwindled to nothing but tremulous sighs. Only then did he gently ease her into the crook of his arm. Fully aware of Laurel watching him with her heart in her eyes, he unfastened the few buttons down the front of her nightgown. The bodice parted easily and he looked his fill.

Savage emotions attacked his mind and his senses. The perfection of her skin was marred, bruised blue and scraped raw. The sight sickened him. If he could have suffered in her place, he would have taken her pain a thousand times over to have spared her.

Swallowing past the aching pressure in his throat, he lowered his head and pressed a kiss to the slope of her breast.

Laurel savored the kiss. In its simplicity it was as healing as any medicine, wiping away some of the horror. More touched than she could begin to express, she laid her hand along his cheek.

"Forgive me," he choked out, caressing the top of her head with his cheek.

She couldn't find any cause for his words. Emotionally spent, content to remain resting in his arms, she could barely think to question. "Forgive you for what?"

"For not protecting you better."

"You couldn't have known."

"It's my job to know. You were in danger and I didn't do anything to keep you safe."

His self-reproach was confusing. It wasn't warranted, nor was it logical. Leaning away as far as his encompassing arms would allow, she sought to assuage his guilt. "Brett, you can't assume responsibility for my actions."

"I know, but I could have prevented the outcome of your actions."

To have done so would have meant his crossing over the invisible line he had drawn for himself. He would have had to step from the realm of soldier to that of man who loved her. And she knew how he felt about that.

Pushing away with gentle, yet indomitable force, she lay back against the pillows and gathered her bodice closed, her expression guarded. The gaze she lifted to him was direct, even if it was shadowed with pain.

"What will happen now? Are you . . . are you here to arrest me?"

He regarded her attempt at dignity with tender eyes. To the bitter end, she was truly noble and straightforward. "No."

"When?" Her expression creased with flashes of anxiety and irritation before resuming its former control. "I will need to settle things with Hope and Tess. I wouldn't want to simply abandon them. If you . . . could give me a general idea of when I'm to be . . ." Appallingly, her voice dried up.

The tenderness in Brett's eyes spread to encompass the rest of his face.

"Why are you smiling?" she asked, hurt and not a little taken aback.

"Because you have always had the most annoying habit of making assumptions."

"I have not. And what am I supposed to have assumed?"

"That you are to be arrested."

She blinked at that, thoroughly bewildered. "I don't understand."

"It's quite simple. No one is going to arrest you."

The shock of that was stunning, knocking the breath from her lungs. Disjointed murmurs slipped past her lips until she finally corralled one into something meaningful. "Why?"

Brett inhaled deeply and came to his feet. He paced to the window and took up a stance there to face her.

"I chose not to pursue the matter," he said quietly.

Laurel could only stare in abject wonder. "But what of Jack? Didn't he accuse me of—"

"Repeatedly."

"Then the army knows what I've done. How can you simply let me go?"

"It was my decision to make."

"And your commanding officer agreed with you?" By the second her eyes were growing wider and wider.

"In the end."

That sounded ominous, and it frayed her limited composure. "Brett, please explain what this is about."

He had disturbed her when it had never been his intention to do so. Returning to her side, he clasped one of her hands between his own. "Rest easy, love. Major Belton is aware of the entire situation, and he agrees with me that nothing will be served by locking you up."

"But you said Jack named me as his accomplice."

"He did. I had my suspicions all along on that matter, but to your great fortune, no actual physical evidence was ever found that could be used against you."

She gazed at him in dawning disbelief. "But you know differently."

"It's Diego's word against yours."

This was beyond imagining. She better than anyone knew how he felt about his principles and yet he was about to compromise that which he held most dear in life. "Brett, you're playing with words. I should know, I've done it often enough."

"I thought you'd be overjoyed," he intoned, a little stung by her reaction.

"I am, *I am.* But I don't understand why you would knowingly overlook my actions."

"Don't you?"

"No! I've been nothing but a source of trouble to you."

Quietly, ever so tenderly, he whispered, "You've also been the single most beautiful person to enter my life." Cupping her face in his hands, he peered deeply into her eyes. "I love you, Laurel."

Overwhelmed, she could only stare at him for a long moment, feeling as if the balance of her life shifted. "You love me?"

"More than you'll ever know." He lowered his mouth to hers and sealed the vow with a deep kiss that stole straight to her heart and touched her soul. "It works out rather nicely, don't you think? Me loving you and you loving me."

She clung to his wrists and searched his eyes, all the while drawing his breath in as her own. He loved her! Stars and garters, he actually loved her. "Hope told you."

"She did, and I will always be grateful." He slanted his mouth over hers again, drinking in her sweet response, made all the more sweet for the love they shared. "Knowing you would sacrifice your life to ensure my sense of honor . . ." He brushed his lips over hers. "No one has ever loved me that way, no one has ever made me feel the way you make me feel. I knew then that I loved you."

"I can't believe this is happening," she sighed, resting her forehead against his chin. Too ecstatic to think of anything else, she repeated the only words of any real importance. "You love me."

"And I intend to marry you."

Shocked again, her head came up, her gaze seeking his. His views on marriage were deeply rooted, and not to be taken lightly.

"Is that what you want?" She made her inquiry with special care.

"If it wasn't, I wouldn't have said anything." Studying the play of emotions on her face, he frowned. "Aren't you happy?"

When it came her reply was cautious. "You've been adamant in your thinking about marriage. I have to wonder if you want to marry me because of some misplaced sense of honor."

He reared back, his annoyance surfacing at once. "What the devil do you mean by that?"

"I mean now that you know I love you, you might feel obliged to do the honorable thing by me."

His jaw hardened and his mouth thinned. Taking hold of her by the arms, he lowered his head until he skewered her with his gaze. "I want to marry you because I love you, because I can't live . . . I won't even *think* about living without you by my side." He dragged her against him, his mouth hovering over hers. "The sound of your scream will live in my mind until I go to my grave."

"I don't want your pity, and it can't be the basis for marriage."

"That wasn't pity, you little termagant, it was anger that someone would dare to harm you, and terror that I would be too late to save you— terror that I would never see you alive again. I knew then that my life would be meaningless without you."

He kissed her with all the passion coursing through him,

melding her to him for all time. "I love you. I didn't know I could feel this way about any woman, but I do." Brushing his mouth over her brow, he confessed, "You were right about so many things."

"I was?" His mouth traveled to her temple and then to her jaw making coherent thinking difficult. "What was I right about?"

"I'm not like my father. There is room in my life for a wife and for my profession." He trailed a line of kisses over her cheek. "I don't have to sacrifice one for the other."

"I'm glad."

"Then say you'll marry me."

"Are you sure, Brett?" His tongue made a pass at her lips. "I won't be a biddable wife."

"I wouldn't want you to be." His lips caressed the corner of her mouth.

"I would want to continue on in the shop—" His teeth found the lobe of her ear and she gasped. "At least for a while . . . to help Hope."

"Whatever you want."

She sighed in profound happiness and pleasure. "I want you. I want you for my husband, my love." The kiss she gave him put a stop to his pleasurable teasing, and spoke of the love that filled her.

Happier than she had ever been, she rested comfortably in his arms. "Did Major Belton really agree to let me go free?"

"He did after I told him I intended to marry you."

"You told him that?" she asked in genuine amazement. "Why?"

"As an insurance. I gave him my word that you would stay out of trouble. As your husband, I would see to it."

The arrogance of that made her laugh. "You beast. You insufferable beast."

"Perhaps, but a beast who loves you."

Her humor gave way to love, pure and boundless. "As I love you, my beast. As I love you."

Dear Reader,

*Illicit* is the result of my life-long fascination with the South and my twenty years of living in Virginia. As a transplanted Yankee, a term still prefaced with "damn" by a few Southern folks, I have found that it's impossible to reside anywhere below the Mason-Dixon and not be charmed by the sense of history, the elegance and splendor that is so typified by Charleston, South Carolina.

Laurel and Brett are the result of my appreciation for strong-willed people. Life seems to be more vibrant for them, colors more exciting, problems more profound, relationships more passionate. What better setting for two such characters than dazzling, enduring Charleston? And what better conflict for Laurel and Brett to overcome than equally strong convictions carried out in two extremely different methods? For Laurel it was truly a case of doing all the wrong things for all the right reasons. As for Brett, well, it was more a question of what he wouldn't do for love.

It is my hope that you enjoyed *Illicit,* just as I hope you like my next Zebra release, *Of Sapphire Dreams.* On the following pages you'll meet Gabriella Spencer, a far too modern-thinking woman, out of her element in Regency London, and Adam Drake, the intensely passionate man who dares to love her.

I wish you many happy hours of reading. You may write to me c/o Zebra Books. A self-addressed stamped envelope is appreciated if you wish a response.

Best Always,

Elizabeth Ann Michaels

Please turn the page for
an exciting sneak preview of
Elizabeth Ann Michaels's
next enthralling historical romance
OF SAPPHIRE DREAMS
coming from Zebra Books
in December 1996

Gabriella Spencer shifted the sleeping boy in her arms so that his head rested on her shoulder, and made her way to the front door of the impressive-looking mansion on Curzon Street. At her knock, the door was swung open to reveal a stout, gray-haired gentleman Gabby assumed was the butler.

"Good evening. This is the Earl of Lancaster's residence, is it not?"

The butler's face paled, his eyes nearly popping from his head. "By all the saints, above!" he exclaimed, fighting for breath. "Master William." He appeared to be caught in a terrible mixture of amazement and dread that held him suspended. Then he coughed and choked and brought himself to life with a flurry of activity.

"My dear young woman, come in, *come in.*"

She stepped into the foyer, seeing none of its grandeur. Instead, her attention was held by several servants staring back at her in shock so real and so overwhelming, she felt a moment's pause. Three seconds passed before anyone said or did anything, but when they finally did react, it was to begin exclaiming and shouting and talking all at once.

Their reaction was everything Gabriella had hoped for. After all, it wasn't every day the five-year-old son of an earl took himself off to explore the wilds of London. It wasn't every day that the very same child remained missing for hours on end only to end up on her doorstep. She had hated to think that no one, least of all the servants, had missed the boy. She had very much hoped for the reaction she got, the one that said more than a few people had worried over little William Anthony Drake.

The butler hurried down the hall amidst cries of relief and laughs of jubilation. Through it all, Will slept on, peacefully oblivious to the commotion he had caused. Sweet little thing. He was dead weight her arms and growing heavier with each passing second.

Gabriella shifted him as best she could, only to glance up at the approach of a tall, fierce-looking man bearing down on her as if he had come from the very depths of hell.

The Earl of Lancaster? He could be no other, for all the rage and horror and anguish in the universe were contained within the man's pewter gaze, all the fear and fury of a parent desperate for his child.

"I believe you've been looking for him," she whispered, a sweet smile gracing her lips.

The earl reached out and caught his son, turning him and pressing him close in one sure move. He ground his eyes shut and tipped his head back, his posture one of agony and relief, his bearing seeming to protect and cherish . . . and promise retribution to any who would dare come between them. One emotion after another flashed freely across his face, each more profound and seething than the previous, each expanding and sharpening until Gabriella was caught by the sheer intensity of feeling emanating from the man.

He loved his son, deeply, wholly, with a strength of emotion that brought tears to her eyes. Never before had she witnessed such raw, unguarded love and shivers raced over her skin. To be so intensely loved was rare, moving her in ways she could not begin to define. All she knew was that she wanted to go on watching the pair forever. At the same time, she felt somewhat of an intruder, trespassing on a treasured intimacy.

Collecting herself, she turned for the door and in that second, the earl's head snapped about, his gaze impaling her to the spot. She hadn't thought he would have been aware of her, or anyone, but he stared at her now in complete awareness. Gone was the seething rage that had glazed his silvery eyes. In its place was something that could only be described as a wild energy.

It pulsed, vibrating through him, barely held in check. Instinct impelled Gabriella to step away from the sheer force of it, from the man, but she held her ground, irresistibly drawn to the enigmatic sensations he aroused.

Myriad impressions charged through her mind, the first being his startling resemblance to his son. Like Will, he was possessed of dark umber hair and eyes that rivaled the misty shrouds of winter's fog. But where Will's face was still baby soft, his father's was lean and hard, his lips firmly chiseled, his cheeks a sculptor's ideal.

Tall and broad shouldered, he held his son with a strength that was nearly tangible. Power was part of his nature, although why she knew that, she couldn't tell. It was there, though, in the way he stood and the manner in which he regarded her, like one of the desert sheiks of the East, supreme in his authority.

The realization was unsettling and would have been annoying if not for the vulnerability underscoring all of that. Despite his air of absolute mastery and control, the earl had been greatly shaken by his son's disappearance. He could not hide it, and in that, she found him reassuringly mortal after all.

Her thoughts startled her. It wasn't like her to be rattled so easily by either a person or by circumstances. And it was definitely out of character for her to relegate a man to the realm of ancient Roman mythology, but all too easily, she found herself likening the earl to Mars—tall, dark and fiercely prepared to conquer.

A tremor seized her heart before it raced downward to the pit of her stomach. The reaction was so quick and unexpected, she drew in a hasty breath. And then, the earl pivoted and strode up the winding stairway, releasing her from the force of his will.

How long she stood there, spellbound, she didn't know. Outwardly, the entire episode had happened in a few seconds. Inwardly, she had been besieged by so many impressions that time had become skewed. The sensation was slightly disorienting, sending her heart into a rhythm of painful thuds.

Quickly, she gathered her wits, denying herself further time to wonder about her internal struggle. Once again she became aware of her surroundings, and all the details she had overlooked. At a single glance, the earl's wealth was clearly evident, from the Italian marble tiling the floor to the richness of the mahogany furniture. And yet, there was nothing ostentatious about the setting.

Everywhere she looked, she saw clean lines and open spaces. There was no frivolity of clutter and she imagined that was a reflection of the earl himself. In their brief moments together, she sensed that he was both candid and direct, having neither the time nor the patience for anything he considered trivial.

She, apparently, fell into that category, but she could

not fault him on that. Others might be insulted to have been left to the servants, but it didn't faze her. In fact, she was pleased to see that the earl's obvious devotion to the boy eclipsed all else. Father and son had been reunited and in the final analysis, that was all that mattered.

Satisfied that she had accomplished her task, she turned for the door again only to be stopped by a tall, sandy-haired gentleman emerging from the cluster of servants who lingered to laugh and wipe away a tear of joy.

"You can't be thinking of leaving," he said.

One corner of her mouth quirked into the beginning of a smile. "Well, yes, actually, I am."

"I'm sure his lordship would like to speak to you."

Her knowing gaze traveled up to the landing at the head of the stairs. "I believe his lordship is otherwise occupied, wouldn't you agree?"

He answered her grin with one of his own, the smile adding his rugged features an air of rakish delight. "Of course, but he is going to want to know the particulars of his son's return. He is, we are all, grateful to you for what you have done tonight."

The identity of this gentleman was a mystery and she did nothing to keep the question from her expression. He read it at once and inclined his head in a mock solemnity.

"I am a friend of his lordship. John Graham, Marquess of Hempton."

The name and title meant nothing to her, but then, that was to be expected. She admitted she was remiss when it came to the peerage. "How do you do?" As an after thought, she tacked on, "My lord." She considered the appellation as she did all such labels, vain and bothersome. It took a conscious effort to remind herself that she was in polite society now, not in a barren dessert or rummaging through deserted ruins. "I am Gabriella Spencer."

"*The* Gabriella Spencer? Daughter of Sir Emmit Spencer?"

"Yes, to both."

Recognition and amazement joined forces to broaden his smile. "This is an unexpected—"

He was interrupted by the twittering laughter of two nearby maids. The sound seemed to snap the marquess to some sort of internal attention. Before Gabriella's amused gaze, he turned a frosty eye first to the maids and then to the butler.

"Jeffreys."

The butler, who evidently was just as overwhelmed by Will's return as the rest of the household, had temporarily forgotten himself. It took the single word from the marquess for the man to be reminded of his duties.

Like an outraged rooster puffing up with indignation, Jeffreys made short, silent work of dispatching maids and footmen alike. In no time, Gabriella and the marquess were alone.

"That was very impressive," she laughed. "And all with only a single word."

The marquess had the good grace to join in her mirth. "I apologize if things are out of order. It has been a harrowing day."

"Please don't apologize to me. I'm happy I could have been of help before Will came to harm."

Mention of Will was sobering. The marquess shook his head slowly. "His lordship has his hands full with that boy."

"Don't tell me Will has done this before."

"No, but he is forever getting into one scrape or another.

It's a wonder the man has retained his sanity let alone his sense of humor. However, I'd wager that the latter is in short supply tonight. There is only so much even a patient father can tolerate."

"Will didn't seem the least bit upset by his ordeal." She related the events of the past hour as well as Will's account of his "adventure."

"That is typically Will," the marquess rued. "He is the—"

This time the interruption came from the approach of two gentlemen who emerged from the hall.

"Excuse us, my lord," the thinner of the two said, "but now that the boy is found, we were wondering what his lordship wished to do about the investigation. Should I recall my men?"

The marquess was considering that when Jeffreys approached with a question of his own. "Excuse me, my lord, but Cook wishes to know if you'll be dining with his lordship?"

A knock at the front door added to the momentary confusion. Within seconds, three of the thin investigator's men had joined the small group. Like the others, they too, wanted some direction.

Gabriella observed the scene with humor dancing in her eyes. These rigid formalities never failed to amuse her. Investigators and butler alike were undoubtedly thinking men, and yet they waited for someone else to tell them what to do.

Well, she had no problem with logic, reasoning or self-direction. Will had been restored to his father. Basking in the pleasure of that, she slipped unobserved from the house.

* * *

The bounds of his sanity had been tested. Fear and rage such as he had never before experienced had taxed him to the extremes of his endurance.

Holding a sleeping Will in his arms, Adam fought hard to control the remains of his anguish. Nothing would be served by another scolding. Nor could the remnants of unreasoning fright be lessened by clinging to the boy through the rest of the night. The need was there, though, burning inside him like a cauldron of agony, scorching him with the compulsion to hold Will close and keep him safe.

Until the day he died, Adam knew he would never forget the torment he'd suffered when he'd learned that Will had disappeared. His life had halted for one hideous moment, only to resume with nerve-racking speed. He had hired teams of investigators to search, but as each hour had passed, nothing had been discovered. No one knew where Will had gone to and every hideous possibility had played through his mind. Had Will simply gotten lost or had he been kidnapped . . . or murdered?

Clamping his eyes shut, Adam forced back the thought. Another, almost as disturbing, rose up to take its place. The hours of not knowing had been the worst, frustrating him as much as it had angered him. With brutal clarity, he had been shown that despite his wealth, position, and rank, he was powerless. He never again wanted to feel that way, helpless to help his son.

Rising from the chair before the fireplace, he made his way to Will's bed and gently tucked him up.

"Would you like me to sit with him now?" Nanny Hutton asked from where she stood in the corner of the room.

His gaze fixed on Will's face, Adam shook his head. "Not yet. I'll stay with him for a while longer." To simply stare at the boy filled a hollowness that had been within him all day.

The nanny rolled her lips inward to bite down another apology that seemed ready to burst forth. From the corner of his eye, Adam could see her chagrin.

"You've explained yourself a dozen times over, Miss Hutton."

She openly cringed, her plump face lining with misery. "I'll never be able to forgive myself, my lord."

"That is something you'll have to live with. I cannot ease your sense of guilt." He finally lifted his head to look at her through the shadows of Will's room. "But I've told you more than once, you must accept that Will is largely to blame for today's debacle."

"He is a spirited child, my lord."

Adam didn't need to be told, and for that, he could not in good conscience hold Nanny responsible for Will's disappearance. As always, she had done her best with a child that required more care and attentiveness than most. Will was that eager, that assertive and inquisitive.

Inwardly, Adam relented to necessity. "Perhaps it would be best if he went back to the country."

"Lancaster Park does suit his adventurous nature better than London."

Truer words had never been spoken. Will was a healthy, intrepid boy, full of mischief and spirit. As he had shown today, he was destined for trouble in a city where he could not explore and indulge his curiosity as any child was meant to do.

From start to finish, Adam had gotten the whole story from Will. Again, he shuddered to think what might have happened to the boy. In this Adam had only himself to blame. He wanted his son near him, not shut away in another household, hours away. Unfortunately, government concerns demanded that for the present, Adam remain in London.

In retrospect, his decision to have Will there seemed a mistake. The keen pleasures father and son took from each other's company were paltry compared to Will's safety. Only the timely intervention of "Miss Gabby" had saved Will from tragedy.

Miss Gabby. His mental images of her were tainted by the soul-rendering urgency that had claimed him earlier. What he did recall of her, though, was oddly captivating. Slender, of medium height, she had scarcely been able to hold Will in her arms.

Hair that ranged in color from deep, dark chocolate to the lighter tones of walnut surrounded a face he supposed was pretty. He couldn't tell. In his anguish, he hadn't been able to take in the whole of her appearance. Only her eyes had made an immediate and lasting impression. Those brilliant, sapphire orbs had had the power to slice through the haze of his tumultuous emotions and leave him with the unmistakable impression of sweet feminine strength.

Miss Gabby. He owed her everything.

At the uncomfortable thought, he jerked suddenly to his feet and nodded to Nanny Hutton before taking his leave. John was waiting for him in the library.

"Well?" John prompted.

Exhaling from the gut of him, Adam vowed, "He's doing far better than I. Right now he's sleeping like an innocent little lamb."

John adjusted his casual seat on the edge of the desk to watch his friend approach. "Little, I'll grant you. Innocent, possibly, but I'll debate you on lamb. He's never been one to blindly follow anyone. He's too intelligent for that. This is a pure case of " 'like father, like son'."

"Until this morning, I took a certain amount of pride in that."

"And now?"

"And now I regret we are so much alike." Resting his forearm on the mantel, Adam stared down at the cheery fire in the grate. "I've decided to send him home."

"As a punishment?"

"No. For his own safety, and for my sanity." He didn't explain further. It wasn't necessary. He and John were friends of long-standing. John knew him better than anyone, and would understand the reasons for the decision.

There was, Adam admitted, a great deal that John understood. He was one of the very few people Adam trusted, one of the very few who didn't want anything more than friendship. Adam revered that, for with the exception of Will, all others came his way with hands extended, grasping for advise or help or support, usually in the form of money.

One of the pitfalls of being wealthy, Adam supposed on a sour note. That made him popular with his relations, and with every charitable organization known to man, but it did nothing for genuine kinship and camaraderie. It was a truth he witnessed daily, and a lesson he'd learned in watching everyone from the pauper on the street to even his mother and his wife.

There were great similarities to the women. Both had been beautiful, both had been spoiled, privileged ladies of their class. Both had greedily viewed their husbands as a means of money and used them accordingly.

The memories of Beth's actions still rankled at the heart of him. He took solace as he always did when he let himself dwell on his dead wife, that one of the follies of youth is a certain naiveté. How else could he explain his ridiculous belief that Beth had been different from most people he knew? What other explanation could he have for so foolishly letting himself think that in her, he had found his life-long companion, a woman who truly loved him?

Now at thirty-eight, he knew better.

He stepped back from the fireplace, the move an instinctive withdrawal from his thoughts. "The house is in order. Thank you for that."

"You're welcome," his friend returned. "I handled things as I thought you'd like, but you'll need to contact the investigators tomorrow."

"And Miss Spencer?" He gazed about, realizing for the first time that she wasn't there. "Where the devil is she, any way?"

John scratched at his chin. "Gone. It was the damnedest thing, too. One minute she was here, and the next . . ." He spread his hands wide to indicate thin air.

"You mean she walked off without a word?"

"Nearly. Did Will mention who she is?"

"Other than 'Miss Gabby', no."

"Well, 'Miss Gabby' is Gabriella Spencer."

Adam recognized the name immediately. "Sir Emmit's daughter?"

"The same, and a very charming little anthropologist she is. Very fetching."

The glint in John's eyes gave Adam cause for a laughing scoff. "Your lust is showing, John."

"It can't be helped. From all I've heard, she's a remarkable young woman. Her actions tonight only bear that out."

"No woman is that remarkable."

"You say that because you have the damnedest luck with the women you've met."

"The women I've met and a good portion of the men, too, are constantly vying for more in life, usually at someone else's expense."

"If anything is showing now, Adam, it's your cynicism."

It wasn't a flattering assessment, but Adam could not refute it. Being cynical, and suspicious, were part of his nature. On more than one occasion, during and since the wars with Napoleon, the combination had kept him alive.

He shoved one hand deep into the pocket of his pants as he turned fully to face John. "We've had this discussion before."

"True, and normally, I wouldn't try to dissuade you, but in this instance, I think you're wrong."

"Everyone is after something. Miss Spencer is no exception."

"I wouldn't be too quick to assume that. She was ready to leave here without even telling me who she was. As far as I could tell, she wanted to see Will home and then be done with the entire matter."

"I find that hard to believe." So hard in fact, he intended to treat Miss Spencer as he would anyone in this instance, with courtesy, gratitude and the compensation of a sizable reward. Miss Spencer would be sure to appreciate the monetary gesture, but more importantly, it would restore balance in his life.

He was accustomed to rewarding people. It was what they expected and wanted and what he had become comfortable doing. To break with the habit was unthinkable if for no other reason than he had no intention of owing Miss Spencer a damn thing.

He would be grateful to her for the rest of his life, but

there was a difference between gratitude, even one of the immense degree he felt, and indebtedness. The first he would accept. The latter was preposterous.

First thing tomorrow, he would send his solicitor around to see Miss Spencer and express his *gratitude.* He trusted then that he could begin to put this day behind him. In rewarding Miss Gabriella Spencer, he would see his life back on an even keel.